# Castle of Villains

L.N. Reagan

ISBN: 9798218635411

Book Cover by Obsi Art

First Edition 2025

# Contents

# Trigger Warning

This story is a dark romantic fantasy and may contain darker themes, those who may struggle with certain topics should take time to read these warnings.

This book contains talk or graphic detail on the following items: Death of all kinds, Blood, Sex, Curse words, and struggle of self worth.

If you find yourself struggling with your mental health, please know that you are not alone. You are loved. You can get through this.

Mental Health hotline: 988

# Pronunciation Guide

Ruellia- (Roo-ell-ee-uh)

Vreilwreth- (Vrail-wreh-th)

Shadowfall- (Shadow-fall)

Calix- (Cal-ix)

Skarlette- (Skar-let)

Kai- (K-eye)

Ethan (Ee-than)

Louissa ( Lou-ee-sa)

Kasira- (Kuh-seer-uh)

Veeling- (Veel-ing)

Elijah- (Ee-lie-juh)

Janella (Juh-nel-uh)

Map of Aurenda
Ruellia
Human Lands
Calix
Vreilwreth
Shadowfall
N
W
E
S

To all of us in our villain era.
The ones burning bridges and building walls to keep our
peace.

# Chapter One

## SKARLETTE

My feet leave the rooftop, my body free falling through the air until I land on top of the man waiting for me below. He grunts from the impact, but I refuse to pay him any attention. Pushing myself up off of him, irritation courses through me that he is even here in the first place.

"What the fuck, Skarlette?" He hisses, trying to keep quiet as we linger outside of the front door of this house. I need to get out of here. Get away from the murder I have just committed. Kai is only making my job ten times harder by tagging along.

"You shouldn't even be here." My feet begin moving, quickly carrying me down the road and away from the crime scene. "I can do this on my own."

The night air that surrounds us, is cold. Winter will soon cover the grounds in snow, but tonight the moon is shining high above us as the howls of wolves echo in the distance. Wrapping my hood tighter around my body, I shield myself from the icy bitterness.

I really hate that Ethan sent him. I am fine. I have been doing this on my own for a long time.

Kai annoyingly falls into step beside me. "He sent me because he feels that you're starting to get sloppy." His words echo in my brain, like a chant telling me I will never do anything right or be good enough.

"I am not getting sloppy," I grumble before gritting my teeth at the hold the fae prince and his family have on me.

"You're a half blood. It's expected that he doesn't trust you." There it is again, another reminder of how I am different. How imperfect and undesirable a creature like me is. The fact that the Goddess let a creature like me be born in the first place is a sin against nature.

I bare my sharp teeth at him in hopes of scaring him off. A laugh bubbles up and out of me when he stumbles back a few feet, his nervousness evident in the expression on his face. The way is eyes widen, his pulse racing in his veins. It's as if he is meeting me for the very first time.

His blood calls to me, begging for me to drain him and be done with it all. "Flee, little princeling," I tell him before he can get hurt.

"Just because my older brother sent me, does not make me *little*. We are the same age, Skarlette. We grew up together." He takes a step towards me, putting away his fear that had a hold on him just a moment ago.

"Ah, yes. We *grew up* together. You the back up prince, and me your family's pet—your family's monster." His face flinches as my words lash out, hitting their mark. My mind flashes through our childhood, remembering all the times I wanted to be equal to them, but I was simply a stray the family brought in.

*'Don't touch him!' The nursemaid barks at me, raising her cane and bringing it down upon my back. 'I don't know why they insist on keeping you in the house. Soon enough, you'll prove them wrong and show them the monster you truly are. And then they will finally put you back in your cage where you belong!'*

A shiver runs down my spine at the memory. She constantly forced me to sit in the corner of the room, playing by myself. The king had in fact put me back in my cage when

I was freshly thirteen. The hormones surging through my body had made the craving for blood stronger, too strong to ignore without the proper teachings on how to control it. When the day had come and the blood lust was too much to bear, I sank my fangs into one of the boys in the school village. The school I was sent to because I wasn't good enough to join the king's children in their tutoring lessons. Maybe if I had been kept closer and under supervision, the boy would still be here today.

I inwardly cringe when my thoughts take me deeper, remembering all the times Prince Ethan came to my cage, his face in a cruel sneer. He would taunt me, starting by throwing rotten food at me before cutting himself and shoving his hand in my cage, daring me to drink from him. *"Drain me, Skarlette. Drain me like you did that little village boy,"* he would mock. He may have been a mere three years older than I, but he was a hell of a lot meaner than the rest of us.

"I know he hasn't always been the nicest," Kai says, pulling me out of my thoughts and back to the present.

Kai is the sweet one, always seeing the good in people, even when there isn't any. He will defend you until his last breath. He wouldn't hurt anything, even if it would have protected his life. Just like tonight. He should kill me, stop what I was slowly becoming.

"The whole faerie kingdom is terrified of me." Some of the sharpness in my voice slowly fades away. I always have a hard time being able to stay mad at him for long.

"I'm not scared," he says, confidence radiating from him.

My feet stop moving as I turn towards him, ignoring the voice inside my head that tells me this is a bad idea. "The world is changing, Kai. The vampires are being swept from this world. As we get older, you're going to learn I am the villain in this story and that's exactly where I want to be."

"Skar—you're…." Kai's voice trails off as I close the small distance between us. My hands take hold of his head, tilting it to the side and lining my fangs up with the sweet spot on his neck. I breathe him in, his scent flooding me. Alarm bells ring in my head that this isn't what I want to do. Kai is my friend, even if I hate the rest of his family.

Behind him, I watch as the wheat fields dance in the night breeze. I close my eyes, savoring the feel of him close to me. His stubble scrapes against the sensitive tips of my pointed ears, making a shiver slowly crawl down my spine, like a spider leaving it's web. Sinking my fangs into his soft skin, I feel the warmth of his blood on my tongue before I taste it. A groan rumbles through me as my tongue laps up his delicious taste. It is like a gulp of my favorite faerie drink, spiced apple wine.

This is not a good sign. It is a terrible sign. One I do not want to believe.

The voice in my head is telling me to stop. If I continue at this rate, I will kill him. But is that not what I should be doing? Killing Kai and freeing myself of this terrible family. It is what I should have done. Send the crowned prince a message by killing his brother, but something in me can't do it. Kai is the only friend I have ever had. When the rest of the kids would run from me in fear, he would come closer. I can't kill the only person that has ever meant something to me.

His blood is unlike anything I have ever tasted. He is sweet and spicy all at the same time and I groan again with the pleasure it brings me, but his body has gone limp in my arms and if I don't stop soon, he will be gone forever.

Finding the strength, I force myself to cease drinking and lower him to the ground. I pull him off of the dirt road, leaving him in the soft grass at the edge of the wheat field. I need to get out of here. I need to put as much distance as possible between Kai Eveningglow and myself.

Drinking from him has opened my eyes to something I have wished for all my life. But now that it is true, I don't want it. I can't do that to Kai. I will send word to Ethan that I have cleaned up his messes for the last time and then I will flee Ruellia for good. I will hide away in another city and hope that it is far enough away that eventually the royal family will forget I ever existed.

# Chapter Two

## KAI

*Three years later......*

My arms shake as they push up, then fall back down, holding the weight of my body. I hop to my feet, running to the edge of the training area and grabbing one of the large stones. My legs burn with a delicious ache as I carry it around the training ring, heart thumping as sweat pools on my lower back.

Louissa's voice calls from the edge of the ring. "Why put yourself through all this torture, brother?"

I let a grunt escape from me as the weight of the rock tests my limits. Ignoring my sisters words, I continue on with my training. I will be stronger. I will fight for her.

Three years is a long time to hold a candle for someone, but something deep in my bones tells me she isn't gone forever. My brother and sister hate how I wait for her. I have gone so far as to pretend I don't care anymore so they leave me alone.

"Brother wants us in the throne room," she calls, shaking her head as she walks away from me. I throw the boulder to the ground, dusting my dirt covered hands off on my pants before following her inside.

The hall is quiet. It's too early for many of the servants to be moving around. In fact, it should be too early for my siblings to be up and moving around, yet here we are.

In the throne room, my brother is lounging on his throne. I hate how lazy he looks. He is the crowned prince, he should have more respect for the seat. His hair is a disheveled mess, telling me he hasn't even gone to bed yet.

"Ah look, my brother and sister's shining faces," he calls to us, far too chipper for this early in the morning. Especially with the events happening all over our kingdom, but once again my father has practically left him in charge.

"What is it, Ethan," I drawl, having no patience for his mind games.

"You two." He points his bony finger towards me and Louissa. "Are going on a voyage." His smile is almost too gleeful, a kind of gleeful that makes my stomach twist with anxiety as he tells us the news. "A ship will be waiting for you to leave at noon today. Lord Veeling is awaiting your arrival in Vreilwreth."

My sister and I give each other confused looks. It is faster to travel to Vreilwreth by horse and carriage, but with all the vampire sightings as of late, my brother must have thought it safer to travel by sea. Our heads whip back to the throne where Ethan's eyes are intensely focused on me, telling me the words he dare not say out loud.

"We need this alliance." That's what his eyes are saying to me when his words can't. I had protested when my brother and father had thought of the idea. They would marry off Louissa to a lord with a large army, to help us control the rogue vampires entering our territory. I knew my sister would hate this, she wanted to marry for love. My father knew it too and I could see in his eyes that he wasn't completely sold, but my protest was in vain. They have apparently been planning this without me.

My head bows, understanding what has to be done. He carries on. "The lord is looking to strengthen our army, and with the vampires being more reckless, we are going to need them."

"I don't understand why I have to go," Louissa whines and I wince. I know what her whining does to Ethan. The prince's hand moves, his thumb and forefinger pinching the bridge of his nose. When his eyes pop open and he looks back at us, anger resonates in his eyes like a tornado busting at the seams of his pupils.

"You go because I say so, Louissa!" The way he barks her name makes her jump back.

"Louissa," I hiss under my breath, urging for her not to fight him.

She looks between us, betrayal evident on her face. "Fine." Her teeth clench as she spins and walks out of the throne room.

"I see you're leaving me to deal with this again." He always seems to make hurting Louissa's feelings my problem. "And what does our father say about this?" My questioning tone is bored, because I already know the answer, our father has agreed.

"He agrees with me. Louissa's union with Lord Veeling will help the whole continent." He picks at the invisible dirt beneath his nails, clearly done with the topic of discussion.

"How long shall we be gone?"

"That, dear brother, is entirely up to you." He pauses,

making sure no one else is around to listen in on our conversation. "I have another small matter I would like you to take care of while you're in Vreilwreth. I need you to find me the chaos bringer. I am tired of trying to put out the fires this villain keeps bringing to my doorstep." He leans forward his elbows resting on his knees. "I need you to bring *her* home brother." His words are like a hammer to my bones.

My throat contracts around the large lump I'm trying to swallow. "We don't know that it's her."

"You and Louissa can pretend all you want, but I know her work when I see it." Ethan leans back and resumes to lounging on the throne.

He doesn't know what his words are doing to me. Hope blooms inside my chest, blossoming like a Ruellia flower. Hope that after three long and torturous years, we have finally found her. My brain shoves down the thoughts of her being a downright menace to the continent, happily content with the fact that we may be bringing her home soon.

I practically run from the throne room, immediately starting to prepare for the voyage ahead. I am going to find the villain. I am going to bring her home.

The sea churns beneath us, my body lurching over the rail of the ship as my stomach mimics the ocean's movements. I'm not meant to sail. I'm meant to stay with the land planted firmly beneath my feet. A passing sailor claps me on the back, my stomach grumbling from the jostled movement. Bile and breakfast crawl up my throat, destined to feed the fish, but I swallow it back down.

"You look terrible." Louissa stands beside me, the sea breeze blowing tendrils of her hair out of the braid flowing down her back. She doesn't look bothered by the rocking motion at all. Dare I say, she is even prettier in the sun's rays that shine off the water.

"I feel terrible. I hate traveling by ship." A large wave rocks the ship and my knuckles go white with the force of my grip on the railing.

"And yet you didn't fight our brother when he suggested this little trip." Her eyes narrow, lips pursing with a suspicious glare.

The words and secrets don't leave my mouth. They won't. I'm not ready to tell her about the marriage and I sure as hell am not going to tell her about hunting down a villain. She huffs out a breath of frustration when I don't respond, spinning on her heal and leaving me to be sick alone.

When the ship finally docks in Vreilwreth's port, my body is relieved, my stomach unknots itself and my food no longer threatens to make an appearance on the deck. The sun is just disappearing below the horizon as we descend. My feet wobble on the gangplank as I fight to remember how to walk on land. Six days doesn't seem like a lot, but when the ship rocks underneath you, you learn to adjust your gate.

As the darkness creeps over the land, I wait, standing on the street near the fish processing area for our cargo to be offloaded. I'm a hundred yards away from the ship, talking with one of the sailors when I see a flick in the corner of my vision. As quickly as it begins, the entire ship is engulfed in flames, the heat warming my skin. People panic, running in every direction. But my brain is already ten steps ahead.

My eyes scan the area, looking for our perpetrator as other sailors begin to hurriedly try and douse the wild fires on the ship. There, slinking away from the scene of the crime, is a shadowed figure with a hood covering their face. A night breeze comes in from the ocean and I catch a glimpse of silver hair that peeks out around the edges of the cape's hood. My heart skips a beat.

"Skar," my voice whispers and the figure halts.

The person turns to look at me. My skin prickles, it's hairs standing on end as the feeling of someone watching me penetrates into my nerves, but I can't see past the hood. I swear I see the glow of her crimson eyes emanating from underneath it. My feet move, taking over control of my body and taking one step towards the person before they take off in a full run down the narrow alleyways of the city.

# Chapter Three

## SKARLETTE

The streets of Vreilwreth are wet from a late evening downpour. With the clouds now gone, the moon illuminates everything around me, it's reflection shining in the puddles that I leap over on my way to burn down some lord's ship.

Tonight is just like every other night. Some lord has paid me to take care of his feud. Set a neighboring lord's ship on fire and be paid a hefty price for my services. I don't really pay attention to all the details. They always tell me what the feud is over, but I don't care. All I care about is getting paid and getting out of here. I have spent the last three years carrying out wicked deeds for others. I actually make quite a comfortable life for myself this way. Carry out heinous deeds for others at night, and live my own life the rest of the time. It is a far better way to live than to live the rest of it as a prince's guard dog.

The difference between tonight and any other night though, is the face I see as I dash away from the crime scene, a face I never thought I would ever see again. I thought I had left him behind me three years ago when I laid him down, unconscious in a field after drinking his blood. But here he stands, staring at me with a murderous glare. I falter, taken so off guard by his presence that I am not sure what to do.

My hands tug on the edges of my hood, pulling it closer around my face, feet bolting away from the burning ship and my past. My hesitant pause wastes too much time. The royal guard is heading right for me. I veer left, dodging down a main alleyway. Footsteps sound behind me, chasing after me, and closing the distance between me and them. Luckily for me, the streets of Vreilwreth are quiet this time of night. Most people have long since gone to bed.

My head turns, looking behind me for a split second. I let a curse slip past my lips as I see how close they are getting. But to my surprise, it isn't the guards I see. Kai is only several feet behind me. Quickly, I try to further the distance between us, pushing my legs to carry me faster. I fear that with the condition I last left him in long ago, he will surely try to bring me back home. Something I really don't want to happen.

In front of me, a dead end is quickly approaching. But after three years, this route is like second nature to me. Hanging a right, I slip in the front door of Mrs. Laverne's washhouse.

"Lettie! What have I said about running through the washroom, girl?" Mrs. Laverne shouts, the large woman's fisted hands resting on each hip as she yells at me, her cheeks rosy from the warmth of the steam permeating the air.

My finger presses to my lips, my eyes pleading with her to stay quiet as I slip inside one of the cupboards. Inside, I try to find a way for me to stand comfortably before peering through the crack between the doors. Kai runs through the washroom entrance, his head whipping in every direction trying to find where I have disappeared to. His chest heaves as he takes in a lungful of breath from running so far.

"Who were you talking to?" He demands from Hattie.

"Oh, my daughter. Kids, ya know? They just never listen." Mrs. Laverne takes Kai's question in stride, shaking her head with disgrace at her 'daughter', and chuckling at how silly children are.

Three years hasn't changed me much besides the scar across my face, but it has done wonders to Kai. He stands several inches taller and has more muscle than when we were sixteen. His dark hair is hanging past his ears and his black fighting leathers make my lower stomach swirl as they hug his curves. His navy eyes land on the cupboard where I hide, making my heart thump loudly in my chest. I press my back against the blankets behind me, shrinking myself away from the crease. Through the crack, I can see his hand clench at his side, the anger between his brows filling me with immense guilt.

Of course he is mad. I bit him and left him vulnerable in a field. Then, I disappeared for three years. I can't expect him to chase me down, pull me into his arms and kiss me. Not after what I have done.

A young woman arrives at the washrooms front door. She lingers on the threshold, her eyes scanning the scene in front of her. Her lips turned down in a frown, dark curls swishing against her cheeks as she lightly shakes her head. There is no mistaking her, even though she has grown older, Louissa still looks so much like Kai and Ethan. Born just a year after Kai and myself. She would constantly follow us around, trying to tag along on our adventures.

Louissa's hand wraps around Kai's forearm, gently pulling him in the direction of the door. 'Kai, we need to go."

Their forms slowly drift outside, disappearing out onto the moonlit street.

My breath stays trapped inside my lungs for several long moments before releasing and deeming it is safe to come out of the cupboard. My hands push the door slowly open, peeking out to make sure they are in fact gone and aren't waiting for me to come out of hiding.

Hattie's arms are folded as she gives me that stern motherly look. "I am not even going to ask."

"Thanks, Hattie. I appreciate it." I give her a small peck on one of her rose colored cheeks.

She has become like a mother to me since I moved here. She is older than what my mother would have been, but she and Charles were unable to have their own children, so when she found me wandering the streets, she took me in.

I am grateful for the shelter they have provided me over the years. Though, I haven't really thought about what would happen if Kai or Ethan came looking for me. I preferred to live in peaceful ignorance. Now that Kai is here, I will need to make myself scarce. The last thing I want is to go back home to Ruellia. I have too many secrets hiding in me, secrets that will only hurt Kai more if he knew them.

"Oh, and Lettie," she calls to me as I head upstairs to the room I call my own. The stairs creak under my light weight, the years of use taking their toll. "Charles just got back from hunting. He saved you what he could."

"Thanks again." My voice carries down to her from the landing at the top of the stairs. As I twist the doorknob to my room, I can here Hattie humming to herself downstairs. A nightly routine, as she washed the clothes that had been dropped off earlier that day.

The clock is nearing one in the morning as I descend upon the streets again. I dodge past the city's night watch. The fae men and women with their blue uniforms parade down the streets in pairs, their batons swinging in their hands and wood stakes attached to their belts. Vampire movement near Vreilwreth had been on the rise. Between that and the chaos I have been causing, Lord Veeling had no choice but to form the nights watch. A group of men and women sworn to protect the people of Vreilwreth at night, but a nuisance none the less. They always seem to spend more time getting into trouble than they do saving people.

"Hey—you!" One of them calls to me.

My feet move, running full speed down the street, sliding to the right as I veer off behind a row of town homes. My feet are pounding against the broken cobblestone streets as their pleas for me to stop ring in my ears. A fence blocks me in the path ahead, forcing me to jump on top of a crate and over the top of the fence. The nights watch and their pea sized brains bang on the fence behind me, yelling for me to come back.

Sliding to a screeching halt, I come out between two homes. Across the street, I can see Kai as he closes the door to the royal townhome and adjusts his jacket for the cool night air. His hand runs through his locks of hair, pushing them away from his face. I can't help but admire how handsome he has become.

Behind me, the guards are still shouting, too stupid to jump the fence or go around. The dark haired prince turns his head just as I fall back, pressing myself against the side of one of the houses.

I peak around the edge of the wall, Kai is moving in the opposite direction and then disappearing around a corner. I dart out from between the houses and in the direction of my favorite tavern. I need to get out of here and quick.

# Chapter Four

## KAI

**M**y mind plagues with me with thoughts of Skarlette. I haven't taken the time to really think about her in so long, but something tonight reminds me of her. Three years is a long time for someone to be gone. My brother told me multiple times to forget her, but I can't. Skarlette haunts my mind like a ghost.

I am sure I saw her today, fleeing from the wreckage of the burning ship. The short pause the hooded figure took when they saw me, the whisps of silver hair that peaked out of the fabric. Hell, if I knew Skarlette, she would be the one who set that ship on fire. The kingdoms have been dealing with a villain these past years, one who carries out dark deeds for others; burning ships, stealing, infiltrating shipments. The list is endless—short of murder.

The coincidence of Skarlette's disappearance and the appearance of this unknown villain isn't lost on me. For a long time I thought it was her, but they haven't murdered anyone, and Skarlette has killed many times before without a second thought. So, what makes her not do it now? Or I am completely wrong and this isn't her. It is just a coincidence and I have someone else on my hands.

"What keeps you?" Louissa asks, coming into the library.

"What? Oh, nothing." I rise from my chair, leading us both into the dining room. My feet drag against the green carpet, my mind still lost in its swirling thoughts.

My brother sent me here to help find the perpetrator and put a stop to their chaos. Amazing luck I have that the very ship I sailed in on was their target. Lord Snelling will be sorely disappointed in the loss of his ship. It is hard for me to put together what exactly is happening. The hooded figure doesn't seem to be using their chaos as a weapon for their own needs.

It seems as though they are simply carrying out dastardly deeds for others. It isn't a very villain like thing to do if you ask me. Most villains you read about want something, whether it be revenge or to rise to power, but this one is . . . different.

"The lord of Vreilwreth is dining with us tonight. Ethan is hoping he can give us any leads to the perpetrator's where abouts." I look up to see Louissa staring at me. Her face holding a perplexed look, like she is trying to dig deep to read my thoughts. "I can see where this is going. It's been so long. You already put it all in the past, don't let old wounds resurface." She gives me a sad smile as she enters the small dining room.

Lord Veeling rises from the seat he has taken at the small dining room table. Crossing the room towards us, he smoothe's down his green waistcoat and trousers before approaching. His hand runs through the greasy blonde locks on his head as he smiles at my sister. Louissa bows, the ends of her pink dress splaying out across the dark hardwood floor. When she rises, a sugary sweet smile is plastered across her face.

"Lord Veeling, a pleasure." My smile turns up at edges. "This is my sister, Louissa," I introduce, watching how he looks her over. Unsurprisingly, I still haven't found the strength to tell her about the arrangement to marry her off. She will surely be disappointed. She reads way too many romance novels and is always hoping for the likes of a gentleman from one of her books. Lord Veeling simply wants a wife who can give him heirs.

The man reaches out, taking hold of my sisters hand, and placing a small kiss to the top of it. "A pleasure to dine with such a beautiful, young lady."

I hide my snort behind a cough when I see the sneer that appears on my sister's face. She quickly schools herself, putting her pleasant smile back in place. This is going to be harder than I thought. "Shall we sit?"

I pull out her chair before Lord Veeling has the chance. His hand reaches out for it, but I find my own reaching for it faster. He gives me a critical stare before heading back to his own seat at the table. When we have all found ourselves comfortable, a servant arrives at the table, offering each of us apple spiced faerie wine. The lord sips his wine with a grimace, clearly preferring the mead his own brewery makes, but he won't dare offend us by requesting it.

"I know you haven't just invited me here to eat with you." Lord Veeling is cutting right to the chase before our food has even arrived.

Taking a long drink of my wine, I let the alcohol simmer before starting this conversation. "You are quite right. We are hoping you can gives us some information on this causer of chaos."

"Yes. The *Il Furfante*." My brows rise in question at the name he gives my silver haired menace. "The only information I have is a slight description of them that someone has reported. A scar going from the left eye all the way down to the right cheek. I have no whereabouts, for it is seen everywhere. It's like a shadow. It creeps up along the edges of the darkness, stalking its prey and hiding from everyone else."

Like a faerie vampire who has inherited the faerie powers of shadow magic, I thought to myself. Fae have been known to be bestowed powers. While vampires were strong and could live forever when they drank faerie blood and even their mate's blood. Fae had abilities. Said to be given to us by the faerie goddess herself. I have not inherited said powers, but my brother Ethan is said to be able to know if someone is lying. My father has the ability to teleport items. My mother was able to manipulate things that grew from the earth. Even my sister seems to have gotten my mother's powers and yet I have nothing.

The disappointment of the family once again.

We finish our dinner with the Lord of Vreilwreth. I am beyond grateful when he doesn't say a word about his and my father's agreement. I need a few days to get Vreilwreth's customs to grow on my sister. I also hadn't realized how short Veeling is until we stand at the doorway to say our goodbyes. My little sister stands several inches shorter than I, and Lord Veeling is a whole inch shorter than her.

"Miss Louissa." He grabs her hand again, his lips stretching out to place a soft kiss to the back of her hand. "It was a pleasure dining with you and I hope I can show you around my town."

"It would be my pleasure to spend the day with you." Louissa's fake smile is painful to watch as she bids Lord Veeling farewell and heads up the stairs to her room.

Good thing we will be stuck here for a few days while I wait for another ship to become available. For now, I can spend sometime showing my sister the delights of Vreilwreth and trying to find the person responsible for burning the ship.

"Louissa, I am going out for a bit. Don't stay up," I yell up the stairs, grabbing my wool coat from the coatrack near the front door. The fastest way to track shadows is to begin at night.

The streets of Vreilwreth are quiet at night. It's a stillness unlike the city near the castle. In Ruellia's capitol city, lots of fae men spend their nights drinking in the tavern. There always seems to be a party of some sort happening some where. Here though? It's just quiet. I see the occasional passerby, but they don't seem to be any sort of chaos causing villain.

Finally, after walking for quite some time, I come to a fork in the road. Right at the center sits a small tavern. Candlelight flickers in the windows, calling the nightlife to come inside. I open the door, walking inside and finding myself a seat. I plan to sit here for hours, listening in on conversations and trying to find out anything I can about this *Il Furfante*.

The tavern owner walks over to me. "Sorry laddie', time to clean up and refresh for the next day." I take the hint, leaving with no more information than I came in with. Maybe a good night's rest will help me figure out where to look next.

The streets of Vreilwreth are a wet mess in the spring. Mud covers my boots and the clouds cover us in gray; carriages roll past me as I make my way to the local inn for breakfast.

Once seated with a plate of boiled eggs and potatoes, I listen in on conversations around me. Many whisper about the *Il Furfante*, how it reeks havoc while they sleep. They call it a monster, a villain, and everything of their worst nightmares. It sounds a lot like what Skarlette used to do for my brother when she lived in our kingdom.

When I have filled my stomach and paid the tab, I move outside in search of our hooded figure. I want the villain to be her. My soul needs to see her face again, it yearns for my eyes to get lost in hers.

Strolling through alleyways, I come to rest in front of the wash house. I swear I see Skarlette dart through the back door before it slams shut behind her. Following, I push through the door, the smell of soap and mildew burning my nose hairs.

"Hello, I'm Hattie! What needs washing today?" A large round woman calls from behind a counter. Off to the side is a large wash basin that is filled to the brim with soap and clothes. "Oh," she pauses once she looks up from the clothes in front of her, "it's you again. How can I be of service to you today, sir?"

"I'm actually looking for someone. Have you happened to see a woman with long gray hair and crimson red eyes?" I see her eyes light with recognition before she schools her face.

She moves to stack a pile of sheets. "I am afraid the

description doesn't sound familiar."

"That's unfortunate. If you do happen to see her, will you let her know I am looking for her?"

"I will, but what if she doesn't want your company?" The woman named Hattie turns back to me now, awaiting my answer.

"Then so be it. I just wanted to know that she is okay." Turning to leave, I hear Hattie's voice again.

"She is as good as she can be in this world." I leave the shop, the door rings in my ears as I make my way back to the townhouse.

Swinging the townhouse's front door wide open, happiness courses through me. "She is here! She is here!" I chant, grabbing ahold of my sister's arms and spinning her around before tightly embracing her.

"Who is here?" Louissa's muffled voice says against my chest.

I pull her from me, giving her a big smile. Louissa's grass green eyes stare at me with bewilderment. I am obviously scaring her with my joy.

Beaming at her, I'm unable to control the smile that lingers on my face. "Skarlette is here."

"Your boyhood crush still isn't over?" She huffs. "I thought I told you this the other night. Kai—she is gone." Her warm hands cup my cheeks in her palms. "Please don't start this again," she begs and my smile falters.

"She left me in a field three years ago. No goodbye, nothing. I deserve to know why, Louissa." My hands wrap around her wrists, removing her hands from my face and turning away from her. I hate that she can't understand my excitement.

Leaving her, I head for my room and let my thoughts consume me. I have changed since then. Back then, I was soft spoken, always seeing the best in people. But now I have grown. I have seen the horrors of the world and learned how to fight my enemies. Taking my role as the family failure, I made myself a warrior from it.

I want answers—want Skarlette to tell me why she left me. Why she would bite me and leave me vulnerable in a field. Inside, I know it is all selfish reasons for wanting to see Skar again, but I have to. I need to have those crimson eyes searching my soul, devouring me with a single glance. I fear if I don't see them again, I will die forgetting what they are like.

My reflection looks back at me in the mirror, taking in my dark hair and eyes. My gaze travels to the two small circles on my neck, unrecognizable to most, but I know what happened. They stand out to me. In fact sometimes, they even ache for her to do it again.

Before I leave Vreilwreth, I *will* see Skarlette. When the sun sets, and the nightlife takes over, I will find the seediest bar in town and wait for her to find me.

# Chapter Five

## SKARLETTE

Inside the dim basement of the local tavern, humid air filled with sweat permeates the air. A smell I have come to find comforting a few nights a weak. Pushing my way through the large crowd of people gathered around the center of the room, I head towards the bar. In the center of the crowd, two men circle each other, delivering blow after blow to one another. Blood flies across the ring as one man delivers a punch straight into the other's mouth. The scent makes my nostrils flare, my tongue darting out to meet my lips instinctively.

"Lettie, it's good to see you." Jamith calls from the bar as I break from the crowd and head in his direction. Jamith's smile creates dimples in his cheeks and his gold tooth shines in the candlelight, his blonde hair having been freshly shaved on the sides falls across his sweat glistening forehead.

One barstool sits open, inviting me to take the spot between two older fae men. One is snoring in his chair and the other grumbles to himself between sips of his drink. Both men's ears are starting to droop as the pointed ends poke out from their white hair.

"Tell Yousif the job is done." Jamith sets a drink down in front of me, my hand wraps around it and moves the tin cup to my lips. I gulp down the warm liquid before slamming the cup against the bar and startling the old man sleeping next to me. He mumbles something before slumping over and resting his head against the bar top.

"He already saw your handy work and sent this for you." Jamith tosses a bag on the bar top. I take it in my hand, pulling at the strings and opening it to count it's contents. Inside, gold coins sparkle, the sound of their jingle tells me he paid extra for a job well done.

When I feel satisfied with the amount, I count out five of the coins, giving them to Jamith, and entering myself in the competition for tonight's fights. A ritual I started when

I didn't have jobs to carry out and I wanted to feel a little pain.

A few drinks in, my name is finally called. The large ring stands in the center, ropes enclose it so onlookers don't get too close. Tables and chairs linger around the edges of the room, giving a place for someone to have a drink and a show. The man waiting for me in the ring is big, even for a faerie. He is thick and probably stands four inches taller than myself, but he doesn't know what monster he fights tonight. He doesn't know that my mixed breeding makes me twice as strong as any full blooded fae in this room.

We circle each other, giving us a chance to size one another up. With my hood up, hiding my face from everyone in the room, he can't tell I am a woman. But by the smirk on his lips, he already thinks I am a weakling. I throw the first punch, tired of waiting for him to make the first move. Throwing it at about half of my strength, I listen as the burly man before me laughs. He throws the next punch, coming into contact with the side of my head.

My ear rings with the impact, but I quickly recover. The pain reminds me I am alive, that I can feel. I get a few more good punches in before a familiar voice carries through the room. My ears track the sound, my eyes moving right to where Kai is taking a seat, front and center to watch the fight. Pulling my hood closer to my face, I try to hide myself from his view. This gives my opponent time to throw a really good punch straight into my face.

Jamith runs up to my side of the fighting ring, a look of concern etched onto his face. The amount of concern that makes someone get the wrong idea. "You okay, Lettie?"

My head nods, letting him know I am okay, but not daring to speak and have Kai recognize my voice.

The man bellows. "You're going to need more than that hood to hide what I am going to do to your face!" His ego is huge, thinking he has already won this fight, but oh how I will relish in his disappointment.

He throws another punch and I catch it with my hand, twisting it until he cries out. My head tilts back just slightly, letting him see the smug expression on my face. Recognition is like a wave as his mouth drops at the sight of my eyes. Oh good, he has heard of me. I have built a nice little reputation for myself in this ring.

"Damnit, Jamith. You didn't tell me I was fighting the red eyed bitch!"

Fuck. I shouldn't have let him see my eyes, I was too caught up in proving him wrong. Now, Kai will for sure know it's me. How many people on this side of the realm have red eyes? I summon my full strength to deliver one final blow to the man in front of me. He falls to the mat below with a thud, completely unconscious.

Reaching down, I grab the bag of coin from the stool next to the ring and rush my way through the crowd. I pass Kai quickly. His whiskey vanilla scent wrapping around me like a welcome home hug and it makes my body want to falter, but I have to get out of here.

"Skarlette," Kai calls after me.

I force myself not to answer, not to look back at his face. It would prove who I am and I can't stand the disappointed look I will see on his face, the sadness reflected in those navy eyes. The recognition that I am the evil spreading through the town.

The night's cool air is a welcome feeling on my sweat soaked skin as I bust through the tavern door and back out into the city. I'm walking quickly through the street, trying hard not to bring attention to myself while also getting as far away from the tavern as possible.

A hand clasps around my arm, yanking me into an alley-way. I let out a hiss and bare my fangs at my attacker. My shadows encase us, ready for me to take out the person willing to cause me harm.

Surprise washes over me like a cold shower when I see Jamith instead of Kai. "Don't scare me like that." I rip my arm from his grasp, putting much needed distance between us.

Jamith's eyes are wide as he stares at me, clearly shocked at what just happened. "I mean, I knew you were half fae and half vampire—but you've never shown me *them*." His voice trembles slightly. My shadows curl up the walls of the buildings beside us, hovering as they wait for their next command.

"Is this going to be a problem?" Arching one of my brows, I'm ready for him to run away, just like everyone else does.

He holds up his hands in surrender. "No, no problem at all."

"Good, now take me to your place," I purr.

I don't want to go to Jamith's tonight. I want to head back to my room at Hattie's and pretend to sleep like I do every morning from three to six, waiting to hear Hattie and Charles' footsteps on the floorboards. But right now, I need to get out of here. To get away from Kai and keep him off my mind.

Jamith gives me a wide grin as I hook my arm around his, heading off for his small loft above Mr. Wellchester's barn. I try to pretend I am into his touch when we arrive. Placing a few kisses to Jamith's lips, I try and summon my best noise of pleasure, but really my mind is reeling.

How long is Kai intending on staying in Vreilwreth? Why is he even here? The vision of Kai standing in Mrs. Laverns's wash house, spurred my desire. This time when Jamith slams himself into me, I moan. I imagine Kai's hands on me, grabbing my breasts. That thought alone has me completely coming undone as Kai's name slips from of my mouth before I can stop it.

"What was that?" Jamith pants.

"I was just saying, 'wow that was great'." The lie flows easily off my tongue.

"Yeah, it was." Jamith grins at me, proud of his work. He rolls over to his side, propping his head on his arm and looking at me with that puppy love look that I don't want to see from him. It makes my stomach sick to see him look at me like that.

Rolling away from his stare, I lay my hands under my head and pretend to go to sleep. I can't look at him, not after what I have just done. I pictured Kai while I was sleeping with someone else.

Once fully clothed, I jump from the loft, landing feet first on the barn floor. Jamith's snores come in a steady rhythm from the loft behind me as I disappear into the night, back to Hattie's washhouse, where I can run away from all of my problems. At least for the rest of the night.

# Chapter Six

## KAI

That was definitely Skarlette inside that fighting ring tonight. When the fighter had complained about the *'red eyed bitch'*, I had a tingling suspicion that it was her. But when she slipped past me, her heady vanilla scent wrapped around me and begged me to drink her in.

I chased after her, only to watch her leave with the bar man. Jamith, I think is his name. I hate it, but I am jealous of that man. It should have been me that Skarlette was walking with.

Heading back to my family's town house, a candle flickers

in Louissa's bedroom window.

The tip of my knuckle raps lightly on her door, but there is no response. "Louissa, I know you read father's letter today and I know you're not happy, but it's for the kingdom." I try to level with her, but still I get no answer. I sigh, heading to my bedroom and giving up for the night.

Laying in bed, I dream of crimson eyes. My neck starts to burn, but then turns into a different feeling altogether. It feels like euphoria. I want to drown in the feeling, over and over again. Skarlette's mouth pulls away, a grin sliding across her lips as she licks my blood from them.

My eyes fly open, my forehead covered in a cold sweat. Taking in large gulps of air, I try to help settle my mind as I rub at the two small, round scars on my neck. They have that ache that begs for her to taste from me again.

The sun peers through the window, forcing me up for the day. Today, I will hunt the streets for Skarlette.

My sister is already eating when I arrive in the dining room. Louissa looks tired, her fork pushing around the eggs on her plate as she stares at them with boredom. I can feel her disdain for me. She was so mad at me for not telling her, but I was so focused on Skarlette that it had completely spaced my mind.

"Louissa." I nod in her direction.

"Brother," she regards with a sharp tone.

Filling my plate, I take a seat my across from her. "You know I can't fix this. I'm as much of a pawn as you are." She refuses to look up at me, simply continues to push around the food on her plate.

"You know this wasn't father's idea. It was Ethan's!" She slams her fork down on the table, making it clatter with the plate and my body flinches. I am not used to Louissa being mad. Ethan? Sure. My dad? Definitely. But sweet little Louissa? Most definitely not.

"We have to do what is needed for the kingdom, Louissa." I was trying to ease her into it, but she makes it so hard with her stubbornness.

"Ethan controls everything and he thinks we are toys, Kai." Her tears are coming in hot, running down her cheeks and splashing onto the table.

"He is the prince, soon to be the king. We do what he says or we meet the same fate as his enemies. Why can't you see I'm trying to keep you safe." My hands fist around my fork, gripping it so tightly that I am bending it in half. Her eyes flick down to the now l shaped fork in my hands, going wide. "You'd be a lot safer here, married to Lord Veeling and not near Ethan or his games." My hand opens, letting the bent fork drop from my grasp. The clatter as it hits the table, echoes through the room.

Louissa stands, walking to my side and letting her hand rest on my shoulder. "But what of your fate, brother? While you try to save all of us, who is trying to save you?"

Louissa leaves the room, letting me stew with my thoughts. I was the one who had to save them from my demented brother. Skarlette's words whisper in my mind. *"A hero complex is the worst of them all. They think they are doing it for the good of everyone, but really they're no better than the one they call the villain."*

Shoving my plate aside, I slam my fist against the table in anger. I have to find Skarlette again. She is the only one who can help me now. Louissa is stubborn, not as stubborn as Skarlette, but that is probably where she learned it from. I need Skarlette to talk some sense into Louissa and myself. The fate of the kingdom depends on it.

My mind filters back to last night. Watching Skar in the ring, fighting that big brute and putting him in his place where he belonged. I'm sure she thought the hood hid her well, but I knew. My soul felt her—it called to her. When she bumped into me, her vanilla scent wrapped around me like a warm blanket. A welcome home.

I want nothing more than to bring Skarlette home and never let her leave again. But I know if I do that, I will be no better than my brother. I need to find reason within her.

# Chapter Seven

## SKARLETTE

My feet pump underneath me, dodging the tree roots that rise from the ground as they try their best to trip me, but I've memorized every one of them. The way they rise and fall across the ground. I run as fast as my legs will let me until I reach the clearing. Quietly, I approach a herd of elk. They graze in the clearing without a care in the world. If I were a simpler person, I would probably find them beautiful, but I was bred to be a hunter. I stalk closer and closer until one hears me. The animal's head whips around, its ears fluttering as it tries to find the predator, but it's already too late. I jump on the elk's back, listening as it wails. My teeth sink into its fur, drinking from it greedily, but it brings me no relief.

Before, it wouldn't have bothered me. But now that Kai is in the same city as me, it reminds me of what his blood tastes like. Animals that would once bring me a semblance of comfort, now taste like ash in my mouth. I need to find fae blood and that is going to cost me.

Leaving the clearing, I make my way down closer to the beach. The sun is setting low in the sky and night will soon be here as the night market begins to set up. Tents of reds and blues pop up on the open land between Vreilwreth and the dock. The night market deals with a lot of odd and peculiar requests some of the lords made. I had once witnessed a lord purchasing a whipping chain. Slaves had long since been outlawed, so I could only assume it was for bedroom pleasure. The night market is also the perfect place for a vampire in hiding to get a pint of fae blood without raising suspicions.

Night melts over Vreilwreth like a blanket and the flicker of candlelight comes with it. I weave through the cluster maze of vendor tents with a familiar ease, accustomed to its ways unlike those who try and navigate it for the first time. The market is set up in a way that will confuse anyone who doesn't know the lay out. This is done purposefully to keep the royals from collecting exuberantly high taxes on rare goods.

Coming to a stop in front of a deep crimson tent, I note that it almost matches the color of my eyes. The shopkeeper must have redyed the canvas, for it had never been this dark. Though I have been here before, it still doesn't feel right. Something about it makes the hair on the back of my neck stand up with unease.

"Vido," I call to the shopkeeper in greeting.

He greets me with a wide mustache covered smile. His slicked back, black hair shining under the lantern light and his hands sorting an array of bottles. "Ah, Lettie."

"You have something for your best customer?" My eyes scan over the table, pretending to look at the bone handled knives and other wares.

"Of course, of course." Vido pulls a crate from underneath one of his tables, rummaging down to the bottom before he pulls out a sheep skin flask. I can already smell the fae scented blood from where I stand. This one must have come from a woman. They always had a more floral scent than the men.

The leather bag of coin in my hand grows heavy as my hand itches to snatch the sheepskin flask from his grasp. "Thanks again, Vido."

"Skarlette. . ." His voice is serious. So serious, that it makes me uneasy. The only time I have ever heard him this serious was when he was being stiffed by a customer. "I don't know when I will be able to get you more. Prince Ethan is really sending out the hounds when it comes to us collecting. Last time, we had to tear down the tents a whole day early because he sent in the guards."

"I understand." My head bobs, but worry swirls in my gut. I could only live off of animal blood for a short time before I would need something stronger.

Shoving the sheepskin into my cloak, I weave my way back through the tents and out onto the street. My feet come to a halt when I smack right into the side of someone. I almost lift my head to see who it is when my body goes frigid.

"Pardon me." Kai's voice is irritated, as it should be when someone runs into you.

"Sorry," I blurt, keeping my hood down and my face hidden. I try to throw my voice into a calix accent, but fail miserably.

"You should be," Louissa barks, my body recoiling at her anger with a wince. Louissa had never spoken to me like that. She was like a sister.

I try to go around them and scurry off but Kai grabs

my arm, pulling me back. Heat radiates off of him, seeping down into my bones. My head turns slightly, my teeth bared, but he can't see them. Something about the feeling of his hand on my arm has me blurting out my next words before I can stop them.

"Not here." I order, still not showing my face. My brain filters through everyway I can try and get away from them, but his grip is tightening, almost punishingly. I am going to regret showing myself to him, but being this close has me doing things before I can even fully contemplate the consequences.

Kai's hand drops from my arm as I slowly peek from my hood, making eye contact with him. Louissa's gasp sounds next to him, but I don't look at her. I keep my attention focused solely on Kai, on his handsome features that beg my hand to touch them.

"Meet me at the wash house at nine o'clock sharp." I don't say another word before vanishing into the shadows. Maybe I could miss the meeting. Leave him alone in the washroom and flee to another city. Although I crave to be free, I want to see him again more than I want to flee.

I am standing in my bedroom, staring at the small clock on the wall. Waiting. For a moment, I contemplate darting out the window, deciding this whole thing is a terribly bad idea.

Cause it is.

But it's too late. A knock is already sounding at the door. "Come in." When Kai enters the room, I am taken by surprise. I half expected Louissa to come with him, but it's just him.

I feel overly exposed without my cloak and hood. There is nothing to hide me from the heat of his gaze. I am supposed to be a ghost. Someone he thought existed, but no longer did. Something that vanished in the shadows years ago.

"Skarlette," he says with relief and that sound pains me. I don't want to bring him this feeling, because I will hurt him again. There is no scenario where I will be able to come home and act like everything is okay.

"It's best if we keep our distance," I say uniformly. It's more to protect him than me. I can already smell him and it's taking everything in me not to taste him again. To feel that same feeling I did three years ago. I want to give into its calling—live up to my villainous ways. But I can't.

"Okay." His voice is soft, but I can see the excitement buzzing through him. "I thought you were gone."

I keep my voice emotionless. "I am gone. I am not the

sixteen year old girl you remember."

He moves across the floor slowly as the wood creaks beneath his weight. He stops in front of me, his hand rising and letting his finger trace over the scar on my face. The tenderness of it makes me shiver and my eyes close, afraid of him seeing the monster I truly am.

"What has the world done to you?" He whispers, his breath fanning over my face.

My voice shakes as I let the words pass my lips. "It's not what the world has done to me, but what I have done to it."

I can see what's about to happen as he leans in to kiss me. My head turns, his lips landing on my cheek and warming the skin beneath them. He can't know what I know. I have to hide it from him for as long as possible.

He takes the hint, stepping away from me, but the hurt is evident on his face. I have to. No matter how much I would have loved to feel his lips on my own, I have to do what is best for him and that means keeping distance between us.

"You make me weak, Kai." My mouth sets in a hard line. "You need to leave me be."

The hurt on his face quickly morphs into anger. "I can't do that, Skar." He huffs out a harsh laugh. "You see, the thing is, my brother sent me here to bring the chaos maker home. . . to bring them back to face justice for their crimes.

"You wouldn't dare." Panic starts to seep in. This meeting was such a bad idea. I should have never invited him here or shown him who I was.

Shadows dart out as panic rises inside me. They creep across the floor towards Kai, but he doesn't seem to mind. The room is darkening as the shadows move to snuff out any light they can find. I see the sorry look in his eyes. No—he couldn't. He wouldn't do this to me.

"I have to." His face is solemn. "I don't have a choice."

My hand slaps across his face, his head turning from the force. His head tilts as he turns back to me and a cocky smile comes across his face.

"I was going to say we could do this the easy way, but it looks like you have chosen the hard way."

I turn to head out the window, but it's too late. I feel the iron's hot metal as he locks the shackle on my wrist. When had he found time to pull those out? I hiss as my flesh begins to sting, my pale skin already blistering red from the heat of the iron burning my very flesh. While I may only be half fae, the iron still burns like it would a full blooded faerie.

It's then that I notice the gloves upon his hands. Special healer magic infused, leather gloves that keep his hands safe from the iron shackles. If I would have been paying more attention to my surroundings, I would have noticed sooner.

We stare at each other, locked in a battle of wills. I know he wants to see the tears. To see that a part of me is still redeemable, but I need him to hate me more. Stuffing the pain in the back of my mind, I continue to stare at him, no emotions and no words.

"I loved you once." He shackles my other wrist, yanking on the chain connecting the two and tugging me out the door. Those four words hurt me more than the iron ever could.

Down the stairs, Hattie watches me get toted out. Tears stream down her face and blubbering sobs follow us out the door towards a carriage.

"I wonder if they know you used them. They loved you like their own and yet you're the. . . what was it you called yourself again? The 'villain' in their story and that's exactly how you want it." He is trying to throw my own words back at me, but I won't apologize.

The world has made me this way. They created the monster I am and I won't change because someone gives me a sob story. I live a better life as the villain, than I would if I were to follow their rules. I have everything I could ever need.

I stay silent, refusing to take the bait. He is trying to make me angry, make me lash out at him and I won't do it.

The carriage rolls away from Hattie's washhouse, rumbling down the road and towards the royal townhouse. People emerge from their homes, hoping to get a look at the *Il Furfante*. They want to see the monster the prince has captured.

When the carriage arrives in front of the tall gray building-what I can assume is their royal townhouse-Kai steps out first. He waits impatiently as I bunch my cape, hoping to not trip and fly out on my face. I ignore his outstretched hand, lowering myself out of the carriage and following him to the door with my head held high. He may have me shackled, but I will not be seen as weak.

Inside the house, green carpet softens our step. The entryway has stairs going up and another set going down. I have a feeling I know exactly where I am headed, and it sure as hell isn't towards a nice warm bed upstairs. He leads me to the stairs and down into the basement. The air is damp with moisture, a cold chill settling over my skin. Even the roaring fires upstairs don't warm this portion of the house.

I hear the jingle of a key and the locking of the door behind me. "Kai—" I start, but when I turn around, he is already gone. I am once again in a cage made of my own destruction.

Hours, or maybe even a whole day has passed before the basement door opens. A candle dances down the stairs, followed by a girl in her nightgown.

"Skarlette," Louissa's voice calls out.

"You shouldn't be down here." My voice cracks with tiredness, while Kai has sent small rations of blood, it isn't enough for me to feel well.

She takes a seat in front of me, setting the candle between us. It flickers and dances, the wax dripping down it's side. I stare at it, refusing to look her in the eyes. I know the look I will get. That look of disappointment they all carry when they see me.

Tears burst from Louissa's eyes, streaming down her cheeks and splashing to the floor. "They want me to marry Lord Veeling."

"Probably for the best. He could give you a happy life, Lou. And you would be far away from Ethan." She is acting like I'm not a monster, like I never left Ruellia.

"But I don't want to." She sniffles as she scoots closer to me, resting her head on my shoulder. "We have missed you."

"You shouldn't," I tell her softly.

"I know you want to be the villain. I won't ask you to change, but don't ask me to hate you." All I can do is rest my cheek against her head. I can't find it in myself to be mean to her. Her crying has stopped and we seem to have come to some sort of truce. We sit for a long while in silence before we hear the creak of the basement door.

"Stay away from her." I am not sure who he is talking to, Louissa or me.

"She isn't a monster!" Louissa wails, running up the stairs and past her brother.

I can just barely make out Kai's shadow behind the candlelight, but I can feel his eyes on me. It sends a mix of emotions swirling in my stomach. I want him to hate me, but I also want to tell him the truth so bad. My hand itches to reach out, to try and grab hold of him. Just when I have the courage to try, he speaks up.

"We leave here in two days," he announces before he turns on his heal and I hear the door shut again. No blood for me today it seems.

Two days is dangerous. But three days, and then the whole carriage ride? Impossible. I reach in my cloak, pulling out the sheepskin flask they failed to find on me and let the last of the cool liquid slide down my throat. Instantly I feel better, feel more awake and more myself. But there isn't enough. It is a mere drop in the bucket so to speak. I will need more and soon if I am going to survive the carriage ride home.

Day two comes and goes, without Kai ever making an appearance. I itch to get on the road and head back to Ruellia. At least there, I would know I had my ration of blood. It is so hard to tell time down here. No windows and no light shine in to let me know the time of day. I merely keep time by the rations of bread and salted pork that are brought to me by guards.

Sitting in the far corner with my knees pulled up to my chest, I wait for one of them to bring my third breakfast since Kai told me we were leaving, but the faerie that comes down the stairs isn't a guard.

"Get up. We are leaving," Kai barks at me.

With the delay in travel, I doubt I can make it back to Ruellia in one piece.

# Chapter Eight

## KAI

Louissa's wedding is extravagant. The lord has gone to great lengths to prepare such a ceremony on short notice. I apologize profusely for rushing their wedding, but I want to get our prisoner back to Ruellia as soon as possible. I have found a carriage and some coachmen willing to take us back home without having to wait for another ship to be built.

We stand in the small church of Vreilwreth, Louissa in a large white dress and Lord Veeling in his suit. Sitting in one of the pews is Skarlette, her hands chained in front of her as she tries to keep her skin off the iron. A part of me feels sorry for the pain the shackles are causing her, but I know if she doesn't have them on, she will flee.

I motion for the priestess to get this show moving along. Enough people are here to witness my sister's betrothal to him, and I need to get back to Ruellia as soon as possible. The vows are exchanged in haste, the entire church clearing out only an hour after this whole thing started. I hoped Louissa would feel more comfortable here before I left, but we haven't the time. My sister's face glares at me, clearly unhappy with the quickness of today's events.

Giving her a hug, I place a quick peck to her temple. "Make this place your home, Lou."

"I barely even know the man," she huffs, her eyes darting to the corner and giving her new husband a glance.

I hate to leave my sister here with such unease, but I have a villain to take home. I will have to send letters later to check in on how my sister is settling in.

Following the newlywed's carriage across the town and back to Lord Veeling's home, I let my footman grab my bags, and a small sack that contains Skarlette's personal belongings that the maids have delivered from the royal townhouse.

Louissa stands on the porch of her new home, her large

wedding dress hanging over the edges of the steps as the wind blows her veil. The delicate fabric catches on a spot of chipped wood. My hand reaches for the fabric, gently unhooking it before it can tear.

Louissa's voice is soft. "She doesn't deserve this, Kai."

"The girl we remember is no longer in there, Lou. She has done terrible things—things no one can come back from." I look back to the carriage where Skarlette sits inside.

"She is still in there somewhere, I know it."

"Who is the hopeful one now?" I tease her, remembering the way she would tell me not to pine over a woman who had disappeared.

She crosses her arms and harrumphs at me. Clearly she is determined to be a hypocrite today.

My arms wrap around Louissa, squeezing her in one last hug before I leave her here. "Send me letters and tell me that you are okay."

"Of course, and please deliver my letters to her." She doesn't name the person she is talking about, but I know exactly who she means.

Climbing inside the carriage, I take a seat across from my prisoner. Her head rests against the wall, her eyes closed and her breathing slow. My eyes linger on her, watching as her chest rises and falls. My hand reaches forward, brushing her silver hair from her face. I gasp with surprise when a zap courses through my finger tip at the touch of our skin.

Her eyes snap open, her red irises, glowing as she stares back at me. My hand snaps back next to my body, coming to rest on the seat next to me. Turning my attention back out the window, I watch the village grow sparse and then disappear altogether, turning into countryside that blurs past us as the horses run full speed ahead.

My eyes shift, taking in the sunken look of Skarlette's skin through the corner of my eye. She needs blood, and soon.

We have been taught from a young age about vampires. They are our sworn enemies, while also being our strongest allies in trade, it is quite the conundrum. We had once been peaceful with them, but the vampires wanted to control us, make us their slaves and use our powers to their advantages. They wanted to rule over the land as one continent under one ruler. The fae didn't like the thought of being under vampiric control, and so here we are. Trade partners by day, enemies by night.

We are also taught about the vampire's need to feed. A vampire could survive off fae blood for up to a week, depending on the amount they consumed. They could live off a mate's blood for longer, but the timeline was a little blurry. Vampires who chose to consume animal blood would only last a few days.

The vampires are good at keeping their weaknesses a secret, but we have learned a few things here and there. Having Skarlette with us helped, but she is still so different from the rest with her being a half breed. Where the vampires preferred night, Skarlette has no preference. It is like she has gotten the best of both worlds.

Looking at her now, I can see the toll of what being locked away has done to her. I am no better than my brother. I locked her away in a cage, angry with her for keeping her emotions hidden from me. Now here I am in a carriage, forcing her back into the very prison she had run from.

Skarlette whimpers, drawing my full attention towards her.

"What's wrong." I try to keep a bored tone, not willing to show her my own emotions.

"It's nothing," she says in a low growl that rumbles across the carriage. Her hands cup her face, showing me the pain she is trying to hide.

"What caused the scar on your face?" I hope my thoughts are wrong. If that scar had been made by iron, she probably doesn't feel the pain of it until she goes without blood.

"Doesn't matter." Her teeth grit together, fangs digging

into the skin of her lips.

"Damn it, tell me!" I roar at her.

"A fucking iron axe!"

Shit, shit, shit. The pain of iron wounds without the help of a healer, would drive any faerie mad. The blood helps her to hide the pain, but now she is starving and the pain is coming back to her as if it had just happened today. I need to think quick, I'm already her captor, I don't need to be a monster yet too.

"Let me give you blood," I offer.

"No," she groans. "Any blood but yours."

Her words are like a slap to my face. She would drink anyone else's blood but not mine? What the fuck is wrong with my blood? I'm just as good as anyone else out there.

"Fine, than starve." I ignore the rest of her whimpers even though each one is like a slice to my heart.

The road to Ruellia makes the carriage ride unbearable. We rumble down the road, seeming to hit every rock and root on the way.

The carriage jerks, making me fall forward in my seat and my hands land on the wall behind Skarlette for stability. I should push away, but I am entranced with her being so close. Her eyes look up at me, darting to the pulse in my neck then back to my eyes. I want to offer again, to tell her to take my blood, but she already said no. She is too stubborn to take it and I am too stubborn to offer it again.

Breathing deep, I take in her sweet scent. My eyes catch on the way her own pulse flutters in her neck. My body begs for me to taste her, but I hold strong. In my mind, I know that once I do kiss Skarlette, it will all be over. I will be ruined for any other woman. Shit, if I am being honest with myself, I already am ruined. Even with Skarlette mad and wishing I didn't exist, I want her. No—I need her more than I need air to breathe.

Shoving myself back onto my seat, I move to the far side and put as much distance between Skarlette and I as possible. My hand clenches in a fist on my thigh in annoyance.

I hate all of this. I hate being the one to let my family down. I hate being the one to let Louissa down, but most of all I hate to be the one to let Skarlette down.

Skarlette's gaze looks out the window, her fangs are peeking out as she bites into her lower lip and it makes my neck tingle, like the scars want her to bite me again. The sensation is odd, but the feeling of wanting is more.

I don't remember much about the night Skarlette bit me. I only remember the feeling of something piercing my skin and then the world going dark. I woke up a few hours later and she was gone. Every day since, I have worked to be stronger for her. I know she needed me to stand up for her when she was a child, but I tried to convince myself that my family wasn't capable of such cruelty.

My thoughts turn quiet when I feel the carriage slowing to a halt. Peering out the window, I can see the dark sky and the moon that hangs like a sliver in it. Our driver has pushed as far as he can before having to stop for rest. The horses are tired and we can not go any farther without putting them in danger.

The small inn that sits on the edge of town is glaringly bright white with light purple shutters. Flowers line the front windows and a black sign with white letters sits above the door. It almost looks unrealistic.

I push the door open, listening as a tiny bell chimes above the doorway when we enter the establishment. A tall man with a large mustache stands behind a desk in front of us, his smile warm as he greets us.

"Welcome. How can I help you today?" I can see the incredulous look Skarlette gives him out of the corner of my eye.

"We have traveled a long ways and need a few rooms for the night." Taking out a bag of coin, the royal emblem makes the man's eyes light up with excitement.

"Your Highness." He bows. "I did not recognize it was

you. It has been quite some time since the young prince has visited us." The man flips through several books that sit on the desk in front of him, his smile faltering more and more the longer he flips between the pages.

"What is it?" Skarlette barks at him, making him startle.

"I am afraid I only have two rooms available tonight." The man looks between me, Skarlette and the two coachman behind me.

"It's alright. Give us the keys and we will sort it out when we get up there." I lay my palm out flat in his direction as he places the room keys in it.

Our group ascends the stairs, walking until we find the first room available. Inside sits two single beds, the other room across the hall sharing only one larger bed.

Skarlette folds her arms across her chest, an annoyed look crossing over her face. I turn to talk to the groomsmen, but they have already taken the other room and shut the door behind them.

My shoulders shrug as I chuckle, but Skarlette isn't amused. "I guess this is our room."

"Great," she says with so much disgust that it physically pains me to hear it.

Once inside, we quietly shuck off our boots before crawling into the single bed and laying there like statues. Neither one of us dares to move and disturb the other. Tension swirls around us, making the air crackle with unspoken words.

Sleep consumes me before I can find the courage to break the silence.

The carriage is finally rolling into Ruellia on our fourth day of travel. Skarlette is looking worse for wear, but for some reason I feel numb to what she wants right now. I need to get her in the castle, see my brother, and get some rest. Four days of being this close to her is driving me absolutely mad, especially when we spent most of the ride in silence.

The carriage rolls to a stop outside of the castle. "Welcome back to Ruellia, Skarlette."

Ethan stands at the top step, waiting for us. When Skarlette takes too long, I reach in, grabbing her hand and pulling her out of the carriage.

"I should have known." Ethan's voice runs up my spine like a snake, reminding me of his cruel nature. I hold onto Skarlette's upper arm, guiding her along with me. "I can take her from here, brother."

I tug her towards me. "That's okay. I can take her to the

dungeons."

"Oh, she's not going to the dungeons. . . when she has her very own cage right in the throne room." My eyes dart to Skarlette, but her face is like stone. No emotions can be found, even in her eyes.

Ethan takes hold of Skarlette's other arm, yanking her from my grasp and leading her away from me. The further away she walks, the more unsettled I feel.

What have I just done?

# Chapter Nine

## SKARLETTE

My cage is exactly how I remember. The gold bars are iron infused, so any touch of my skin against its warm metal will singe into me. It sits on the left side of the throne room, adjacent to the throne itself. It reminds me of a cage someone might try and keep a bird in, with it's dome top, but big enough to fit a person. Oddly enough, It does seem smaller than I remember, but I guess that is what growing up does to you.

I sit patiently in the very center, knees pulled to my chest, somehow having managed to convince one of the wait staff to bring me wine, which helps ease the pain of my scar. I was put back on my ration of one cup of blood every other day, enough to keep me alive, but too little to give me much strength.

Ethan enters the room, a long black fabric hanging from his hands. I hate to think of who that is for, but I already know it is probably for me. He does love it when I put on a show for them. He loves dressing me in frivolous clothes that bares my skin to others. It is a skill he learned from his father who did the same thing the minute I turned fifteen.

"I have a present for you." He holds up a black dress, its skirt falling all the way to the floor, a slit in the fabric reveals a gap that will travel all the way up to my hip. "Isn't that nice of me?"

I curl my lip in disgust. "You shouldn't have."

"You should be grateful. I could have provided you with no clothes at all. I am sure our guests would rather stare at your naked body," he snaps, his patience with me wearing thin.

Reaching his hand inside my cage, he runs the back of it against my cheek. "You will make such a pretty prize."

Someone calls for the prince, making his hand abruptly jolt away from me as he gives me one last look over. Something about the way he is looking at me is different than before. Like he see's me differently. He turns, walking away from me without another word.

A maid arrives shortly after with a guard in tow. He argues with her about unlocking my cage, trying to convince her I can undress here, but thankfully she refuses. She guides me to a guest room where she helps me dress in the gown and do my hair. She curls and pokes at the hair on my head, ending with a look that is half up–half down, with ringlets of silver running over my shoulders.

The mirror reflects back at me; a woman I don't recognize. The dress barely covers my breasts, and the slit exposes most of my hip. My hair is perfect and the maid even added a layer of kohl to my eyes. If I was going to a ball instead of being locked in my cage like some show exhibit, I might have felt pretty.

I stare in the mirror for too long before the maid reminds me it is time to go. I can see the pity in her eyes as she leads me back to my gilded cage.

Back in the throne room, inside of my cage, I can do nothing but sit and wait. Wait for whatever they have planned. I watch as servants bring in the Ruellia flowers, their purple color bringing life to the gray and white of the castle.

It takes the castle staff no time at all to have the throne

room ready and filled with people. Guests from every edge of our realm. I even see Louissa and her new husband, Lord Veeling. It feels like a lifetime since I have seen her, when really it has only been a week. They must have left not long after us if they were arriving so soon.

My attention draws towards the entryway as Kai enters with a beautiful blonde haired woman on his arm, a sting of jealousy courses through me at the sight. I will have to tamp down my emotions if I am going to live in this castle again. Moving towards the edge of my cage, I wrap my hands around the bars and hiss from the pain.

"Oh look, it likes to cause itself pain," one lord announces to another with a chuckle.

"This is great entertainment, watching this foul inbred thing writhe in pain," another responds.

Their words are nothing to me. You can't hurt someone who has fully accepted that they will be hated no matter what. That's the best part about being the villain. I know they will be disappointed in me. I don't have a false sense of hope.

A younger man comes closer to my cage, studying me. His eyes are completely black, shining like onyx gems. They are unlike anything I have ever seen before. His hand reaches inside my cage, sliding up the slip of my waist until his hand lands on my bare hip. I step back, but his hand holds me in place with unnatural force. My stomach twists with an uneasy feeling. The contact of his hand on my bare skin is making me want to puke.

"Let go of me." I try to shake him off, but his grip is like steel.

He leans in close to my cage, the iron having little to no affect on him. "When you are ready to be free of this cage, you only need call me." A shiver slithers its way across my skin. My eyes zero in on the pointed ears. If he is fae, how are the bars not having an effect on him?

What does he mean? Who is he? He must be a vampire if the iron has no affect on him. Maybe he is like me, a half breed. . . but the iron still affects me. I want him to come back so I can ask him questions, but he has already disappeared amongst the crowd.

The night wares on. People gawk at me like I'm someone's prized possession. Kai spends the whole party on the farthest side of the room, as far away from me as he can get. Which is exactly what I want. If that were true, then why was I having such a hard time of convincing myself that?

Louissa approaches my cage, sending a bread roll flying between the bars. "Here, eat," she whispers out the corner of her mouth. I quickly grab the peace of food and wrap my hand around it.

Slipping away when her husband calls out for her to get away from the cage, she pretends she is just looking. I break off small pieces of the bread, stuffing them into my mouth when no one is looking. My stomach grumbles, begging me to fill it with a delicious meal. While blood gives me power, the faerie part of me still needs the sustenance of food.

"Menace," Kai greets, sliding up to my cage with the blonde girl still on his arm.

Staring at him, I don't say a word. I don't want to speak about his betrayal right now. It is still too raw and we have company. The girl on his arm grows impatient with our game. Her eyes roll into the back of her head before shooting me with an icy glare.

"I want to dance, Kai," she whines.

"Why don't you get something to eat before we dance? I will catch up with you in a minute." She doesn't seem pleased when Kai won't follow her, but she does as he says.

His eyes slide down my body, taking in every inch this dress isn't covering. His navy eyes seem to darken and his tongue licks over his bottom lip. The action lights my soul on fire, like it's been starved of oxygen and he just blew the life back into me. Gripping onto the bars tightly, I let the pain remind me that I don't want him. That everything I have done over the last three years was to protect him from me. Kai has always been the sweet one, but he is a whole new person after the last three years. I almost don't even recognize him. He could be cruel now. The thought of him taking out our enemies is delicious and exciting, but I can't have it no matter how much my body aches for it.

"He picked it for me. Don't you like it?" I twirl around, his eyes following my movement before they land on my raw palms which I quickly fist to hide my wounds. The pain of my fingertips ghosting over the raw skin sends a silent scream through my brain.

"Why do you hold the bars when you know it only brings you pain?" His face holds a pitying look that makes me want to punch him in the face. It is my pain to hold, not his. He doesn't need to pity me.

"The pain reminds me that I am alive. It reminds me they can't hurt me more than I can hurt myself." Laying my hands out flat in front of me, I show him the angry skin. "And it reminds you that you did this to me. You brought me back here and let him stuff me in my cage." The last of my words are cruel and I know it, but the way his face hardens tells me they did their job.

"You know I didn't have a choice," Kai says firmly.

I bare my teeth at him with a hiss. "There is always a

choice."

"Is he bothering you, pet?" Ethan coos, making my stomach turn sour at the new nickname.

"Don't call her that," Kai snaps.

"Still have a soft spot for the monster, I see." Ethan looks between us trying to gauge what exactly is happening between his brother and I.

Ethan's eyes narrow on Kai's neck before an incredulous laugh escapes him, making both Kai and I jump. Worry instantly slithers its way through my veins. Does Ethan know? If he does, will he tell Kai?

"I see now. You let her drink from you." He shakes his head, continuing to laugh. "You thought this monster would actually love you?"

"That is not what happened. I bit your brother and left him for dead, like the monster I am." My words seem to only add to the glee in Ethan's eyes.

"Even now, you two cover for each other. You did it as children too." Then I see the spark in Ethan's eyes. "No fucking way."

"Don't say it." I silently beg, hoping Ethan will see the plea in my eyes.

"You two are mates, aren't you?" I gulp down the lump of anxiety in my throat. This isn't how I wanted Kai to find out.

"Are you crazy? Of course we aren't." Kai is exasperated with this conversation. "Tell him he is crazy, Skarlette."

Kai is about to be so mad at me. I should lie. . . tell Ethan he is crazy, but I can't keep the secret any longer. Maybe letting it out will keep me safe. Maybe telling him now will make him so angry, he will finally hate me enough to see that he is better off without me.

I don't meet Kai's eyes.

"Menace," Kai growls the nickname, sending a jolt of need straight to my core. "We aren't mates, right?"

I still don't say anything. Kai reaches his hand in my cage, grabbing me by my throat and brings me as close as he can without burning my face off.

"Kiss me." His hand squeezes slightly and a sick part of me loves it.

"You don't want this, Kai," I whisper as a single tear slides down my cheek.

"I need to know." He pushes his face closer, close enough so our lips can connect through the slits between bars. His lips press hard to mine and the world implodes around us. The mate bonds inside us sing to each other. He groans, biting down on my lip before pulling away and releasing my neck from his grasp. His face is mad, just like I hoped.

Kai walks away before any of us can say another word. The blonde woman meets him halfway, batting her lashes as he brushes her off, heading straight out the doors of the throne room. Good, this is exactly what should be happening. Now he can stay as far away as possible. But I can't help the ache in my chest as he storms away, the way my soul wants him to come back and tell me this is everything he has ever wanted.

"Well I guess that wasn't the answer he wanted. He doesn't want the monster after all." Ethan chuckles, clearly amused by my suffering. "You see, I am not like my brother. I like my women feisty." Ethan's smile is cruel, just like his soul.

The night slowly dies down with no further appearances from Kai. He is either really unhappy that I have kept this secret from him or he really doesn't want to be mated to a monster like me.

As the last maid leaves the throne room, I sit back down on the cool cage floor and curl around myself, there is nothing else I can do. I wipe the tears from my cheeks, my palms stinging from the salty water that touches my burns.

I may be the villain, I may like being the villain, but I am still a person with emotions. Still a person capable of feeling love and loss.

# Chapter Ten

## KAI

My hand sifts through the strands of my hair as I gaze out at the night sky above me with the twinkling of firelight in the village below. I am having a hard time believing that Skarlette has kept this secret from me for the last three years. She had to have realized when she drank my blood that we were mates, and still she chose to leave. She knew that if I found out, I would protect her to the ends of the world. She chose to leave me behind, because she is yet another person who doesn't want or need me.

"Kai," my brother calls.

He is the last person I want to see right now. He will use this information against us. I wouldn't be surprised if he sent one of us away so we don't have access to each other. Knowing my brother, he will be as cruel as possible with this information.

"There you are, I thought I'd find you lurking here." Ethan takes a seat beside me on the roof top. His clothes are disheveled and he obviously had a good time at the party tonight.

This is my favorite place to go to get away from it all. It is quiet up here, and I have the perfect view of Ruellia. It feels like a lifetime ago when Skarlette would join me up here and we would talk about what life had in store for us. She always knew her life wouldn't amount to much and I wanted to change everything for her.

"What do you want?" I grumble.

"I'm going to offer the little monster a chance to come out of her cage. If she works for me again, that is." I wait for the catch. It's never this simple with my brother. "And you are going to get married."

"You know I can't. I have a mate."

"Yes, a mate you can't even be with. She is an abomination and that will not sit right if one of the fae princes is mated to a half breed." My temper rumbles under the surface. I know he is right, but Skarlette isn't an abomination to me. She is my beautiful menace.

I can't stand to sit here for another second and listen to him talk. Rising from the rooftop, I bid my brother farewell, walking away from my him and what was once my favorite spot. Just like everything, my brother has ruined it for me. Making my way down the hall, down the stairs, and into the throne room, I find Skarlette. The candles are all doused for the night, the entire room dark but a sliver of moonlight coming through one of the windows. The light illuminates her silver hair as it drapes over her legs.

Her lithe body is sitting in the very center of her prison, legs hugged to her chest and face buried in her arms. The slit on her dress has her entire left leg exposed, all the way up to her hip. Being this close to her, now that we have kissed, the mate bond surges, wanting me to put my hands on her skin. To free her from that cage. To tell her I am a fool for running away earlier, but my brain reminds me that she is the one who left me first. Plus, freeing her from that cage will not only get me in trouble, but it will hurt her far worse than keeping her in there.

My mind goes back to her burnt palms and that's when it happens. Before my very eyes, my own palms begin to glow, heat radiating off them. I can't believe it after all these years, my powers are finally showing themselves.

I am a healer.

Creeping closer to the cage, I try not to scare her. "Skar," I whisper.

Her head rises slightly, her eyes sunken into her head with rings of dark black circles around them. The dark kohl that lined her eyes earlier is now running down her cheeks. Her fangs peek out from between her lips and her hair is a mess. It is like I am looking at the ghost of Skarlette. The strong and courageous villain who carried out bad deeds for others is replaced with a girl who is broken and hurt.

"What," she croaks, her throat dry.

"Give me your hand," I say, holding out my own in her direction.

She hesitates for a moment, before slowly reaching her hand towards mine. I take hold of it, pressing it between my hands. A soft glow illuminates her cage as my hands heal hers. I'm careful to keep her hand steady so as to not burn her again.

"Your power is healing?" She stares at her hands, where her palms were once red and raw, they are now smooth and pale.

"I guess so." I am just as amazed as she. The crackling of power in my veins has never shown itself to me until tonight. I remember begging the goddess for my powers, to make themself known like everyone else's.

"How long have you known?"

I give a small laugh. "Since right now."

"That explains a lot, actually."

"What do you mean?"

"When I bit you three years ago, I felt so rejuvenated after. It was like I was a whole new person. The mate bond was in there, so I figured that's all it was, but from all the stories I've heard over the years, no one has felt that good after drinking from their mate. Though, it makes sense now that you are a healer, your blood was healing me."

I let her confession settle. She had felt so much from drinking my blood, and still she left me there. The anger resurfaces like a storm inside of me. How could she have left me after all of that?

"Why did you do it?"

"Do what?" She asks, but when I meet her eyes, I can tell she knows what I am talking about. "I bit you cause I was angry. I didn't want you following me around like I was a pet on a leash—but then when I felt the mate bond sing to me through your blood, I knew I couldn't stay. I'm not supposed to have a mate. You don't deserve to be tied down to a mate that will bring you so much shame."

"You could never bring me shame." Resting my head against her bars, I forget for a moment that they are made of iron. My skin hisses as the iron scalds me.

Rocking back on my heels, I position myself farther away from the cage. Her hand slides through, her palm resting against my cheek.

"I will not stop being a monster. Even with our bond, I will not stay here and take the lashings they will doll out to me," she whispers.

"I know."

She pulls her hand back in the cage and instantly, I miss her touch, the coolness of her skin against the heat of my own. "You can't free me. It will only get you in trouble."

"Ethan is going to offer you a deal. You can be free of the cage, but you will have to work for him again and I have to marry." Silence wraps around us as the reality of our situation sinks in.

"I will take his offer." Her quick decision pangs an ache in my chest. She so easily gave me up to be free. She just said she would not stop being a monster, I just wasn't quite yet ready to be thrown under the wagon like that.

"Menace, you can—"

"I am so glad to hear it." Ethan's voice echoes off the throne room walls.

"Don't make her do this." Taking a stand as my brother approaches, I try to keep myself between him and her.

"Too late, she has already said she accepts." Ethan crosses over to the cage, unlocking Skarlette and letting her out.

He sneers. "You can have your old room in the attic."

"She can stay in mine," I blurt out without thinking. Both of their heads whip in my direction, staring at me with bewilderment.

"She will do no such thing, you are engaged to be wed. That would be highly inappropriate."

"It's okay, Kai." Her hand rests on my arm, giving me the comfort of her cold touch. "I will take my old room. Anything is better than the cage."

"I will walk you there."

Ethan doesn't protest this time, just waves us off like we are some sort of annoyance. Skarlette and I walk side by side down the halls, making our way up to the highest point of my family's castle. Arriving at the little attic door, we hesitate. On the other side, Skarlette will find a room full of boxes of items long forgotten. Amongst that stuff, she will find a pile of blankets in a very far corner where Skarlette had curled up as a child.

Her hand twists the knob slowly. She steps into the room, taking a look at the sad and decrepit area around her.

"Thank you. I should let you get to it."

I can see what she is trying to do. She wants to shut me out. Ignore the mate bond that is running through our veins. But I am not going to let her do that. No matter how evil she thinks herself to be, I want to give her my love.

"Menace," I growl at her.

She spins around, taken aback by the sudden irritation in my voice.

"Don't you dare think for one minute that I am going to let you walk into that room without marking you as mine." I stalk closer towards her.

"That's not fair," she whimpers. "You get to mark me and then be married. Marking me will keep me from ever finding someone for myself."

"Exactly, because you're mine." I grab her face in my hands, lowering my lips to hers and consuming her.

She moans into my mouth as my tongue swoops in. I purposefully nick my lip with one of her fangs, so she can drink. I may not be able to marry her, but I will provide her with the blood she needs to survive. I move from her mouth, down her neck and to her collarbone. The taste of her is like a drug. I need more. My body vibrates with the urge to bend her over and claim her in more than one way.

"Kai, stop," she says, pushing at my chest and waking me

out of my animalistic urges.

Taking a step back, my breathing is ragged. It feels as though I have been starved for her all my life and now I have finally gotten a taste, a taste of what I need.

"You should go." She pushes me out the door, closing it as soon as I am across the threshold. I can't stop the smile spreading across my face, because I know I affect her too, it's why she pushed me out so quick.

Leaving her room behind me, I make my way down the hall and back to my own room. I want to turn around and head back. I need it in my very soul to be close to her. But I don't turn around. I keep heading down the hall to where my dark blue room sits. Falling onto the bed, my eyes focus on the ceiling above. Skarlette would like this bed. It would be comfier than the stack of blankets on the wood floor of the attic, but I know if I go to her and ask her to sleep in here, she will refuse.

My mind replays the memory of her lips on my own as sleep washes over me.

# Chapter Eleven

## SKARLETTE

**M**y hands press against Kai's back, shoving him out the door. I quickly lock it behind him, taking a seat on the worn out blankets on the floor. My fingertips brush against my lips as the memory of Kai's mouth on my own haunts them. If I hadn't stopped him, he would have made sure to mark me enough for no man to ever touch me again.

Something far more haunting swirls in my mind. How could I be capable of loving someone when I was still too mad at the world for the way they treated me? How could someone love me when I was burning rage and nothing else?

Tomorrow, I will get my job from Ethan and make sure to stay as far away from Kai Eveningglow as I can. I need time to think and get myself together. It will be easy to avoid him if I stay busy. At least, that's what I convince myself before I try to get some rest.

"You will be accompanying my brother this morning. He has some business to attend to in the village and I have a name for you." Prince Ethan slides the piece of paper with his next victim's name in my hand. The paper is yellowed, and Ethan's hand writing hasn't gotten any better over the recent years. "You know what it is you have to do. He owes me money and I don't like waiting."

I read the name quickly, balling up the paper and throwing it into the fire on my way out the door. I made it a habit long ago to remember the names and not have a single speck of evidence on me. Even if I knew I would not get in trouble, it was for the best.

Entering a carriage with Kai is the farthest thing from staying away from him. His whiskey scent lingers in every corner and I'm unable to be more than a few feet away from him. The bond and my own raging hormones urge me to get closer to him, to climb in his lap and let him envelope me. I stay on the opposite side of the carriage as far down the seat as I can get. I beg for it to be a swift ride into town, where I can manage to go off on my own for the rest of the day.

The carriage rumbles down the road, hoofbeats pounding to the beat of my heart. I can't help myself when my eyes flick up to Kai. It is like my eyes have been attached to a magnet and he is the other piece.

His voice grumbles towards me. "Menace, if you don't stop looking over here like that, we aren't going to last long."

I force my eyes to look out the window, to watch the hills as they pass us by. "I don't know what you're talking about."

He scoffs, offended I would try and play off my stares. "We are trapped in this carriage together, I can smell you as much as you can smell me."

I pull my hood over my head, hiding my face and crimson cheeks from him, hoping that if I just ignore him, all the feelings and tension will go away. Keeping my face towards the scenery for the duration of our ride into town, I count down the seconds until I am out of this carriage.

The carriage has barely rolled to a stop before I flee as quickly as possible, darting down an alleyway.

Evan Charles. The name repeats over and over in my head. Ethan said he doesn't want him dead, but he wants me to send a message. So, a message I will send.

I make my way to the closest tavern. The easiest place to gather information. Between the drunk patrons and a bar keep who will happily give me the information for the right amount of coin, it is the perfect place to get information on my victim.

"Javier," I greet the bar keep. The tavern is dimly lit, but I can see clearly thanks to vampire sight.

"Skarlette. How good it is to see you again." The large man smiles at me.

Setting a bag of coin down on the bar, I show him I mean business. This isn't just a friendly house call.

"I'm looking for Evan Charles." At that, Javier's face downturns.

"I don't think that's a good idea." Javier pushes the bag of coin back in my direction.

"You know I don't have a choice. Ethan has given me the name and if I want to stay out of my gilded cage, then I will obey." Javier nods, he knows what it is like to have to stay in the prince's good graces.

"At least take Kai with you. Evan knows the prince is coming for him. Has hired himself some bodyguard." I snort at that. I don't need anyone protecting me and some fae bodyguard doesn't scare me.

"I won't be doing that. I don't need Kai to rescue me. I'm not a damsel."

"The old Jenkins house." At that, my stomach turns sour.

The old Jenkins farmhouse brought back terrible memories. It was the first time I had to kill someone. Ethan was there to make sure I had done the job right. When I hesitated, Ethan screamed at me, telling me I would never leave my cage again if I didn't kill this man. I had cried for a weak after that. I was only fifteen years old. In our practically immortal lives, I was just a baby.

I turn to leave, but a familiar pair of eyes are watching me from a dark corner of the room. I sit down across from the strange man, my eyes roving over his tan skin and short black hair.

"What are you?" I whisper.

"I'm just like you," he says, white teeth flashing with his smile.

"There isn't anyone like me. Plus, the iron affects me, it didn't seem to hurt you any." I have more questions than answers at this point.

"I am afraid I do not have an answer as to why the iron affects you and not me, but I would like to talk to you more." His eyes scan the room. "Just not here. There are too many prying eyes and listening ears." He slides me a piece of paper, closing his hand around mine. "We aren't safe here, Skarlette. Meet me when you have time, I will be waiting in room four."

Rising from the table, I walk on wobbly legs out of the tavern, my mind racing with thoughts. I open my hand, smoothing out the crumpled paper and reading the elegant hand writing.

*"I wasn't supposed to exist. It was always meant to be you."* What the hell did that mean?

I try to push the note from my mind and focus back on work as I trudge my way up the hill. I spend most of the day staking out the house, watching the coming and goings. It did look like Evan had hired some sort of bodyguard. The man is tall. Some might say he is half ogre—if you believe those types of creatures exist. Still, he will be no match. I am much stronger.

When the sun has left the horizon and the moon is but a sliver in the sky, I make my way closer to the house. I peer in the window where I see Evan sitting in a chair near the fire. If I can find a back door, this will be an easy job.

I tiptoe around the corner of the house, making my way through the empty sheep pen and towards the back door. Pushing the door open slowly, I cringe when it makes a loud creak, alerting them to my presence.

"Who's there?" A male's voice calls from inside the house.

I stay silent, urging the shadows to envelope me and keep me hidden from sight. I don't know the exact time that my powers had come in, but they have helped hide me from so many situations. Right now, they keep me secluded. They are like a fog roaming from the very corners of the room.

Creeping up to Evan in his chair, I pull the red handled dagger from my boot. I reach forward and— *bang!* Something hard smacks against my skull, making my brain bounce around in my head. I spin, the shadows dropping away and coming face to face with the tall, ogre looking man.

Flashing him my teeth, I jump forward, sinking my fangs into his throat. Greedily, I drink from him until he loses consciousness. Evan takes the opportunity to bolt out the door, putting distance between us. Dropping the body to the floor, I run after him, my legs fast after the new blood from the big faerie.

I can't see Evan anymore, but I can smell him. Tracking

his scent is like a game. It brings me a thrill of adrenaline that courses through my veins. "Come out, come out. I can hear your heart beating," I call out in a sing song voice.

Peering around a tall stack of hay, I look right at one trembling Evan. My teeth shine in the reflection of his teary eyes. The blood dribbling down my chin drips to the ground below, making the man quiver with fear.

"Prince Ethan has requested I send a message. Pay what is owed by the full moon or I will be sent to do a lot more than to threaten you." I pull his hand forward, biting into his wrist. Evan screams, trying to rip his wrist from my hold, but I am stronger.

The blood hits my tongue and instantly I spit it on the ground. The man's blood tastes awful, like something has died within his very skin. He's obviously been on Ruellia in high concentrated amounts. I have only ever tasted blood like this one other time. I don't normally mess with the junkies, they usually end up taking care of themselves.

Ruellia is poison, but when strained down and mixed with other things, it becomes a drug. It keeps you floating through life as though you are a king in this mere pissant world. Weak women and men will chase that high for their entire lives.

The man laughs. "Guess you don't like the sweet Ruellia

I took earlier." I could see it now. The way his pupils stay small despite the lack of light.

"Guess I'll just have to punish you another way." Giving him a sinister smile, I call to my shadows. They lick the floor in front of me, making their way to his feet and started to climb.

"No!" Panic swirls in the man's eyes as he looks between me and the magic that makes it's way towards him. "Please!"

I slow the shadows as they reach his waist. "Beg harder," I demand, the shadows pushing him to his knees.

"I'll give you anything you want—!" He holds his hands up as if he is praying to the goddess herself.

"What do you have that I could possibly want?" I was getting bored of this game already, but I did like to play with my prey.

"I…I have." He tries hard to find something, anything that he might have, but fails. Like most junkies, he has given up everything for the sweet relief of Ruellia.

"You have nothing that I want. I am already quite happy. I mostly get to live in peace while doling out punishments." Crouching down close, I whisper my next words in his ear. "You think you fae would learn. I am the villain of this story."

My shadows climb quickly now, reaching up and wrapping around him in a tight squeeze. Liquid pools on the mans pant's, clearly he has pissed himself. When I feel like he is good and scared, I drop the shadows, letting Evan drop to the floor.

"Pay the prince or pay the price," are my parting words before I leave the piss soaked faerie.

When I step outside, Kai is waiting at the gate. I pull the vial of Ruellia oil and matches from my cloak. I douse the stacks of hay in front of the barn and light my match.

Kai is walking slowly towards me, his steps cautious, like he is approaching a wild animal. "Don't do it, Menace. You already scared the poor bastard."

"Why should I? They hate me, Kai. They don't even give me a chance. So why would I give them one?" His lips are in a full downturn and I can tell he doesn't know what to say. "If they are gonna hate me, I am going to give them a reason to hate me." I flick the lit match into the hay, watching it go up in flames. A coughing and sputtering Evan runs out from the barn, slumping to the ground outside the house. He heaves as he tries to catch his breath.

I don't linger around to watch it burn, no matter how much joy it will bring me.

The moon illuminates the path in front of me. Frogs and crickets singing me the song of their kind. I'm tired from how much of my power I used today, the exhaustion is starting to creep into my bones. I need blood, dinner, and a nap.

"Skar, wait up," Kai says as I pass him.

I slow slightly, but don't stop walking. He catches up quickly, his gate coming into step with my own. I know he wants to talk about my anger, but I don't think I am ready—if I'll ever be ready if I am honest.

"You don't have to talk about it, I can feel your anger. I get why you're angry. It's not fair. It's not fair that everyone has cast you aside and shown you how cruel the world can be from such a young age and still continues to do so. But don't be angry with me. I have been there for you." I get what he is saying, but the last part of his sentence plucks the chord of my anger.

"You have been there for me?" I stop walking, spinning to look at him. "You fucking brought me back here. You know how these people feel about me and you brought me back anyway!"

"I know," he says, not even apologetic for it. "I am no better than my brother." He rubs at the back of his neck, trying to fight the guilt.

"You are nothing like your brother." I hate to say something nice when I am so angry, but I can't let Kai think he is even an ounce like the monster living in that castle or like the one standing in front of him.

Turning away from him, I continue my way back to the castle. The one that is looming before us, growing in size as we approach it. I hate this feeling deep in my chest, like I will never have a place in this world. I feel like whether I am the hero or the villain, I'll never belong. It's almost as if fate hadn't expected me to survive this long.

# Chapter Twelve

## SKARLETTE

Traipsing through the front gate, I make my way through the gardens and towards the front door of the castle before coming to an abrupt stop. Standing in the entryway is Jamith and Ethan. Kai charges past, coming to stand a few feet away from his brother, his eyes scanning the man standing at the door. I know he recognizes him from the bar in Vreilwreth. He probably saw the exchange between us, when my ring mate had managed to land a punch.

"Let her go. I know you brought her here," Jamith spits

in Kai's direction.

"Jamith, you need to leave." Jamith spins around his eyes snapping towards me. He scans a look over my body, looking for any sign that I have been hurt.

I slide past him, careful to avoid his touch and move to stand between Kai and Ethan. They both stand, arms crossed like they are protecting their little sister. Inside, it makes me laugh slightly, for once we are all standing together against something.

"I won't leave here without you," he says, trying to take a step closer to me, but Kai stops him.

"She won't be leaving here with you," Kai's voice is lethal.

Jamith's eyes land on the bruise on my face. "Are they hurting you?"

"You need to go now. You don't know anything about this." Jamith's hand slides past Kai, trying to caress my cheek.

"I love you." I recoil at his words. "We were going to get married," he cries.

"I was never going to marry you." His hand falls limply by his side as I keep my composure, showing him no emotions. The hurt of my words making his face twist. When had it gotten this far? When had he started believing that we were settling down, getting married? Somewhere in this transaction, I had gone terribly wrong.

Jamith tries to grab my arm, but Ethan moves in closer to me and Kai, creating a barrier in front of my body. If we had been actually family, it would have seemed endearing for them to act so protective. Instead, it is two royal faeries, guarding what is theirs, keeping their treasure from someone who wants to steal it.

"I think you heard her. You need to leave." Kai's voice sends sparks exploding in my stomach. It is like I have been lit on fire. "Menace, I think you need to go upstairs." I can see that he is restraining himself. His need to protect me is strengthened by our bond. The closer I am, the harder it is for him to hold back.

I scurry up the stairs, listening as Kai and Ethan escort Jamith out of our home. I tuck myself inside of Kai's bedroom and wait. When I think the coast might be clear, I slowly open the door, peeking out into the hall. Kai and Ethan's voices filter towards me, heading in my direction. Quickly closing the door, I leave it ajar so I can listen in on their conversation without being seen. My body presses against the wall, my eyes peering through the crack as I watch them argue. "You need to control yourself," Ethan chastises.

"I am and it's killing me. The bond inside me is calling out for her and I am doing everything I can to keep it at bay." Kai runs his hand through his hair with frustration. "You have no idea how much I want to kill him for touching her."

"Well do better. Your bride will be here the day after tomorrow." Listening to Ethan's footsteps recede, I hold my breath, hoping Kai will head somewhere besides his bedroom.

"Come out, Menace." I hesitate, wondering if I should pretend to not be here before pulling open the door. "Snooping?" He says with a half-cocked smile.

"No. I hid in here while you sent Jamith away. I was trying to come out when you and Ethan arrived outside the door." Stepping out into the hallway, I softly close the door behind me.

Kai moves towards me, pushing me against the door and resting his arm above my head. His breath fans across my face as he speaks, sending a thrill down my arms.

"I'm going to have a terrible time sleeping now. With your scent in my room." My skin pebbles with his words. I hadn't even thought about my scent lingering in his room. That's probably how he knew I was here. His head bends, his nose running along my jaw as he breaths in my scent. His eyes return to mine with a heat that we both know is bad.

We stare at each other for what feels like forever before he reaches around me and opens the door. I stumble backward, catching myself with one hand on his dresser. Waiting until he passes me, I dart out of the room and down the stairs, not stopping until I make it outside. Gulping in the fresh air, I try to rid myself of the tension that lingers in my bones.

Hunting always seems to clear my mind. I take off at a quick pace, making my way to the forest where I know I will be alone with the animals. The act of watching and stalking my prey before I jump, gives me a thrill any predator would have—a sensation to temporarily sate my desire to take and drink the essence of life from a living creature until it's last breath. The large pitiful animal falls beneath me with a shriek as I sink my fangs into it's neck. But while I drink, the animal's frantic limbs kicking to escape, slows to a mere twitch. I know that no matter how much I feed or just how full my belly will be, it's warm blood won't be able sate my truest deepest desire. It is simply therapeutic to me.

Returning to the castle, I am met with a navy blue dress laid out across my desk. It is almost identical to the black one I wore in my cage. It takes me by surprise that it is the choice for dinner tonight, for the dress matches Kai's eyes.

I slide it on, feeling exposed from all the places it doesn't cover. A knock at the door makes me jump, but a small part of me hopes it is Kai, back to finish what we almost started earlier. But when I open the door, Ethan stands before me. His eyes roam over my body, a devilish smile spreading across his lips. I crush the urge to crinkle my nose at the way he eats me up.

"You do look marvelous," he purrs.

Stepping out of the room, I close the door behind me. Looping my arm through his, I bite back the uneasy feeling it gives me to be this close to him. "I take it I am your guest for the evening."

"Kai's betrothed decided to make an early appearance." I keep a small smile on my face, refusing to let him see the disappointment that is blossoming inside of me.

It is at this moment I start to connect the dots. Ethan bought me a dress the color of Kai's eyes to keep us in this weird state of uncomfortableness. I will show up in the room, dressed like a whore on Ethan's arm while Kai is forced to ignore me all night and focus on his soon to be bride. It is all a game. A wicked game to see who will break first. Ethan's favorite kind.

Turning my head in Ethan's direction, I give him a tight lipped smile. "Sounds like a wonderful evening."

The ballroom matches me. Everything in front of me is the same color as my dress. Am I supposed to blend in or stand out? Tonight is getting more confusing by the second. Ethan tugs me along behind him, passing the food and drinks and heading straight up to where the King and Kai sit.

Ethan pulls out a chair at the long table, signaling for me to sit. He slides the chair in as I take my seat, the chair scraping against the floor with a loud screech. Instantly, I become incredibly uncomfortable from all the eyes and whispers. I think every set of eyes in the room are staring at what is happening up here. My eyes are pulled to the one person who makes me the most uncomfortable. The King is watching with rapt curiosity, a warm smile gracing his lips as Ethan greets him.

"Father."

"Ethan. Skarlette," the King greets back.

I know better than to greet him myself. Instead, I give him a nod and a warm smile. It had taken me many years growing up to learn that responding to him only got me lashed. He is allowed to address me, but I am not allowed to speak to the King.

Glancing down the table to where Kai and his new bride sit, I take in her short stature and bright blonde hair. She has a prim smile and twinkling eyes. She is pretty, but seems like she might be a stickler for the rules. In fact I think I remember seeing her a few weeks ago at the ball that was held in honor of my return. She turns her head in my direction, meeting my gaze and tilting her nose to the sky.

Well fine then, if she is going to be that way, I will try and kill her with kindness. I give her a beaming smile. If only she knew the things I did to people who underestimate me, who look down on me like I am a stray dog.

Ethan's arm slips around my chair, pulling my attention away from Kai's bride to be and making my stomach knot. Pushing away the uneasy feeling, I lean into his touch trying my best to play the part. I bat my eyelashes and rest my hand on his thigh. Kai looks towards us, his eyes traveling to where my hand sits on his brother's leg. Anger swirls in his navy irises before he quickly looks away. I can't help the small smile of victory. I have managed to get under Kai's skin.

It's not long before the King excuses himself from the table, making his way down to the other tables lining the great hall to greet his guests. People buzz with excitement to speak with the king and it makes me want to scream at them, tell them the kind of villain that he is behind these walls.

"Get you're hands off her." Kai seethes.

"I hate to tell you brother, but I think her hands are on me." Ethan's grin is villainous. It's big and cheesy with his pearly whites shining in Kai's direction.

Kai's hands ball into fists that rest on his thighs. "I know what you're doing."

My voice comes out sickeningly sweet. "You haven't introduced me to your bride to be."

"Skarlette, this is Kesira." She turns towards me, that fake smile spread across her face. "Kesira—"

"Skarlette. I have heard so much," she interrupts, her voice as prude as her outfit.

"All bad I hope."

Ethan barks out a laugh at our greeting. "That's our Skar. Always the funny one." Kai's eyes roll as Ethan says 'our Skar', like I am their best friend.

"Skarlette, let's dance." Ethan says, rising from his chair and holding out a hand for me to take. Reluctantly, I place my hand in his and smile up at him as he pulls me from my seat. He leads me out into the center of the room where people have started to dance. I can hear their whispers. The sound is so loud to me it is like a swarm of flies.

*"Can she really dance?"*

*"How kind of the royal family to teach the beast our ways."*

The floor beneath us has recently been waxed, its surface reflecting the light from the candles above. People float around the room, like they are floating above the shiny floor. I can feel my dress flowing behind me as Ethan spins us around the room. If I had been dancing with anyone else, this would be magical. . .but I know Ethan is doing this to drive his brother crazy.

Halfway through our third dance, a guard approaches, whispering something in the prince's ear. I see the furrow of Ethan's brow before he nods his head.

"I am afraid I must go. Don't have fun. Do you understand me?" The polite Ethan that sat next to me at the table and danced with me in front of this large crowd, is now completely gone. Replaced with the harsh prince I know best.

When Ethan is gone, I move to the the outer edges of the room, observing like the trained assassin I am. It is safer here. I am closer to the shadows, which means closer to my power when needed. Watching Kai and Kesira twirl around the room is bitter sweet. Her cheeks are pink and she laughs way too hard at the littlest thing he says. But he also smiles at her. She is what he needs, a perfect match for a royal prince. Forcing myself to look away before I puke, I stuff my face with donuts and spiced apple wine.

When my cheeks are hot and the room is starting to spin, I decide I am long overdue to head back up to my room. I'm almost out of the ballroom when a hand wraps around my arm. I stumble, my legs wobbly from my consumption of copious amounts of wine. The hand's grip his rough and when I try to yank away, they only hold tighter, making me stumble more.

"Woah," the voice says. I try to place where I have heard it, but it's not coming to me, my brain is too muddled.

"So…sorry." I hiccup, trying again to pull my arm free, but they don't let go.

"I always wanted to meet the *Il Furfante*." Alarm bells start to ring in my head, but I am too drunk to get anywhere fast.

"I am not a prize to be looked at," I snap. The hand releases it's grip on my arm, making me fall to the floor. Apparently we have been walking, for I land upon the grand staircase steps.

"You are a bastard half breed that thinks she is something special," they spit. Their saliva raining down upon my face.

Rubbing at my eyes, I try to get the swirling under control so I can see my attacker. Blond hair, vibrant blue eyes, and cheek bones that could rival a statue. I don't remember seeing this man a day in my life, so how does he know who I am?

Rising to my feet, I pretend I am ready to fight this guy. I raise my fists as shadows creep from the corners of the room, coming closer in order to try and protect me. Double doors swing open behind the blond haired man, and two Kais' walk in our direction.

*Two?* That can't be right. The wine is still affecting me.

Kai's voice booms across the open expanse of the grand entryway. "Did you touch her?"

"What's it to you?" The other guy puffs up his chest, ready for a fight.

"You touch her and I end you." Kai's stare is menacing, if he was the one with shadow powers, this entire room would be consumed.

We stand there in this awkward triangle, waiting for someone to make a move. A laugh begins to echo off the walls. The man's head swiveling to look between Kai and I.

"Well isn't that rich. She destroys thousands of lives and gets the protection of the fae King's family." He stops laughing, looks dead at Kai and says, "I bet you're fucking her too." I can feel the flush of red on my cheeks from embarrassment. I'm not embarrassed about this man thinking I had sex. No, I am embarrassed and angry that this man thinks I would trade sexual favors with the prince to keep me safe.

Kai's betrothed picks that exact moment to make an appearance in the hall, her face blanches with what she hears, but she takes me by surprise when she stays silent. Kai doesn't say anything, he motions to the guards and has them escort the man out of our home.

Kesira approaches Kai and begins to whisper, but I can hear every word.

"Are you really fucking her?" She questions. "If you are, you will have to stop. She doesn't deserve your attention." She throws a glance over her shoulder at me.

I don't want to be a part of this conversation, I want to be in my bed, sleeping off the effects of faerie wine. Ignoring the rest of their discussion, I let my feet carry me up the stairs, the wobble from drinking long gone and replaced with the adrenaline that is running through my system. When I am sure no one is coming to check on me, I open the small window that leads out to the attic roof. I squeeze myself through it, carefully placing my feet along the slim ledge.

I have done this so many times, the fear of falling is almost non-existent. The wind blows my hair as my hands hold onto the spiked columns on the roof with white knuckles. Approaching the end, I jump down onto the balcony below. My feet pump underneath me so I can leap across to the next balcony. Down, down I make my way to the ground.

The minute my feet hit the gravel below, I keep running. Faster, faster as the wind whips my ponytail. The dagger in my boot is rubbing against my leg, but I keep going. Following the river as it winds and bends along the edge of the village, I follow it all the way out into the clearing.

The meadow is a welcome sight. A place where I can sit in the early morning hours and contemplate everything. Everything that has happened the last few weeks replays in my head. I throw my arms open, screaming to let out all of the rage I've been keeping inside. My shadows burst forth, crawling across the ground faster than I have ever seen. The meadow is cloaked in darkness before I even stop yelling.

When my arms drop and my mouth closes, I hear someone behind me.

Spinning to look at the intruder, my eyes widen with shock. I had no idea he had followed me. Worry instantly slices through me. My eyes do a quick scan of his body, making sure my shadows didn't harm him.

"What are you doing out here?"

Kai shrugs. "I heard you leave and thought I would come make sure you are okay."

"I am fine." I just need a little peace and quiet for a minute.

"That doesn't seem like someone who is fine. Also, I am now highly aware of just how much power is running through your veins." He says it like he is concerned, but his face doesn't show it.

"I know. The more I drink from faeries with powers or Ruellia in their systems, the stronger I get." I rub my hand on my arm, self conscious now. I wonder if I should tell him how much it scares me. How the power flowing through my veins sometimes feels like more than I can handle.

"Are you sure it is their power fueling it and not the anger you feel when you drink from those people?" He questions and his theory completely rocks my world.

He is right. It is the anger fueling my shadows. They grow anytime my anger or fear overtakes me. So when I drink from people who anger me, it makes the shadows stronger.

My powers had just engulfed an entire meadow, every beautiful flower gone as they drank the life source from them and I haven't had a single drop of blood all day.

"I can't always control it," I admit softly.

Kai closes the distance between us, pulling me into a hug. His arms wrapping tightly around me, infusing me with a warmth I didn't think was possible. I take in a deep breath, trying to steady my thoughts.

His chin rests against my head. "We will figure it out."

If only I could believe him. No one wants to help me, they only want to use me for the very powers that are starting to consume me.

# Chapter Thirteen

## SKARLETTE

I am going to take down prince Ethan if it is the last thing I do.

This morning has started off rough. I am grumpier than usual and I can't put a finger on exactly why. I hadn't rested well. While I don't technically need sleep, I still like to lay down and rest. I need time to shut my brain off from the thousands of thoughts that zoom through it daily.

Ethan is already on one when I arrive in the ballroom, handing me a list with three names and why they had wronged him. One poor man just walked the wrong direction at the wrong time, another wouldn't let the prince have relations with the man's daughter. Honestly, I don't mind being the one they call the villain when it pays my way in this world, but this is just downright stupid.

The prince is having me hurt, kill, or scare anyone who doesn't agree with him. If I wasn't around, I bet he would hold public lynching's of these poor people.

Taking the list from him with a little too much force, I grumble under my breath about how stupid this is. In response, I am quickly met the back of his hand to my face. My cheek stings from the impact as I immediately bare my teeth in his direction, my body on high alert from the threat.

"You do as I say without hesitation or grumbling, or you will see yourself burned like the rest of your kind," Ethan sneers at me before walking away. Clearly we are both grumpier than usual today.

He spoke of my people, but I don't really belong anywhere now do I? I don't have people. As far as I know, there is no one else like me. The vampires don't condone half breeds and neither do the fae. It is the reason I have always felt alone, even in a crowded room of people I had at one time called my friends. I was naive then.

The man I saw at the ball pops into my mind. I had met

someone like me though. Shit how many days has it been? I scramble to search my brain. I had been so busy with my own life, I had completely forgotten about the mysterious hybrid. I will make a stop at the tavern today and hope that he is still in town.

My first stop this morning will be at the blacksmiths. While I have no money to give him, I am a very skilled thief. Approaching the smith's anvil, I watch with pretend curiosity as he beats a piece of metal into just the right shape, length and width. Taking my chance while he is hard at work, I move around to his side, pretending to still be watching him in awe. While really I am positioning myself just perfectly so the hands behind my back can reach for one of his already completed pieces. By the time he realizes it is missing, I will be long gone.

Grabbing a freshly finished dagger, I wait until I am around the corner to shove it into one of my black leather boots. It will weigh down my cape too much to leave it in my pocket.

I run through the streets, searching until I come upon the small house. Peering inside one of it's front windows, I can see my first target. He is a short man, with a bald head and fat round belly. His daughter was working her fingers to the bones, sewing a pile of his old clothes. I could see the bruise on her cheek from where he had more than likely backhanded her. The man had control and he hadn't wanted to give it up to get in the prince's good graces.

My knuckles bang against the wood, giving three hard knocks on the door. Inside, I can hear the chair as it scrapes against the floor followed by the sound of footsteps as he comes my way. He opens the door, his eyes wide with shock as he studies my crimson irises.

"Prince Ethan sends his disappointment." I thrust the knife into the meaty part of his belly. I finish the job quickly, wanting to be done with my assignments so I can go to the tavern. My excitement about learning more about myself buzzes through my body like a swarm of bees.

The large man falls to his knees, his hands wrapping around the handle of the dagger as blood drips from his wound. I leave him there without another thought, ready to move on to my next victim.

This time, I stop long before I have approached the house. I can see a boy reading his story book on the front lawn. When his mother sees me and calls his name from the window, I feel a hint of disgust. Ethan wants me to hurt this young boy just because he ran in front of the prince's carriage, scaring the horses and delaying the prince by all of ten minutes.

I may be a villain, a monster even, but children don't deserve to die. They can still learn from their mistakes.

Turning, I walk away from the house for I can not find it in myself to harm this young boy. Even knowing that I will get the boy's punishment instead doesn't have me turning around. I will take it for him with dignity.

When I see the tavern, I stop. Maybe if I just make a quick stop inside, I can meet the mystery hybrid and be on with the rest of my list. The hum of excitement in my body makes my teeth chatter. I still don't know this persons name, but today I will be sure to ask. I climb the steps two at a time, making quick work to get to room four. Knocking three times, I wait for a response, but when I am only met with silence, I push open the door.

The door barely opens, blocked by something behind it. With the door now cracked I am instantly hit with the strong scent of blood as it overwhelms my senses. I push harder on the door. Someone has put a large blanket to block the scent from filtering through the crack beneath the door. It splinters with my final shove, pushing my way in and falling to my knees. Laying there in a puddle of scarlet liquid is the other half breed. His eyes are open wide, staring at the ceiling above him.

All the giddy happiness drains out of my body. I'm left

with a numb anger that is filled with sadness. This was my chance. I could have learned more about being a half breed, seen the similarities and differences between us. Now it is all gone, like sand filtering between my fingers.

I ransack the room, looking for any information that will tell me why this man was here and looking for me. But even with the room turned upside down, there is nothing. Like someone took it all or he didn't bring it, because he knew this would happen. I pull the crumpled note he gave me weeks ago from my pocket, reading the words over again.

*I was never suppose to exist. It was always meant to be you.*

I need to get out of here. I have a final name on my list and sitting here wondering what could have happened isn't going to help me any.

My third target is not as surprising. Ethan really hates it when the women don't like his company. I enter the brothel, making my way down the hall. Moaning, grunts and bangs fill the air around me. No one has even noticed my presence, they are far too busy being wrapped up in one another, which is why this was the best time to take care of this. Going to the fifth door, I kick my boot against it, busting it open. A half naked woman sits on all fours on the bed, her boobs bouncing with the impact of the man behind her as he thrusts.

I throw my hood on my head, not wanting the man to see me, because what Ethan wants me to do to her is monstrous. Stepping closer to the bed, I grip my blade in my hand, ready for what I have to do.

"It's twenty coin to watch." She just finishes her sentence when my blade slices her throat. This is where I become monstrous, killing people who merely displease Ethan so that I can have a place to sleep and eat. But I am fighting a bigger war behind the scenes. I am biding my time, hiding under the prince's nose so I can take him down from the inside.

I want my freedom. I want to carry out dastardly deeds on my own time to people who deserved to die. A small part of me craves for people to respect me, for people to look up to me and say, "I hope to be as strong as her one day."

"What the fuck, man! I paid for a full hour," the man spews behind me as I move towards the window, opening it wide and sliding through to stand on the roof. I jump, falling to the ground and landing on my feet before taking off into the woods.

I finally stop running and take a look at my blood covered hands, the memory of the other half breed flooding my mind. I shake away the thoughts, remembering I am being timed. I need to make it back to the castle before midnight or Ethan will have a lot more in store for me than just the young boy's punishment.

A small spring greets me, the perfect place to wash my hands and blade before securely tucking the dagger in my boot again. A twig snaps in the distance and my ears zero in on the noise, listening for whatever may be out here.

"Who's there?" I call out, but there is no response.

Another twig snaps and then a breeze rushes up on me. I see the vampire with his fangs out before I feel them dig into my flesh. I shove the creature off just as they seem to realize what I am.

"Ow, asshole." I rub at the two small puncture wounds.

"You…you're." My eyes roll as he stumbles to find the words. I have never met such an incompetent vampire.

"Yeah, I am part vampire too. Maybe you should watch a person before you bite them. How are you even out here anyway? The King made sure to burn all vampires when the treaty expired." I pretend not to know about the vampire sightings.

The vampire in front of me seems to hesitate for a moment. "I live in a cabin out that way." He points north of us.

"You're coming a little close to the village, don't you think?" I should be ending him right now. Ethan will kill me himself if he finds out I let a vampire live. He will go and tell the king of what I have done and they will rejoice in my death.

"I'm so hungry, I got a little crazy." My eyes scan him. His eyes are crimson just like mine and his pale skin seems almost luminescent compared with his pulled back long, dark hair.

"I'm Keenan." He holds out his hand, but I don't take it.

"Lettie," I grunt.

A smile spreads across his face, not a cruel one like I have seen on most faces, but one that reminds me of how Kai used to smile at me. Like he is excited to see me after a really long time. Maybe even like a friend.

"Well, Lettie, seeing as you are a vampire and I am a vampire, I think we are going to be really good friends." The goofy smile across this vampire's face and his easy going demeanor is making it hard for me to not trust him.

"I don't have friends." I move to walk away, finding myself annoyed when he follows. I stop, shooing my hands at him. "You can't follow me."

"Why not? You're in hiding too, right?" His voice is too excited and it makes my teeth feel on edge. There is nothing to be excited about right now.

"No, I have somewhere to be and you can't be there. If

they knew I let you live, that would be the last of me." I have said too much, I know it.

His eyebrow arches with curiosity. "Who?"

"No one." I throw my hood on, ready to start running when his hand grabs my arm.

"Please come back and see me." I rip my arm from his grasp and take off.

It's late when I return back to the castle, making my way towards Ethan's rooms. The hall feels like it's three miles long, the distance lengthens with each step I take. It takes me forever to get there, the events of today replaying in my mind like a nightmare that just won't let me be. I didn't harm the boy Ethan asked me to and then I ran into another vampire. I am going to be completely and utterly fucked.

My feet halt in front of the prince's office doors, my hand is ready to knock until Kesira's sugary sweet voice filters out into the hall. My senses bristle at Kai's fiancé being in Prince Ethan's office so late at night. Something deep in me tells me this isn't right, that she isn't here for just business.

"Why do I have to marry the shy one?" She pouts. I can see them through the opening crack between doors, their bodies inches from each other. Her hand is plastered against Ethan's chest, her eyelashes fluttering up at him. "I wanted you."

"Well you won't get me. If you want to be married to a prince, my brother will have to do." Ethan removes her hand, but she moves quicker, moving it down until her hand is resting on the mound in his pants.

"But don't you like what I have to offer?" Her whiny voice is grating on my already frayed nerves.

Taking a step back, I knock on the door, pretending that I wasn't just eavesdropping on their private conversation. The door opens and Kesira is standing on the other side, glaring at me.

"Fucking one prince isn't enough? You have to have them both?" She screeches. I give her a bored look, walking past her and taking a seat across from Ethan's desk. I'm not in the mood to deal with this harlot.

"Kesira, I have business to attend. If you could close the door on your way out." Her jaw drops as the prince dismisses her. I can tell she wants to say something, but decides better of it before she storms off, slamming the door behind her.

"I don't think she likes me very much," I state and Ethan barks a laugh in response.

"I take it you did what needed to be done." He doesn't look at me, just keeps scribbling away on the papers sprawled across his desk.

"I took care of two of them. The other is just a boy, Ethan."

"I told you to take care of it. You do it, no questions asked, *Skarlette*." The way he bites out my name makes me flinch.

My teeth clench, my jaw hurting from how hard. "He is a boy."

He turns his head to me. "I take it you are willing to take his punishment, then." Ethan stands, smoothing out his coat jacket.

"I am." I stand as well, looking Ethan right in his cold eyes, showing him I'm not going to back down or change my decision.

Ethan rounds the desk, grabbing me by the arm and pulling me out of his room. He leads me all the way out into the courtyard, and down to the where the royal blacksmith has his hot fire starting to burn down for the night.

Looking back at the castle over my shoulder, I look to the window I know connects to the younger prince's bedroom. I can just make out the silhouette of Kai, watching as his brother mutilates my body. Some kind of mate he is. Watching while I take a brutal punishment.

Ethan pulls a small brand off the wall. Its shape is a swirl with two lines crossing each other. He sets it in the fire, waiting for the metal to burn red hot while his other hand still grips my arm tightly. When the metal is bright red, he pulls it from the embers, shoving me against the anvil.

"You know what to do Skarlette." Muscle memory has me pulling up my shirt and the waist of my pants down slightly.

Ethan takes the brand, pressing it into the skin right over my hip bone. I try to keep the pain inside, but its too much. My skin is sizzling and an agonizing yell slips when I'm unable to hide the pain it causes me. Heat is a vampires worst enemy. That is why they burned us. When they have no stakes to take us out quickly, they tie us up above the fire like the witches they extinguished years ago.

The brand is removed and I can here the crunch of shoes on gravel. When my eyes open, the prince is gone. Looking down at the new brand that sits right next to the other two, I fix my pants and let my shirt fall back into place. Every step back to my room makes my new mark ache. I want to douse it in water, but after the second brand, I told myself I would live through the pain. I will take the pain I keep from others. I will suffer, because that is what I deserve.

# Chapter Fourteen

## KAI

Standing here, watching as my brother mutilates Skarlette's body is hard. The urge to bust through the window and push my brother's face into the fire is making me itch. It makes me wonder what she did to earn such wrath from him. They both stand there like they have done this before and that makes me feel sick to my stomach. How many times has he branded her?

My eyes track my brother as he crosses the lawn and heads back inside before they fall on Skarlette. She wavers at the blacksmith's station before limping her way back inside, the pain is obvious. She isn't one to normally show her pain. She believes it shows her weaknesses, but right now she thinks no one was watching.

Leaving my room, I am hoping I will meet up with her in the hall. I find myself pleasantly surprised, when I find her on the first set of stairs. Her head rises when she hears me approach and immediately she straightens, pretending that the pain isn't affecting her. Trying to hideaway her pain under all the layers of her thick skin.

"I watched the whole thing, Skar." Pity seeps from my voice and makes me wince, because I know that my words are only going to make her defensive.

"I don't need your sympathy, Kai," she snaps.

Rolling my eyes at her stubbornness, I try to help support her, but she just shoves me away. "Obviously."

She continues walking to her little attic room. I follow closely behind her, practically nipping at her heels like a herding dog. Her long, stick straight silver hair dangles near her lower back. Her black leather pants cling to her every curve and the way her hips sway has me salivating. Fighting off the thoughts that make myself go hard, I curse to myself. I am a monster for thinking of her in that way while she is hurting. Only a monster would sit in his room and watch from the balcony instead of going out there and stopping my brother.

When Skarlette tries to shut her door, my hand flies out, stopping it from closing. Her face drops into a scowl, her beautiful pink lips in a full downturn and she looks like she wants to punch me. Good. She should punch me. I deserve it.

"Let me help heal it a little," I offer.

"I don't want it healed." She's being short with me, her arms are crossed and her boot blocks the door so I can't open it further.

"Don't torture yourself like that." Using all of my body weight, I shove against the door, putting her off balance and stepping into her room.

Every step I take towards her, she takes a step back. It's like we are locked in a dance.

Halting my advancing steps, I stand in the center of her room, my hands held up in a signal of truce. "Skar, I can't live like this. I can't live with you hating me for whatever reason."

"I don't hate you. I'm a bad person who does bad things and you are a good person who does good things. We aren't meant to get along." Her voice is soft as she takes a step towards me. That step is like a peace offering. She is finally giving in.

Dropping to my knees in front of her, I wrap my arms around her legs and pull her into me. Her hands press against my shoulders, trying to hold herself from falling over. Her scent is so good, it makes my mouth water. My lips press against the spot on her pants where her new scar sits just underneath, sending a jolt of healing through our bond. It doesn't take long for her to realize what I am doing. She shoves me away, anger clear in her expression. I have just done the exact thing she asked me not to.

"You didn't deserve the pain," I say softly, knowing my words will not help me.

"I deserve all of the pain." Her words are harsh as she uses her shadows to push me out the door before slamming it in my face.

The wood door stares back at me as I blink my eyes. I deserved that. I had gone against her wishes and tried to heal her. But still, the slam of the door and her words stung.

I slink back to my room where I lay in my bed, unable to sleep. Skarlette's words ring through my mind. '*I deserve all the pain.*' What did she meant by that? If my brother makes my menace feel like she needs to be the one hurting, I will burn this castle with him inside. She doesn't deserve it. She doesn't deserve my brother's anger for not completing the cruel task he set for her. She has never deserved the way my family and the people treat her. My brother is the one who deserves to suffer.

In fact, that isn't such a terrible idea. My brother will become a tyrant once my father passes or steps away from the throne. He will rule as he practically does now. He sends Skarlette off to be his assassin, to be the name everyone fears, while he sits back here in his lavish home, reaping the rewards she provides.

I must be crazy for this. If my plan doesn't work, I will be beheaded—or worse, Ethan will make Skarlette kill me and that will only hurt us both. He may even decide to put my head on a stake and use me as a symbol to all of those who dare try and take him down. I can not afford to fail. Skarlette is counting on me. The whole of Ruellia is counting on me.

Tomorrow I will begin planning. I am going to make my brother pay for every ounce of hurt he has forced upon others who do not deserve it. I am no longer going to sit by and watch my family treat the people of this kingdom like their slaves. I am going to stand up for what I believe is right.

I'm going to be the one to change the continent of Aurenda forever.

# Chapter Fifteen

## SKARLETTE

*D*<sup>ay one.</sup>

Today, I will begin to exact my revenge. I am going to kill Prince Ethan Eveningglow. I want to show him the villain he has created over the years, prove to everyone that I am the monster they have created. I am truly sorry to everyone who thought my story was going to be different. If they wanted to see the badass female save everyone...well that isn't me and that's not my story. I am, and will always be the villain.

Pulling myself up off the small bed of blankets, a bed I

have been sleeping in since I was old enough to be out of the nursery, I cross my tiny room. This is the only place they deemed safe to keep me from everyone else. There is a lock on the outside of the door, something made to keep me in in my younger years when they were scared my urges would send me down the hall and to their rooms. Later, when I had become an adult, I added my own to the inside. It isn't a huge extravagant area like the others have, but it is still my own.

Brushing out my long pale hair, I throw on some leather pants and a long flowy red shirt before finishing wrapping the corset around me and pulling the strings tight. I slide the dagger I stole into my boot and head off for the day. I will need to earn some money and get some supplies if I am going to be successful in killing the prince.

My plans come to an immediate halt as soon my feet hit the bottom of the staircase. The royal doctor is talking to Kai and Ethan, a solemn look across his face. The doctor's eyes dart in my direction, his face turning pale with terror. I may have bit him as a child when he tried to give me an exam and obviously he still remembers it very clearly. I give him a feline smile, wiggling my fingers at him in hello. He pales more, rushing his words with the princes in front of him.

"I am sorry, but I have to go." The doctor hurries out the door, throwing one more glance at me before disappearing completely.

"What was that all about?" I question as I approach Kai and Ethan.

"Father is ill." Ethan's face holds a painful look of sadness, but in his voice I can hear his glee. It makes me sick that he is excited to see his father ill. While I too would like to see the king dead, It is a whole other thing for your child to be happy about your sickness. Soon, Ethan will be the king of Ruellia.

A chill runs down my spine at the thought. Visions of spiked heads lining the walls of the castle flood my mind. A ruler who is benevolent and throws a tantrum when he doesn't get his way will soon be the harsh reality of this place. A wicked king, they will call him.

Kai looks at Ethan with an icy glare. "Don't get comfortable in the throne just yet, brother."

"Just keeping it warm while father is away," Ethan sings as he walks away from us.

Kai paces in front of me, his hand running through the short strands of hair. I awkwardly stand there, not sure what I can or should do. I need to get out of here and start putting my plan into place. It is more important now than ever.

Walking away from him, I focus back on the plan I originally set for myself. While I may be the villain, I do not relish in the mass genocide that will ensue once Ethan has complete control. If there is no one to walk this earth than there will be no need for a villain and if I'm not a villain, than who am I?

"Menace," I hear Kai growl behind me. "Where do you think you're going?" His tone is firm, making the bond inside me light like a flame.

"I have things to do. I am sorry about the king, but I can't sit around all day." I continue walking towards the door, but Kai's hand wraps around my wrist, tugging me to a halt.

"I don't think you have sat still a day in your life." His thumb rubs at the soft skin on the inside of my wrist. It brings me a comforting feeling that I am unsure how to handle.

It all feels too comfortable. Too much like a loving gesture and that makes my skin warm, but also makes my nerves spark on high alert. I need him to keep me at a distance. This plan will only work if he hates me. I am the very person who will be responsible for killing his family. I don't want to see the heartbreak in his eyes when I finally finish my plan.

Ripping my arm from his grasp, I scowl at him as I leave through the doors. Outside, the sun warms my skin, bringing me a comforting warmth, while others like me would have burned. I am grateful my half fae lineage makes me able to walk in the sunlight. It is one thing I do not take for granted when it comes to being a half breed.

Taking in a long breath of fresh air, I refocus on the task at hand.

I am thinking of trying to poison the prince. While I have no chance of getting the poison through the taste testers, I could whip something up on my own and give it as a gift. Though, he might find that a tad suspicious, seeing as I have never offered him anything before.

Killing Prince Ethan will be no easy task, no matter how much I wish it was. I want nothing more than to set that castle ablaze. In fact, I barely care who is inside when I do. While I don't want Kai or Louissa dying over the acts of everyone else, I will have to take my shot when the time is right, whether they are there or not.

In the village, the streets are lined with vendors. The first weekend of every month, vendors line the streets of Ruellia, selling wares of every kind. They always have beautiful items, hand made vases, yarns of every color, and foods from distant lands. Spices, breads, and other delicious food that sometimes is only made one weekend every month. My mouth waters from the sights and smells of the street market.

I remember my very first market like it was yesterday. I was twelve at the time. The king wanted to take us to see the village, flaunting me around, reminding the kingdom that he had a pet they should fear was more accurate, but us kids were excited.

*I stare in awe at all the beautiful things, the tables packed with items. I come across a one with large wooden stakes, my eyes glued to the one thing that could kill me besides fire. The vendor must have seen the fear in my eyes, because she lets out a chuckle. Running through the market, I urgently trying to escape, bumping into a table with loads of different foods not from our kingdom, some of them spilling to the ground in my haste.*

*"Woah there little one." The vendor holds up her hand, stopping me.*

*Her eyes go wide with shock when she looks me in the eyes. My crimson red irises giving me away. A smile I hadn't been expecting creeps over her lips. It wasn't a smile I felt scared of, it was warm and welcoming, like a mother smiling at their child.*

*She turned around to grab something off the table before holding it out to me. "Here—I think you will like this."*

*Hesitantly, I take the round red fruit from her hand. I roll it back and forth in my hands, taking in it's bumpy outer texture. I wasn't sure if I was supposed to take a bite or not. It wasn't like* any fruit I had seen in Ruellia before.

"Go ahead, try it. It's from your lands." The woman said. If only she knew. Shadowfall wasn't my home and neither was Ruellia. I may call it home, but I had no home to speak of. I wasn't the same as everyone else. The fae were tied to the land, the vampires tied to the shadows of night. I existed in both.

I bit into the fruit, red juice spilling over my lips as the sweet and tangy taste melts over my tongue. It was the best thing I had ever eaten. I greedily, sucked down the rest of the fruit, wiping my red stained hands on the beautiful blue dress the queen had picked for me to look the part.

The red stains on the skirt of my dress probably made me look like the true blood sucker I was. People stared at me in horror as I walked back to the royal family. The queen's face looked down at me with disgust at the state of the gown.

"Gladice, take Skarlette back to the castle. Her outfit is no longer appropriate for our outing." The queen dismissed us, moving on to the next stall in the market.

Gladice grabbed hold of my upper arm, dragging me back to the carriage, my little feet barely able to keep up with her. The entire way back she grumbled to herself about having to keep eyes on me. How I ruin everything and how I was a freak of nature. How could the goddess have been so cruel as to let me be born? She prayed in her seat across from me on the way back to the *castle, begging the goddess to take me back and rid Ruellia of the monster the devil had created.*

*Back at the castle, she threw me in my gold colored iron cage, leaving me in the fruit stained clothing before walking away.*

I shiver at the memory. I should be glad for it. It made me who I am today, but it also has me thinking of what my life would be like now if only they had been kind.

Making my way to the very stand that started that memory, I pull the hood of my cloak over the majority of my face. My hands hover over the variety of items. All from Shadowfall.

"Can I help you find something?" A hand comes into my view, pointing at specific items.

"Just looking." I hope my voice carries through my cloak.

Spotting exactly what I need towards the back of her table, I look at the rest of the items all placed strategically so only someone looking for the item may find it. My finger stretches out, pointing towards it.

"How much?" I keep the tone of my voice monotone, not wanting to give away my identity.

"Probably more than you can afford." I can hear the laugh in her voice. She thinks I am a peasant. My lips quirk up in a smile.

Letting my hood fall, the surprise that takes over her face

is joyous. I reach into my cloak pocket slowly, my hand wrapping around the bag of coin as her face morphs from surprise to downright fear.

"You." Her hands shake a little as she reaches for the bottle. "They tell stories about you all over the continent. The crimson eyed faerie. A beautiful enchantress with deadly secrets." .

I bark out a laugh. "Is that what they are calling me?" Silly fae with their silly stories.

"What should they call you?" There it was, her way of trying to get my true identity.

"I have many names: Enchantress, *Il Furfante*, Monster. But none shall know my true name." I take the pouch of coins out of my pocket and drop it on her table.

"For the bottle." I point to the bottle wrapped tightly by her white knuckled hands.

She holds it out to me, hands shaking like the leaves on a tree as I snatch it with a smile, depositing it into my cloak.

"I saw you once, long ago. You were kind to me," I whisper to her before leaving the market behind me.

# Chapter Sixteen

## SKARLETTE

My feet move, carrying me in a different direction than my head. I planned to go back to my room, sit on my blankets and figure out what exact poison I just purchased. My feet have a different idea. They move me through the forest, moving over logs, leaves, and grass, taking me past the small pond and arriving again at the small cabin in the woods.

Knocking, I secretly hope he doesn't answer and I will be forced to go back to my room where I belong.

"Hi," he says with a bright smile on his face. "I am so glad you came back." He moves away from the door, offering for me to come inside. The front of his brown tunic is hanging open, exposing dark chest hair and his black pants hug his legs. If my heart didn't already belong to someone else, I probably would find this man very attractive.

I hesitate for a moment on the threshold of the door before heading inside. Taking a seat at a small table that is cluttered with dishes and cups, my eyes roam over the cabin, taking in the small area of room. A bed sits in the corner farthest from me while a fire warms the room from the wall closest. It is a cozy place, I can't doubt that, but how did a vampire come to acquire such a dwelling?

Keenan stands, staring at me with expectant eyes. Oh right, I was the one who came here unannounced, I remind myself.

"I don't know why I came here. I guess I just needed a friend?" I have no idea if I could call this man my friend, I only met him yesterday.

"Here I am." He holds out his arms and gives me a warm smile. "Though I do have somewhere to be. You are more than welcome to tag along if you'd like?" He moves towards the door, throwing on a jacket and a hat.

I hesitate, worrying my lip between my fangs. I would hate to burden him with my company, but I am always up for a little mischief.

"I'll come," I respond, following him out the door.

We head into town and my stomach twists with anxious worry. If someone were to see me hanging around town with a vampire, it would mean my death. Surprisingly, he sticks to the shadows well. We dart down alleyways and hide behind crates as we try to make our way through the village without being seen. I urge my own shadows to help and keep us secluded from any watching eyes.

Keenan slips into one of the local taverns, making his way to the back and into a secret room. Inside, he takes a seat across from one of the fae noblemen.

"Do you have what I need?" The nobleman asks, leaning forward in his chair with expectant hands.

Keenan slides a small wooden box across the table. I can't see what is in the box from my position in the corner, but I assume by the large bag of coin that he receives in return, it is something worthy.

Once the nobleman has agreed to the exchange we make quick work to leave, slipping out the back exit and out into another dark alleyway. Fae guards flank both sides, boxing us in. I throw my hood over my head to help hide my face. My hand slides inside my boot, wrapping around the cool hilt of my dagger as I draw it.

"I can't be seen here with you," I hiss in his direction.

"We'll have to fight our way out then won't we?" He looks at me with a wide grin.

The guards are closing in. I can practically smell the blood that runs in their veins. The vampire urge to drain them of their blood sings to me like a siren, but I ignore it, just like I always have. My back presses against Keenan's as we stare down the guards on either side. In the blink of an eye Keenan's presence is gone and I hear the sound of blood raining down at the same time I hear the first guard yell. He has already taken the first one down.

Looking ahead, I see one of the guards coming for me. I lunge forward, plunging my blade into the man in front of me. Another comes up on my side, trying to get a swing in with his sword. Pulling my blade from the body in front of me, I duck, missing the swing meant to decapitate me. That's good. They think I am a vampire. They have yet to realize who they are dealing with.

Jumping on top of a large crate that sits in the alleyway, I fling myself over the largest guard and slice my blade across his neck. He crumples to the ground. One more to go. Looking down the alleyway, I make eye contact with the last guard. My hood has fallen off with all the fighting and I am so in the heat of the moment, I don't even notice.

The guard's mouth drops, and I can already see that he is going to try and run back to the castle and betray me. But I don't let him get away. My shadows are faster than his feet. They wrap around his ankles, dragging him back to me.

"Please! I won't tell anyone. Please don't kill me," he cries.

I smile down at him. "How naive you are, to think I will let you live after you saw me here." My shadows wrap around his neck, cutting off his air until he finally falls into the forever sleep.

Turning away from the dead guard in front of me, I find Keenan feasting on the bodies of the other three guards. I can't find it in myself to drink from them. It had always been that way. While I did sometimes bite people when I was on mission, I never went out of my way to eat them. Something about it made me feel gross. Funny thing for a monster to feel bad about eating something.

I wait, with my arms folded for the vampire to be finished with his meal before I follow him back to the cabin, I can't help but feel a sense of friendship growing between the two of us. We just took down six fae guards together.

"I'm going to poison the prince," I blurt out. My eyes widen and I slap my hand over my mouth. I'm unsure of what it is that makes me feel like I can tell him my plans.

"Prince Kai?" Keenan has a sparkle in his eye, one that tells me he is thirsting for the prince's blood. I guess I won't be telling my new friend about my oldest friend. We enter the cabin, where Keenan flops down in a chair at the table.

"No, Prince Ethan," I correct, now feeling slightly uneasy for telling him all of this. Taking a seat across from him, I can't get my eyes to look away from the blood that soaks his shirt.

"I would love nothing more than to see the whole royal family go down. In fact, I would take pleasure in eating them myself. I am sure they taste delectable." My face twists at the thought of some vampire drinking Louissa's blood, her face going ashen as the vampire drains her life source.

Luckily, Keenan doesn't seem to notice my expression. He rises from his chair, moving around the small kitchen to grab some food as well as two mugs of blood. The smell of it wafts towards me, reminding me of just how long it has been since I indulged in more than a thimble of the sweet red liquid. When he hands me one of the mugs, I greedily gulp it down. The taste is definitely faerie, but I am not going to ask where he got it from. It really isn't any of my business.

Setting the mug down on the table, I wipe my mouth on my sleeve before looking up at Keenan with a sheepish smile. His face doesn't look surprised, nor is it angry that

I drank all of the blood. Something else resonates in his crimson pupils that matches my own. Like he is looking at someone he admires.

"Sorry, it's been a while since I have had that much blood." I feel it pulsing through every vein in my body, restoring me to my full strength. Keenan's smile doesn't waver, he merely pushes his own mug in my direction.

"You'll need it," he says, motioning for me to take the second mug of blood.

"No, really I can't. One mug was more than enough." I pop a grape in my mouth, hoping the change of food will get him to take the mug back.

"I insist, Skarlette." Immediately, warning bells ring in my head. I have never told him my real name.

"How…" My mind goes fuzzy, my eyes begin to water and my words aren't coming out like I want them to. I try to stand but I can't get my legs to move out from under the table. The blood was poisoned.

His voice coos at me, sending slithering sickness deep down in my stomach. "That's the sedative I snuck into your mug. The vampire king wants to meet you, Skarlette." I slide from my chair, trying to crawl across the floor, but it is no use. My limbs are going numb and my vision is getting dark.

Blinking my groggy eyes open, I can feel that my body is laid out on a cold hard floor. It takes a moment for my eyes to adjust to the pitch black room around me. A holding cell of some sort, I assume. There are no skeletons or other people, which tells me it probably isn't a dungeon cell.

My vampiric sight makes it easier to see in the dark room. The walls and floor are dirt, and the door in front of me seems to be made of some sort of metal. I stand on wobbly legs, my head spinning from whatever poison Keenan slipped me. Making my way to the door, I rise up on my tiptoes and press my hand against the metal, trying to see out the small window.

"Shit," I hiss as the metal sizzles against my skin. The door is made of iron. If I had been a regular fae, I probably would have stumbled across the dark room, unable to see in the pitch black conditions and then burned myself terribly on this thick iron door. This is a holding cell specifically made to keep a faerie. Though the fae could live many years, iron weakened them, causing their skin to burn from the inside out, making this the perfect holding cell.

Stumbling away from the door, I hold my burnt hand against my chest. Turning a pointed ear in the direction of the door, I listen closely for any sound. There in the distance, coming closer towards me, I can hear footsteps. I stumble backwards as the footsteps close in right before they get to the cell.

The door swings open in my direction and a man stands looming on the other side. With the light coming from the other side of him, it's hard to make out his features, but I can tell he is taller than any man I have seen before.

"Come," he demands.

"Where?" I spit back at him, not moving from my spot at the back of the cell.

"The vampire king is waiting." I move my feet slowly, wary of what lies before me on the other side of the door.

The man waits for me to stand beside him before he starts walking me up the stairs. At the top, we are greeted by a ginormous hall. Beneath us, the floors are red and white marble, the red swirling in intricate patterns throughout the white. Pillars of the same color rise from the floor and into the ceiling.

My eyes move away from the swirling marble, they roam around the large space before landing on my captor. The man next to me has to be at least seven feet tall, with shoulder length dark hair and broad shoulders. He wears a black shirt and pants that hug his form. On his arm is a large tattoo of wrapping vines with hanging bats and tiny red flowers.

My eyes find his as he gives me sideways glance. His crimson orbs tell it all. He's a vampire. He grumbles something under his breath about 'filthy half breeds' before looking away from me. I am just about to give him a piece of my mind when large double doors with beautiful gold patterns greet us. They creak as they slowly swing open, revealing a large dark room before us.

Inside the large room, I am in awe of the chandeliers hanging every so many feet with a ring of candles all a flame. Their light providing just enough brightness for someone to see, but just enough darkness to keep the vampires comfortable. It is nothing like at home. At home, there are windows galore, providing ample amount of daylight. But here, I do not see a single window. Probably to avoid the sunlight.

I have never been one to feel self-conscious. The king and queen had tried many times, but I shut off that emotion long ago, to protect myself. Now though, standing before the vampire king in his red robes and golden crown, the women in beautiful dresses on either side of him. I feel as though I am underdressed.

"Your Majesty," I say as we approach. The body guard next to me makes a weird noise, something like a strangled laugh.

The vampire king's voice rumbles deep across the room. It's almost like he is speaking directly into my mind, but I can see his mouth moving. "No need for the pleasantries."

"I'm confused on why I am here." The guard next to me lets out a snort this time, making me turn towards him with a cocked eyebrow.

"She has no clue who she even is," he barks at the king and now I am wondering if he is just a guard.

"She will find out if you just shut your trap," the king shoots back.

I am the one to laugh this time. Watching them bicker like an old married couple is delightful and I barely even know them. The king's attention returns to me, making me freeze.

"Hello, Skarlette." The way he drags out my name, like we are meeting for the first time after a long time apart.

"I'm sorry, I know you are the vampire king, but have we met?" I question.

"We have not. I knew your mother long ago." I instantly

prickle at the thought.

"Oh, don't tell me I am your child." Disgust roll's from my voice and the women on either side of the king take on disgusted faces.

"You are not, but you were my brother's child." The king's voice fades off, his eyes looking towards the ground with longing. "Unfortunately, he is long gone."

"Okay." I drag out the word, waiting for the king to explain more.

"Again, this story is filled with misfortune. You see, most vampire kind are unable to birth children, myself included. Your father though, he was blessed by the goddess herself and he managed to get a woman pregnant. Albeit, a fae woman. He is one of only ten vampires to ever have succeeded, our father was another." He paused, turning to the ladies seated on the arm of his throne and order them to leave. Once the last one has disappeared from the room he continues. "I am dying."

"Vampires can't die." I cross my arms, wary of the game these vampires were trying to play.

"It is true, but I have been alive a long time. Thousands of years and I am done. I am choosing to die." My mouth drops open at his confession.

"Okay, but this still doesn't answer why I am here." The

guard rolls his eyes at me.

"You are the sole heir to the vampiric throne." The words spin around my head like a cloud.

"Me?" I was shocked. "B-but I am just some half breed mutt," I stutter.

"See, she agrees with me." The guard says, earning himself a glare.

"You may not be a full vampire, but you are a true born heir and maybe with your breeding, you will be able to unite the people once again." The king rises from his throne, walking up to come face to face with me. "You are our only hope."

"I am a villain, not a queen." The vampire king takes my hands in his.

"Who says you can't be both? Be the villain you are needed to be, but lead like a queen." There was that wisdom he had gained from living a thousand more years than myself.

"Why can't he do it?" I throw my head in the direction of the guard.

"I am afraid that Elijah, while he may be my son from turning, is not what the fates want." Elijah grumbles at his father's words.

Elijah looks at me like he wishes I didn't exist. "I wasn't born a vampire. You were."

I have prepared myself to live out the rest of my life in a small village creating havoc. Not living in a castle. I am planning on burning the castle I currently call home to the ground as soon as possible. "And what if I don't want to be a ruler?"

The king sighs. "Skarlette, there is a prophecy." He pulls the scroll from somewhere beneath his robes, holding it out for me to take. Rolling out the parchment, I read the scribbled handwriting on the page.

*Come time, there will be a child born of two. This child will wield the greatest and most powerful powers known to our kinds. The child will have the opportunity to do great good or become great evil. This child will unite the two realms, whether it be in darkness or in light.*

I roll the scroll back up and hold it out to him, not wanting to reread it. There is no way I was the child of this prophecy. Surely there is someone else out there born of two with great powers.

The king loops my arm around his, walking us out of the large hall. "You play the part of the villain because you receive comfort in living that life. You take the things you need to survive. In a castle, you will be given all the things you currently take. You could live in this castle and never have to see another soul beside your guards. You will live as you wish."

We walk through the castle until we come to a large window overlooking the world beyond. It is a pleasant surprise to find such a large ornate piece of glass in a castle without windows. My eyes travel over the dark forest that lays before the castle, but they catch off to the right of the castle, where homes sit nestled in the half bowl-like shape of the mountains. On the far side of the forest, sits the faerie castle and village. The place I currently call home. The place I loathe more than anything else in my life.

I can see everything from this window.

"What happens to the fae who enter the forest?" It's been a tale told to faerie children of all ages. If you went into the dark forest, you never came out. It's said there lives a wild beast who takes you to the vampires who then drain you of your blood.

"Some were fed upon." The king points to an area of the village with brightly colored homes. "Others have made a home amongst us."

"Why not let them come back to Ruellia?"

"*He* burned us at the stake. The minute a vampire steps foot on the other side of the forest, we are crucified. How could I let him believe I am showing his people mercy, when he will not show that to mine."

I nod in understanding. He is doing the very thing I am doing. Being the villain to bring his people comfort. Protecting the very ones he loves, even if it means others see him as a monster.

It makes me wonder if we are really the villains. Aren't we all slightly evil to get the life we want?

"I need time to think about it," My brain feels like mush. I can barely form thoughts, let alone make such a huge decision in this moment.

His head bobs in agreement. "You have until the first frost on the Ruellia petals."

Three months. Three months to decide if I will be a villainous queen or a villain with a disguise.

# Chapter Seventeen

## KAI

The minute I realize Skar is missing, I retrace her steps. I am not going to let her get away from me again. I find a small cabin in the woods that reeks of vampire. Skarlette's scent is different, she smells of sweet vanilla and Ruellias. . .but this, this smells like death and decay. A common scent of full-blooded vampires. Something about draining people of their life source, just makes you smell like shit.

I immediately ride through the night to reach the dark forest. The roots of the trees stretch, winding up and down, and incredibly hard to see when the canopy above blocks all sunlight from touching the ground. My horse hesitates, pushing back when I try to urge her forward. I refuse to push her more, dismounting and leaving her to graze in the small meadow outside the forest. I will have to go on foot.

The roots grab at my feet, trying to trip me every chance that they get. The stories I had been told as a child, trickle in from a small space in my memory. The monster that hunts the woods for fearie children. The vampires waiting for the monster to make its sacrifice to them. My skin pebbles, the feeling of someone watching me making me unnerved. I have to keep going no matter how much this forest wants to keep me from getting to the tall black castle on the other side. My menace is in that castle somewhere and I need to find her.

My left foot steps out of the forest first and instantly the crawling feeling of something creepy, eases. I stand in front of beautiful iron gates with trees etched into their metal, taking in their delicate detail before darting off behind the large trunk of a nearby tree. I wait patiently for an opportune moment to pass the guards. A wagon full of supplies is rumbling up to the gate, a perfect place for me to sneak past. I quickly hop in, hiding between the large stacks of crates. The wagon's bumpy ride jostles me around and I can hear the guards through the wagon's canvas.

When it rolls to a stop, I climb out, trying to make myself as unseen as possible. In front of me, the large castle looms over, it's black brick towering over everything else within it's radius. I search around the grounds, hoping to find a secret entrance. Clinging to the shadows, I dart around walls and slither into corners when guards or other vampires pass by. Finally, I find a small door, sliding inside before I am met with a pitch black tunnel. I walk a few hundred feet, keeping my hand to the smooth dirt walls before coming to a bend.

The area illuminates before me as torches light the new found hall. On my right sits a set of stairs, leading up to a large hall, to my left another set of smaller stairs that lead down into darkness. I take my chances and go with the darkness.

The farther down the stairs I go, the more the cold from the ground seeps through, chilling me to my bones. Fewer and fewer torches light the hall until I am in complete darkness. My eyes take a while to adjust as I approach a cell door, reaching my hand up, I fumble while trying to find the latch.

I call out to her, just as my hand finds an iron lock and I hiss out in pain. "Skar?"

Slamming my boot into the iron lock, I put enough force behind it to blow the cell door open.

"What the fuck are you doing here?" She says, rising from the ground and walking towards me. It is so hard to see her down here. I could curse the goddess right now for giving the vampires all the good eyesight.

"I came to save you," I say before giving her a cocky smile.

"I could have gotten out myself." She stands in front of me with her arms crossed over her chest and a raging fire in her eyes.

"But you didn't, and now here I am." I know my boastful voice is grating on her nerves.

"Thank you, Your Highness. How would I have ever been saved if you had not come to save me yourself?" Her voice is dripping with sarcasm. I can practically see the eyeroll through the dark.

"Don't give me attitude, Menace," I growl at her.

"Oh, I am going to give you a lot more than attitude." Her eyes go wide at the same time a smile spreads across my face.

"I'm hoping so." Even though it is dark, I can see her cheeks turning pink, but her mouth is still in a flat line, not taking the bait.

Picking her up, I throw her over my shoulder, taking her back out through a secret entrance, only stumbling a couple of times. I expect her to freak out, to bang her fists against my back in protest, but none of it comes. She deadweights in my arms, resting her body against me as though I am carrying a dead body.

"I expected you to put up more of a fight." I walk quickly. Getting out of the vampire's territory without being noticed is going to be hard. If anyone was to see me here, it would be the death of me.

She stays quiet, ignoring my attempts at having a conversation. I round one of the bushes, coming in direct contact with a guard's back. With quick feet, I slip back, trying to press myself against the wall and banging Skarlette's head in the process.

"Ow!" She hisses at me, but I ignore her, slowly stepping out of our hiding spot and running towards the forest. Behind me, I can hear the men yelling. They had to have seen us.

Once I feel we are far enough into the forest to be safe I scan her face, looking for any signs of hurt before working my eyes over the rest of her body. When I have determine all is intact, I let out a sigh of relief.

"What happened in there?" I try to take her hand in mine,

but she yanks it away.

"Too much to explain out here in the middle of the woods, or ever." She walks away from me, heading back in the direction of home.

I give another glance back towards where the castle stands, sure I will see a hoard of vampires coming in our direction. But instead, I see a tall figure as it leans against the iron gate, watching us with their arms crossed.

"Menace? Should we be concerned about that?" She turns her head, looking back at me and then the figure. Her shoulders shrug as she continues to walk away. Obviously she isn't concerned so I will try not to be as well.

Quickly catching up to her, I glance over my shoulder a few times, waiting for the figure to disappear. It doesn't until we reach the edge of the forest. My brain swirls with the many questions I have for Skarlette. I know she doesn't want to answer them, but I need to try and ask her.

Following her through town, I hold the door she swings wildly open as it leads us into the local tavern. I take a seat next to her, expectantly waiting for her to tell me what the hell has happened over the past few days. How the hell she ended up in enemy territory and what on earth had made them let her leave?

The barkeep slides her a mug of ale which she greedily

gulps down. My eyes follow as a droplet runs down her mouth, sliding over her curves and continuing down her neck before disappearing under her shirt. I gulp down the lump in my throat that begs me to lick it off her skin. Now isn't the time for my lust to get in the way of whatever is going on.

"Skar. What happened back there?" I stay cautious with my words, knowing that bringing up things she wants to keep secret never ends well.

"Apparently I am a fucking princess and am about to inherit a kingdom," she snaps before taking another large drink of her ale.

"What are you talking about?" There is no way Skarlette is the princess the vampires have been looking for. Her mother was a maid in my kingdom, her father a wayward vampire traveler. Or at least that is what her mother told everyone.

She doesn't turn her head to look at me. Instead, I watch her with an analyzing stare as she looks deeply into the mug of liquid. Looking for the answers to all her problems. "The vampire king had me kidnapped, then told me a long tale about my mother and father having a one night stand and boom—a vampire princess is born. Vampires can't normally have children so there was no need for me, until now."

"That's a lot to process," I say, my thoughts still swirling.

"No shit," she snaps, her eyes finally leaving the cup and looking into my own.

The minute she looks at me, I am lost in her eyes. The way they seem to swallow me whole. I feel like I am swimming in a pool of blood. If you asked me long ago what my favorite color was, I would have said green like summer grass. But now if you ask me that question, I will always respond with red; red, like her eyes. Red like the blood that dribbles down her face after she feasts. Because to me, red embodies Skarlette. When I think of red, I think of her and that is all I ever want to think of.

"What does all of this mean?" I ask quietly.

"I have no idea." Her voice is barely more than a whisper. "Isn't this what I have wanted? To feel like I belong."

"Do any of us really belong?" I suggest.

"I just want to be treated as an equal instead of a freak of nature. But still, it feels like everyone hates me even if I am the savior." She lets out a long sigh as she turns away again, the warmth of her eyes leaving and letting the cold of this dim tavern return. In my mind, I am begging for her to look at me again. I want her to look at me as if I am the savior to all of her problems, but I know that isn't going to happen. One thing Skarlette is good at is saving herself.

The chatter around us begins to grow, the rowdier crowd of drunks shuffling around us and occasionally bumping into our table. Skarlette just keeps sitting, ignoring the commotion all around. She is waiting. Waiting for what, I am not exactly sure, but we continue to sit and wait. Neither a word or a breath is shared between us. She continues to down her drinks while I grab a bite to eat. I hold out a morsal of food to offer her some, but she refuses. I hate seeing her like this. So unsure of herself. Drowning her unsureness and sorrows in alcohol.

My whole life, I have grown up with the crimson eyed girl who doesn't take shit from anyone. She has always been strong and I admire her for that. I was weak before—but when Skarlette left us, I vowed I would become strong just like her.

"Skar," I say gently, "we should go."

She nods, reaching into her pocket to grab her payment. I throw my own bag of coin on the counter before she can even pull hers out. She looks at me with a scowl before dragging herself out of the tavern. Outside, the night air is surprisingly warm. A breeze dances across the meadow as we arrive at the bridge crossing the river. Skarlette stops, whipping around and I can tell she is ready to lay into me.

"I don't understand what you don't get, Kai," she states,

her anger like flames of fire in her eyes. Her shadows leave the ground beneath her feet and slither their way towards me. "I am not a faerie, I am not a vampire, I am a monster created by two people who didn't even want me!" Her voice rises with her emotions, practically screaming at me by the end. The shadows are close, so close that if she gets any angrier, they might just snatch me.

"You are not a monster to me." I reach for her, placing a hand on each of her shoulders, ignoring the shadows that now touch my legs. "You are a beautiful creature who brings fear to her enemies and love to her friends."

She lets her hair fall in front of her face, trying to hide herself from me. The silver strands blow out as she snorts at my words. Her arms cross and she points her head towards the ground.

"Skarlette," I demand, but still she does not look up at me.

One hand leaves her shoulder, moving to her chin and tilting her face to look at me. My other hand brushing away the hair covering her face. Every inch of her is exceptional. Even in her anger, I find her downright sinful. Her red lips match her eyes and beg for me to kiss them. Her scrunched brows leave little wrinkles in her forehead and her eyes look at me like she wants to punch me.

"Kai, I am the monster of everyone's nightmares." She is

determined to make me hate her.

"Menace, you are the monster of my dreams." I can do nothing but love her.

# Chapter Eighteen

## SKARLETTE

If I truly call myself a villain, then why do Kai Evening-glow's words effect me so much? When he said I was the monster of his dreams, my heart leapt from my chest. It gave me a weird feeling, like I wanted to jump from my skin with happiness. When his lips touched mine, performing the perfect motion, my knees practically buckled. It was everything my younger self had dreamed of.

I guess the saying that villains don't have feelings, isn't entirely true. We are just better at hiding them than everyone else.

Crossing the bridge, I am unsure of how long it will take us to get back to Ruellia on foot. We probably need to rest for the night, stay somewhere. But with Ruellia's summer festival soon starting, I doubt we will be able find a place to stay. It's why the tavern had been so crowded.

In the distance wolves howl. A sound that is so beautiful and yet chills you to your bones. Something dark dashes across the road in front of us, making our feet halt in place.

"Skar, we should find a place to rest for the night." It's like he is reading my mind.

Calix is a small fae village between Shadowfall and Ruellia. Many faeries who live inside the village trade wares or hunt inside the dark forest. These fae are far braver than the fae that live back home in Ruellia. They risk their lives hunting down the wild boar in the dark forest to provide for their families, while the people of Ruellia sit in their homes, sipping on faerie wine and living off the hard work of every other village on this continent.

A few small cottages line the streets on either side of us before giving way to the stores. We make our way down the main strip of road and head straight for the only inn in the village. The town is buzzing with people as they make their way to Ruellia for the summer festival.

We enter the the inn that sits higher than all of the other

buildings. Standing under its crooked wooden sign, the door creaks when we push it open. Inside, the run down building greets us with cobwebs hanging in the corners. The innkeeper is an older woman with white hair down to her shoulders, her wrinkled hands shake as they reach for the items on the desk in front of her.

"We need a room for the night, please." The old woman looks up, a smile lighting up her face when she sees the Prince of Ruellia standing in front of her.

Her eyes shift towards me, curious as to who the prince might have with him. Lowering my hood, I let it fall around my shoulders, watching as the panic grips the old woman in front of me. Her hand shakes a little more as she reaches for a pencil.

"I don't want any trouble now," her voice quivers.

"We aren't looking for any trouble. Merely a couple of rooms for us to rest for the night before we head home." My face tries to give her a smile, but it feels more like a cringe and It doesn't really seem to have the affect I was hoping for. She seems to glare at me in response.

Her eyes dart between Kai and I, worried of what might come. Or maybe she is just curious at why the prince is with me? Maybe she fears, I am going to kill him in his sleep. "I am sorry, my prince, but I am afraid I only have one room left for the evening. This place may be old and dusty, but it can be quite busy this time of year."

"That is fine." Kai plops a heavy bag of coin on the desk, pushing it closer in her direction.

The woman's eyes twinkle with joy as she greedily grabs the bag and stuffs it into her pocket. Grabbing a key from the drawer in front of her, she hands it to the prince. As we walk away we can hear her counting the coins behind us. The stairs leading up to the second floor feel like they may give out at any moment. Something about this place, was giving me an ominous feeling.

Upstairs is dark. Most of the doors that line the hall are closed, except for the one that we arrive in front of. The room we have been assigned for the night.

Cautiously entering the room, I check for any sign that someone is lurking in the shadows. I come to an abrupt halt next to Kai as we both stare at the one and only bed. It's ugly yellow quilt feels like an omen for what is to come. We are going to have to share this bed all night long.

"I sleep on the floor all the time. You take the bed," I say to Kai, but then I notice he is giving me this look that is less than enthused when I start to grab blankets.

"You will not and that is exactly why. You sleep on the floor everyday. Sleep on a bed for once." Kai is insistent, his hand stopping me from grabbing any more. He takes a seat in the chair in the corner, taking off his boots and placing them underneath so as not to trip over them in the night. He crosses the room, his frame getting larger the closer it gets and reminding me of what a bad idea this is.

Laying here next to him, I'm afraid that even my breath will call to our mating bond and lead some place we can never come back from. My hand brushes against his, the heat from it, warming me. His pinky rubs against the soft skin of my hand, sending shivers down my spine.

"Do you ever wish things were more simple?" I whisper, hoping he has fallen asleep and won't answer my question.

"Every day of my life." His voice is hushed, our voices whispering out between us like we are telling lifelong secrets.

"I always wondered what it would have been like to be born a farmer's bastard instead of a maids. Maybe I would have had extra work dumped on me, but I wouldn't live the life I do today." Kai's breath is the only sound for a long moment while he takes time to digest what I am saying.

"I wonder too. Then I remind myself, life wouldn't have brought me you if it were different." With that, we let the conversation fall off. Quiet surrounds us, the small chirps of crickets outside the inn window lulling Kai to sleep.

I have too much adrenaline, too many questions pumping through my mind to even attempt a slight rest. Instead, I lay here staring up at the ceiling above my head and wondering how I have gotten here. Yesterday, I was perfectly fine with being everyone's villain, going about my business and sulking in the shadows. Now, I am expected to be a queen. I can barely take care of myself, so how on this magical earth am I supposed to take care of not one, but two races of creatures?

Next to me, Kai groans, rolling over onto his side and mumbling under his breath. I try to listen closely, make out whatever it is he is trying to say, but it seems the sleep has jumbled his words. My eyes scan over his sleeping form. His broad shoulders, the muscle of his arms. I have been back in Ruellia for weeks now, but I'm still not use to how strong he is now.

He had always been such a scrawny kid like Ethan, with a tall frame and slender limbs. But the Kai laying next to me now is a man not afraid of a challenge. A man willing to throw the world into chaos if it means bringing me back to him. Am I still mad at him for bringing me back in the first place? Of course I am, but I also have a soft spot for him. To everyone's faces, I will argue and say the bond gives me these feelings, but it isn't just that. It is so much more. It's a feeling that has been many years in the making.

The way he always cares for me when no one else does. Sneaking me rations of blood when the rest of his family would try and starve me. Taking care of me when the village boys picked on me. Kai had always had a soft heart and I didn't want to get wrapped up in it when he inevitably saw the villain I was and became disgusted by it.

Shoving my feelings down I curse the goddess for making the world so cruel.

My thoughts linger back on the vampire kings words. I could rule them all, show them that the way they treated me was wrong. If they still chose to be cruel to me without care, then I will be crueler. I will become queen, but I will be the villainous queen they all think I will be.

The morning sun rises, shining through the window and blinding me in the eyes. When I fling my hand to the side, expecting to come into contact with Kai's body, it instead falls flat on the mattress. After coming to terms with the fact I am going to be ruler of a whole lot of people, I found myself relaxed enough to sleep.

"Figures. Probably running off to tell his brother," I mumble to myself.

"Tell my brother what?" Kai asks, coming through the door.

I let out a little screech, taken aback at his entrance into the room when I thought he was long gone. My screech makes him bust up with laughter. He is practically bent over and unable to breathe from the loud laughs that spill from him.

"What was that?" A few more chuckles as he closes the door. "You're a vampire assassin and I just scared you, didn't I?"

I can't help the scowl that comes across my face. "Of course you did. I can get spooked too, you know. I thought you were gone, so it wasn't like I was focusing on listening for anyone." I fold my arms across my chest, the metal of my corset digging into my ribs.

"It was the cutest noise I have ever heard you make," he teases, bopping my nose with his large sausage fingers.

"I don't make cute noises. I'm a scary assassin." Rolling my eyes at him, I'm annoyed that any sound coming from me would be considered 'cute'. "Now if you will excuse me, I have orders to take." I try to move around him, but he stops me.

"I bet you do make cute noises." His voice seems to drop an octave, like he is thinking about things he shouldn't be thinking about. Like I am about to be in a whole lot of trouble.

His body comes closer, forcing me to step back until I am pressed firmly against the bedpost. My breath begins to quicken as his eyes bore into me.

"I bet you'd make the best noises if I was buried inside of you while your teeth are buried in my neck." My breathing halts, images of his words float in my head and I know I am in so much trouble right now.

I need a way out of this. Kai is engaged, I am still emotionally unavailable and we haven't even talked about the fact we are mated to one another.

"I bet you make the best sounds with my knee in your gut," I quip back at him, making him instinctively look down to make sure my knee wasn't ready to take out his prized jewels.

With that, he backs away, hands held up in defense. I know I bit back too hard, I can see the embarrassment in his face, but I am all bark and no bite when it comes to Kai. I don't know how to be anything different. I want to tell him I want him too, want to sink my teeth into his skin again, but I need to keep my distance. I told myself it is because of

Ethan and the fact that Kai is engaged. But if I were truly honest with myself, it is because I am scared of how it all makes me feel.

If I wasn't the villain in this story, than who was I?

# Chapter Nineteen

## SKARLETTE

We manage to find horses for the ride back to Ruel-lia. Riding back is going to give me a lot of time alone with my thoughts. The horses body sways beneath me, it's feet padding against the ground. Looking over at Kai, he meets my glance and gives me a smile. I'm not the woman Kai needs, I am dead set on getting the peace I crave even if it means sacrificing the people he loves. It makes me sad to think of the pain I might cause him. I'm only going to end up hurting him in the long run. Then just like my mother he will leave me.

My legs are aching from the amount of riding we have done the last two days. You'd think an assassin who runs around all day, wouldn't be sore, but riding horses was a whole different ball game. I almost wish I could have been knocked out again for the trip home. I much enjoyed falling asleep in Ruellia and waking up in Shadowfall.

The large stone castle comes into view, its luxurious gardens sprawling out before the double doors. I fling my leg over the horse's back and dismount from the saddle. A shriek of surprise escapes me when I feel Kai's hands land on my hips, his fingers digging slightly into my clothes. He guides me away from the horses, pressing me up against one of the gardens tall shrubs to keep us out of the guards view. The shrubs leaves and branches scratch into the back of my neck, tangling in my hair and keeping me from being able to get away.

My voice comes out breathily. "Kai, you can't be with me." The look I see in his eyes is like heat from a flame, a hunger that can only be quenched by our touch. We have been in close proximity for too long. The need is calling to us both and we have to make it stop.

"I laid next to you all night, listening to your whimpers as you dreamt. Smelling the scent of you waft around me like the smoke of cigars. I need you, Menace." His hand slides up, resting against the side of my neck as his lips come down on my own.

His tongue darts in, swiping across my own before leaving. His taste is like heaven, I want—no, I *need* more. It feels as though my life will crumble if his lips do not touch mine. My palms lay flat against his chest, giving him a light push to put some much needed space between us. I start to walk away, but Kai's hand grabs my own, pulling me through the castle doors and up the stairs.

Halting in front of Kai's bedroom door, I once again pull away from him. "Kai, I am serious. We can't do this." I'm losing my bluster. The words are starting to fall as the need pools between my legs. The thought of him bringing me up to his room with the pure need to see me naked has me a complete mess.

He tugs me inside and closes the door behind me. "I know of a thousand reasons why we shouldn't, but Menace, you are my mate. The bond will only grow stronger the longer we live in this castle together, and when you are away, it is excruciating to know that you are not near."

"That's all it is, some bond telling you that you want me." Yanking my arm from his grasp, I cross them under my breasts in hope that he won't try and pull me close again.

"Forget the fucking bond, Skar." His voice booms, making it clear that he is done with me trying to push him away. "I love you. I have loved you ever since I was a hormonal teenage boy. And no, not because of the hormones, but because of you. Menace, you are the most beautiful creature I have ever laid eyes on. I admire your strength and your ability to not take shit from anyone. I want more than just some mate bond. I want you, Skarlette. I want to go to sleep next to you every night and wake up next to you every morning. I want to kill the men who lay there hands on you, even though I know you can do it yourself."

I can't look away from him as I stand there letting the words sink in and mix with the blood that runs cold in my veins. I have never felt love before, but I know this is it. Taking one step closer, I wrap my arms around his neck, and press my lips to his. This is such a bad idea, but oh, how it feels so good.

His hands slide up my waist in slow movements. Taking his time to unsnap each of the hooks on my corset before letting it fall to the floor. His eyes roam over me, making me feel naked even when I am completely clothed. His hands make quick work to discard the rest of my clothes, baring me to him.

"Skar, all I want is the taste of you on my tongue." His tongue drags across my nipple, sending a lightning bolt of pleasure to my core.

One of my fangs sink into my lip as I throw my head back from the feeling. Everything is so heightened with the bond. His hands feel like they are searing my skin and his tongue sends tingles through my entire body.

His mouth comes back to mine, his tongue darting inside my mouth and running across my fangs. My teeth are so sharp that a small trickle of blood spills from his tongue and into my mouth.

"Kai," I moan. "You're bleeding. We can't"

"Take it, Skarlette," he demands.

"I don't know if I can stop," I admit to him, worry lacing through my veins.

"You will." His hand slithers down my body, moving between my legs and sliding through my center.

My back arches under his touch, my lips hovering over his neck as my hand cups the back of his head and pulls him in closer. He slides two fingers inside me just as I bite down. The mix of those two actions send me into a completely different dimension. I am floating. The world around me disappears and all I can feel is intense pleasure.

Before I register what I am doing, my feet are moving, pushing both of us towards the bed. I let my fangs ease out of his skin, licking away the blood that dribbles down his neck.

His fingers slide out, slow and agonizingly steady, making me miss their touch. My hands press firmly against his chest, pushing him down on the bed before I climb on top.

Once fully seated on his lap, I push him inside of me, rocking back and forth in a steady pace and letting my head fall back as he places kisses on my chest. His hands are plastered against my back while I come completely undone, shuddering from the feeling. It feels like a long gone out spark has been lit. Inside of me feels warm, like the bond is humming to my heart. More like my soul humming along with his. It is like nothing in the world matters or exists when we are together.

Lifting me off his lap, he lets me curl into the soft blankets on his bed. They smell like him and it brings me a sense of comfort, a sense of home. My eyes shoot open, the realization of what we just did comes crashing over the blissful afterglow of my orgasm.

I marked Kai. I smell like him now too. Both the fae and the vampire mating rituals now seal our bond. This is a mistake we will surely pay for.

This wasn't supposed to happen, not like this. Kai is still engaged to Kesira and I am Ethan's assassin. *Shit. Shit. Shit.* Ethan will smell Kai on me tomorrow when I go to get my assignments.

"It will be okay." Kai's hand reaches up, softly rubbing his thumb against my cheek. He clearly must have seen the panic stricken look on my face.

"How is it going to be okay? We are going to ruin all of the plans." Rising from the bed, I dress quickly. "Kai, you realize we just completed both mating rituals, right?"

"I'm aware." His voice is grim. The strange part though, it doesn't feel like he is mad about the mating ritual part. It feels like he is mad at me.

"You know I am not mad it was you. Our plans to take down your brother are going to be ruined if he knows we mated. We are supposed to be keeping a low profile." I slide my dagger back inside my boot, making my way for the door.

Kai grabs hold of my wrist, pulling me back towards him and hovering his lips above my own. I could easily be pulled back into the spell of him if I let myself.

"I will fix this." He says before placing one last kiss on my lips. Letting my wrist drop from his hold, he watches as I leave.

Opening the door slowly, I peer around it to make sure no one can see me leaving Kai's room. One foot is halfway out when Ethan's voice echoes down the hall. I slip back inside, slamming the door closed behind me.

"What in the world are you doing?" Kai spins to look at me, a bewildered look across his face at the slam of his door.

"Ethan is out there." I lock the door behind me, running across the room, and flinging open the window. Throwing one of my legs over the sill, I climb out the window.

"Don't be in such a hurry to leave, would ya," Kai says gloomily.

I let my feet dangle as I hold on to the window's ledge. Below me, about five feet, is a patio—one I can land on without breaking any bones. I wait a few seconds before letting myself drop. My boots land with a thud against the stone and I take in a sharp inhale of breath from the impact. Continuing to move quickly, I open the french doors in front of me and quietly make my way through the study.

An all too familiar voice calls out to me from the dark recesses of the study, making me freeze.

To my left, seated near the warm fire, is the king. His cough rattles through the room as I approach. His body is covered in a blanket and his form is slouched slightly from the coughing fit.

"Your Majesty," I greet with a small bow.

"Why are you sneaking through?" He questions. Though sickly, his voice still holds a level of assertiveness that makes the little girl in me scared.

I give him a sheepish smile. "Just playing a game with your sons."

A laugh turns into another fit of coughs as the king chuckles at my joke. "I'm sure you are," he responds when the fits have ceased.

I pull the blankets closer around his shoulders. "You should rest."

"You fool them, you know. They think you are a fun toy to play with. . .but if only they knew you are so much worse. You are destined to be something neither of them can handle." I'm speechless at the king's words.

"Wha…" My questions are abruptly stopped when a nurse maid enters the study, her beady dark eyes narrowing in on me.

"Get out of here. You shouldn't be anywhere near the king right now," she hisses at me, her disapproving glare looking me over for any sign of blood.

Baring my teeth at her, I growl as I walk past. When she jumps away from me, I can't help but laugh. They always like to torment the beast until it comes back to bite.

Now I'm off to deal with the consequences of my actions.

# Chapter Twenty

## SKARLETTE

The large double doors to the throne room sit before me. I stare at the light green color, looking for some sort of imperfection, but they have none. The only horrors are in my own mind. Letting out a sigh, I push open the doors and stride towards Prince Ethan who is lounging upon the throne as though it were his bed. His hair is a rumpled mess and his bony fingers trace along the edges of a bowl of grapes.

"Finally come to get your assignments?" His face widens into smile when he sees me approach, his fingers ceasing their current movement before grabbing and popping a grape into his mouth. He chews it slowly, taking his time and keeping me locked here for longer than I would like.

"Yes." I bow my head at him, impatiently waiting for the paper with names. I want out of here. I want to flee this room and put as much distance between the two of us as I can. Part of me worries he will see it written on my face or he will read my thoughts. My mind chants, telling me he already knows about my plan to kill him.

"I have nothing for you today." Shock reverberates through me. He really has nothing for me to do today? No one to hunt down who gave him the wrong thing or who crossed his path when he didn't like it? "Nobody has irritated me lately." He winks. "I guess my guard dog is working."

My head bobs, turning to leave the throne room when Ethan's voice comes again.

"Oh, and Skarlette. I know what you did." I refuse to turn around and let him know how much his words shake me to my core. Hesitating slightly before simply walking out the doors, my back is rigid with the ominous parting words.

Having a free day is great, but I am so used to people telling me what to do, that I find I am having a hard time deciding it on my own. I need to find enough Ruellia juice to blow this place up. I'm sure if I talked to the Havard twins, they will know exactly where to get something like that. For years they tried to blow things up at school before finally getting expelled. The only problem with that plan, was that I had no idea where the Hagar twins lived. I wasn't allowed to walk home like the other children. I was picked up in a royal carriage with the curtains drawn so I would not see.

This meant I would need to divulge my plan to someone else, someone who knew where they lived. I racked my brain, trying to think of someone I could both share this information as well as someone who would actually talk to me. I am left with little choices.

One girl comes to mind. Her long red hair and freckled face made her stand out amongst the crowd, but she was always kind to me. Janella would know where the twins lived and she would be one of the only people willing to talk with me. Though, telling her my plan might just cost me everything.

I knock three times on the old farmhouse door. Pigs grunt as they root around in the pen to my left while chickens squawk and dart around my feet. A woman appears on the other side of the door, looking like a replica of Janella if she had gained a few pounds.

"Can I help ya?" She looks at me with tired eyes, the baby on her hip happily squawking at the toy it chews on. At first, I think she might be Janella's mom, but clearly she isn't old enough for that, even in fae years.

"I'm looking for Janella." I keep my hood up, worried that if this woman sees my true identity, she might send me away with a door slam to the face.

"Janella!" She yells, leaving the door open and walking away. Inside the small farmhouse, another small child plays on a worn rug with his wooden train. The sink is over-flowing with soapy water, and the hallway that leads back to what I assume would be their bedrooms, is dark.

When Janella comes to the door, she quickly steps outside. The door closes behind her and she ushers me around the corner and into the barn. I lower my hood, watching as her brows rise a little with recognition. Obviously, I was not who she was expecting.

"Skarlette?" She looks me over, her eyes tracing the scar across my face, her brows scrunching with confusion at why I have arrived on her doorstep asking for her.

"I hate to bother you, but I need help." Concern instantly

morphs the confused look on Janella's face.

"What do you need?"

I rush my words, worried that someone will find us or over here our conversation. "I am planning something—something big and I can't really tell you all the details, but I need to know where the twins live."

"They live down by the river. Close to the old Craigstan place." Her finger points to the old windmill, it's broken sails limply spinning in the slight breeze.

I start to head in the direction she points to when her hand comes up, halting my steps. "I'll go with ya."

A weird feeling crawls through my chest. I have never had someone want to come with me before, besides that time Kai came because his brother told him to.

Janella takes the lead as we approach the farmhouse, readying her fist to knock on the Havards' door when voices filter out through the window. My hand grabs Janella's arm, yanking her back and pulling her around the corner to listen in on the conversation.

"What is it you need from us?" The voice is deeper than it used to be, but I can still easily recognize it as one of the twins.

The voice speaking back to them is familiar, but I can't quiet place where I have heard it before. "I need as much

Ruellia poison as I can get my hands on. How is it going with adding it into the smoke?"

"It is working out beautiful, but we haven't really been able to test it's full potential."

"There is a small vampire village on the other side of the river, ones who don't take kindly to the vampire king's rule. I am sure it would be no problem to test it on them. We wipe out an entire village to see if it works, and the vampire king is none the wiser."

Chairs scrape against the floor and I push Janella back farther, pressing my back against the cool stone of the house. Finally, one of the speakers comes into view and I realize why his voice was so familiar.

Damien. The King's general. The man that controls the entire fae army.

We watch as the general climbs onto his horse. When he is almost out of sight, I pull away from the wall, walking away from the house and down the road. I have no idea what Ethan is planning, but I have to find out and quickly.

"Wait, don't you need to talk to them?" Janella calls, trying to catch up with me.

"Won't do me any good. They are preparing to wipe out the vampires." I can feel Janella's nervousness as she follows me back to town. She buzzes around at my side like a fly stuck in a bottle. She isn't sure what to say to me, so I take the plunge to break the silence.

"Thank you for your help today," I say as we approach Janella's door.

"Skarlette, you amaze me. You do these heinous things for the prince, yet here you are being nice to me." Her words needle under my skin like a knife.

"I guess the world isn't as black and white as people want it to be. I can do bad things for someone else or even do bad things against the people who show me their true colors, but the people who have shown me kindness don't deserve the villainous side of me."

"You want people to see you as the villain because then they leave you alone—but deep down, you are a good person, Skar." Watching Janella's form disappear behind the door, I ponder over her words of wisdom as I leisurely take my time walking back to the castle.

I don't know what to do with her. Was she being friendly? I am not even sure how to act around someone who isn't trying to kill me or pretend I don't exist. I mean, I know how to talk to Kai. But someone else? Not in a million years would I have expected this.

I kick the dirt as I walk, slowing when I see a shadow at the edge of the forest. Its orange glowing eyes stare at me with an intensity that shakes me. I make quick work of grabbing my dagger, ready to fight off whatever animal has its sights set on eating me.

The large wolf takes slow and calculated steps towards me. I take in every sign the large animal is giving me. Its teeth aren't bared and the furry ears atop its head are upright. I think it is more curious than anything.

Continuing to walk back to the castle, I try to ignore the large beast. It's walking beside me, following me all the way. Closing in on the gate, I don't know what to do. I need to get rid of this animal before the guards try and kill it.

"Shoo!" I yell, waving my arms and trying to get it to flee. It stares at me, its head turning sideways as it listens to my orders. It takes a bit, but finally the animal leaves, disappearing back into the forest.

Several guards rush past me with clanking armor as I enter the castle, running in the direction of the throne room. Curiosity kills me, forcing me to make my way there. Inside, I find Kai and Ethan wrestling on the freshly polished floor. At first, I think it is some sort of training exercise, that is until I watch Kai punch Ethan right in the face.

"Kai!" I yell.

His head snaps in my direction, looking up at me and giving Ethan time to push Kai's body off of him. He stands, raising his fist and landing a punch right in Kai's cheekbone. Blood instantly blossoms along the open wound. Ethan tries to throw another punch, but Kai ducks, throwing his shoulder into his brother's torso and taking him back down to the ground.

Ethan yells at his brother, his lip swollen and bleeding from the fight. "Get off me you brute!"

"Kai," I say again, hoping he will stop fighting, even though I really enjoy watching Ethan get his ass handed to him.

He stops for a moment. This time he doesn't look at me, only stares into his brother's soulless eyes.

"She has you on a leash already, brother." Ethan's teeth are blood soaked as he smiles.

Kai's fist pounds into the marble floor beside Ethan's head. "Talk about her like that again and I will end you."  He stands and the guards rush to Ethan, helping him up and taking him away to his room.

Ethan raises his hands, making the guards halt in front of where Kai stands. "I will make your lives hell when I am the king of this castle." His hand drops and the guards begin to move again, escorting the prince to his room. The castle workers that had been standing here gawking at the events, scatter like roaches, retreating back to their duties.

Kai is walking towards me, determination in every step when Kesira comes running up to him. She attentively wipes at his blood stained cheek with her handkerchief.

"Are you okay?" Her high pitched voice askes. "Let's go get this washed up." She loops her arm in his, spinning before she see's me standing in the doorway. "Haven't you done enough today?" She snaps at me as they pass.

Narrowing my eyes at her, I walk farther into the throne room where a maid is trying her best to clean the blood from the floor. The tap of my boots against the floor echo. The evening light filtering through the large windows, casts an orange glow over the throne. I sit down, placing my hands on the gold arms and letting the coolness seep into me.

"*This is what it would feel like to be a queen,*" the devil in my head chants. The angel says nothing, she gave up on me long ago. I straighten my back, looking out across the room and pretend I am in Shadowfall. "*You could make them bow to you. Show them what a merciless queen could be like.*" He slithers in my ear.

How in the world am I supposed to bring together two species that loathe each other? How am I to bring the fae in, when I would be the one to burn their beloved castle to the ground? It will be a feat, but I am the chosen one. I have been made for this.

My shadows creep amongst the darkness of the throne room, filling in every corner, before rising up the walls. I urge them higher, raising my head and making the ultimate decision.

I will be reborn through the ashes of this castle. I will burn it down a monster and rise from the ashes a villainous queen.

# Chapter Twenty One

## KAI

Kesira follows me all the way up to my room. I wish to talk to Skarlette, but Kesira never gives me a chance. She whines about the fight, scolding me for starting something over a 'filthy half-breed', as everyone likes to call her.

Once inside my room, Kesira looks at me with utter disgust. "You can't be with her, you know? You are the prince of Ruellia and she is simply a weapon for our disposal." She takes a damp cloth, trying to dab away some of the dried blood on my cheekbone.

My hand shoots out, grabbing her wrist in a punishing

squeeze as her eyes snap up to mine with fear. "Get. Out," I say to her, slow and menacingly as to get my point across. At this point, I would rather never see her again.

Kesira rips her wrist out of my grasp, storming out of my bedroom door and slamming it behind her. Good riddance. She is the last thing I want to be dealing with. My face is already healing, but my brother's words run deep.

*"You need to get it together. Skarlette isn't yours,"* Ethan said to me in the throne room after Skarlette had just walked out the door. *"She is my weapon and I will use her as I please. In fact, I wouldn't even bother getting close to her. I have a mission for her soon—and she won't be coming back."*

Ethan's words chilled me to my bones. What in the world is he planning? I hate myself for standing there and listening to him threaten her like that. I should have exploded. Instead, I waited a beat too long and he took the opportunity to egg on my temper. The way his fox like face sneered at me, his navy blue eyes glowing. He did like to cause mischief, even at the suffering of others.

*"I know you bed her last night. You guys reek of each other. Maybe I should have my go with her too, before she leaves us forever."* The smile that came across my brother's face had me fuming, but the twinkle in his eye, the way his mouth quirked up on the side in that smug expression, made me

lose all self control. I lunged towards him, knocking him to the ground and throwing my fist into his face.

They say hitting won't make you feel better, but hitting my brother in the face, watching his smug expression fall, made me feel fucking great. Skarlette can't seem to see it, but I am just as bad as her, if not worse. She doesn't hurt the people she loves, but I feel amazing while punching my own brother in the face.

We were rolling around the floor, grunting and cursing as more and more castle workers joined the room. I smelled her before she even called my name. When her voice rang out, my eyes immediately snapped up to hers. I knew I should let my brother go, but seeing her there had his words digging deeper. When the fight had finally finished, I felt calmer. I knew that in just a moment, I would walk over to Skarlette and I would feel better. Until Kesira showed up anyway.

Walking into the bathing chamber attached to my room, I look at myself in the mirror over the sink. The cut where my brother punched me is practically healed already, dark circles underlined my eyes from lack of sleep, and my hair is a disheveled mess. I need some sleep, but I need to warn Skarlette about my brother's plans.

A knock comes from the door, her vanilla scent wafting

around me before I even open it. It is like she is reading my thoughts and came at my call. I swing the door open and am met with fiery crimson eyes. Oh good, she is going to be mad at me too.

"What were you thinking?" She scolds, her hand on her hips and a pointed look in her eyes.

"My brother started it. He is the one that said…" I trail off, not wanting to tell her about my brother's plans like this.

"You can't just go around beating up the prince in charge." She runs a hand through her soft gray colored locks, the anger melting from her face and turning to tiredness.

"I know that!" I snap at her. This shit storm that's happening and no sleeping these last few days are starting to get to me. Her face turns to stone, giving me a bored look like she doesn't have time for my temper tantrum. "I'm sorry, Skar," I say softly. "He got in my head and I just snapped. I will try better to control my self." Moving closer, I try to put my arms around her, but she steps away from me. The distance between us is like a stake to my heart.

"We can't keep doing this." She bites her lower lip with worry. She didn't come here to yell at me about my brother. She made a decision and she is about to tell me the news.

"You are going to fulfill the prophecy." I keep my voice

hushed, in case listening ears are sitting in the hall. She looks up at me with worry swirling in her eyes. "I am so proud of you, Menace."

A small smile plays at the corners of her lips. Like pride is swelling inside of her. I can tell she wants to put space between us. She wants to keep me at arms length but I'm not going to let that happen. I am going to be by her side every step of the way. I spent three years away from her and I can't let anymore time pass without her.

"I will make my enemies pay, but I will be kind to those who earn it." She is sounding like a queen already.

"You will make a beautiful queen." I step closer, testing the boundaries she set earlier. When she doesn't back away, I take the moment to wrap her in a hug and press my lips against her forehead.

"And it's exactly why we can't do this." She steps out of my hold and motions her hand between us. "I have to take down your family, Kai. I have to burn everything you have ever known to the ground in order for me to rise from the ashes. I need to do things that you won't be able to come back from."

"Let me be by your side, Skarlette. Let me help you earn the hearts of the fae people. We are bound together, whether you like it or not."

"I don't want to be bound to anyone else, Kai, but what I am about to do…" She pauses for a moment. "I am afraid you will finally see me for the monster I truly am."

"I have told you once already, but I will tell you again and again if I need to. I love you, Skarlette—I want you no matter who you are or what you do. There is nothing you can do to scare me away, for nothing you do is different from what I myself have done. Menace, it's you and me forever and you need to remember that." Taking her hand, I hold it tightly in my own as my thumb rubs softly against her smooth flesh.

Skarlette's shoulders relax. I can tell it's hard for her to trust what I am saying, but when it comes to Skarlette, I never lie. My hands reach for her, my palms resting on either side of her face.

"Tell me how we are doing it, Menace." I kiss her lips. "Tell me how we are going to burn it to the ground." Another kiss to her lips. "Tell me how I will be begging on my knees for the attention of my villainous queen."

Skarlette's hands rise, pushing my hands away from her face. Disappointment blooms inside me when I think she is leaving, but then she pushes me toward the bed, climbing on my lap and kissing the life out of me.

"I don't know what I did to deserve you," she breathes

between kisses.

She breaks away from me, resting her forehead against mine. "You survived."

To anyone else, those words probably wouldn't have made sense, but to us they are everything. It was a reminder to her that when I asked thirteen year old her to live, she did it. Reminded her that every time she came to me in tears from the abuse my family handed her—that I asked her to stay strong. That one day it would all be over.

She climbs off my lap, making her way across the room. "Skarlette?"

"Hmm?" She hums from where she has taken a seat in front of the window. She seems to be watching some wolf dog that is running along the river.

"What is something you really want?" I realize, I have never heard Skarlette ask for anything before.

She seems to be lost in thought for a long time, searching through her mind for the right answer. "I'm honestly, not sure." She looks at me with a look of sadness in her eyes. "I stopped looking at stuff that I would want a long time ago. Now all I want is peace. As a little girl, I wanted so many things that you and your siblings got. Horses, toys, sweets. I wanted it all, but everyone else got what they wanted except me. I just gave up. It wasn't worth the pain I was putting myself through." She shrugs her shoulders, turning her gaze back out the window to the life below.

Soon, the terror my family reigned over her will be over and I will be standing at her side, watching them burn.

# Chapter Twenty Two

## SKARLETTE

I leave Kai to fester on his fight with his brother and the fact that I will be a queen. Heading to my room, I hope I can get a few hours of rest before heading off to see Janella. The door creaks, welcoming me to the cold, dim room and inviting me to ease my weary mind. I take a seat at the small desk, but something feels off. I scan the room, but nothing catches my eye. Lighting the half burned candle that sits atop my desk, I pour myself a glass of faerie wine from the decanter, still unable to shake the uneasy feeling of someone watching me.

The liquid is sweet with a hint of sour, sliding over my taste buds and down my throat. I take another sip, slower this time, savoring the flavor, but something isn't right about this wine. There's a hint of floral flavor that shouldn't be there. The glass drops from my hands, crashing to the floor with an ear piercing sound. I spin as bootsteps approach from behind. My eyes spin a few seconds behind my body, giving the large fae guard in front of me time to grab ahold of my arms.

The guard's hands are strong, as one of his meaty hands slides down to grip my wrist in a tight squeeze. His free hand moves, reaching for his sword. I try to will my shadows to grab hold of it, but whatever he has managed to slip into my wine is making me sluggish. My shadows barely make an appearance. The man looks at me with curiosity as my brows pinch in confusion. Grunting, I push with all of my soul to get my shadows to rise, but they don't move.

"Not so strong with that special faerie wine running through ya?" His eyes are gleeful and the smile on his face tells me it is having the intended affect.

"I am the crowned prince's assassin." I glare at him, secretly hoping the goddess will bless me with two powers and he will combust into flames just from my stare, but alas I am not that lucky.

"The prince is the one who sent me," he says with a snorted laugh.

My blood begins to boil, my temper rising to the surface. Why is Ethan trying to get rid of me? I thought he was going to use me to take down the entire vampire race. Maybe Kai heard wrong. Maybe Ethan never planned for me to do it, only to get me away from his brother. They need the vampires. Need the alliance with them to get the gold.

I watch in what feels like slow motion as the guard before me pulls his blade. Putting my hand against his arm, I try to keep the blade away from my throat, but I can feel the weakness in my limbs. I should have drank blood this morning.

"Any final words before you leave this earth?" The man taunts.

"No," I choke out as my hand falls and the blade pushes against my throat.

"I have some." A deep voice says from somewhere from behind me.

The guard's eyes shoot up, his eyebrows rising in surprise. "Your Highness," he stumbles to say, but his hands don't leave me.

Kai's voice rumbles over us. "You're touching what's

*mine.*"

The guard's hands falter ever so slightly. I can see his confliction as his eyes dance between Kai and I. Then his eyes drift farther, to something that stands in the doorway. I can hear the wolf's growl as she bares her teeth at my attacker. Apparently Kai had brought me a surprise.

"I'm afraid you didn't hear me." Kai's voice is closer now, just over my head. "Your hands are touching her and I didn't give you permission to touch her."

In the blink of an eye, Kai's sword comes down between me and the guard, the hand that previously held the dagger to my throat falls to floor with a thud. Blood spirts from the man's open veins, spraying across my chest. My mouth waters, and my tongue begs for me to taste it, but I am too sluggish to hit the right spot fast enough.

The guard looks at me with terror in his eyes as my finger comes up, wiping through the blood that sits on my chest and slowly making it's way into my mouth. I suck the finger, letting out a groan at the fresh taste of his blood. My eyes don't leave his as I watch his face turn pale at what he has just witnessed.

"I do love it when you tease them," Kai purrs.

"My prince." The man trembles on the floor between us.

Kai squats down in front of him. "What did you lace her

drink with?"

"If I tell you, will you let me go?"

"If you tell me, I will end you swiftly." The hope drains from he man's face instantly.

"I hope the half-breed bitch dies with me." Spit flies with the force of his words, landing all over Kai's face.

The small amount of blood seems to steady my feet, my eyes are starting to focus, but the room still moves around me slightly. Kai grips hold of the guard's chin, his eyes venomous. If looks could kill, I think the entire room would be dead.

He bites out every word. "What. Was. In. The. Wine." The man groans at the force Kai is putting into his grip. The wolf barks, nashing her teeth at the gaurd.

"Ruellia leaves." I hear the answer leave the man's lips and watch as Kai's hands move quickly. The man's neck snaps, his head lolling to the side at an awkward angle.

Kai's arms wrap around me, scooping me up and carrying me out of my room.

"Clean up that fucking mess," he snaps to one of the servants. Keeping my head tucked into his chest, I try not to look at the people who pass by us. It only seems to make the dizziness worse.

Forcing my eyes shut, I try not to be sick. The rocking

motion from him walking, plus the spinning my own head is doing from the Ruellia poison is unbearable. Walking all the way to his room, I expect to feel him put me down when we arrive, but he doesn't. Instead, he sits down on the bed with me still in his arms.

"Drink. It will help with the sickness." Opening my eyes, I see his neck bared in my direction.

"I don't want to drink from you." I know the implications, the feeling and strength it gives me.

"Drink," he demands.

Nuzzling my nose against his neck, I take in a deep breath, letting his scent flood me before lining my fangs up and sinking them into his skin. The warmth of his blood rushes into my mouth and down my throat, like a cool drink of water after a long day. I feel the affects wash over me like the waves of an ocean.

Moving so I can straddle his lap, I hold his head in my hands. A small part of me is afraid I will drain him, too drunk on how good his blood makes me feel. My right hand grips the back of his head, grabbing hold of his soft hair. I slowly pull my fangs out, pulling his head back and looking at the two small puncture wounds.

Surprise shoots through me when Kai's hands grab my hips, keeping me from moving off his lap. My eyes move from his neck and see him looking at me with need. Like he wants to devour me.

A knock at the door interrupts whatever was just about to happen, making us both let out a low groan. The wolf pup on the floor lets out a growl, reminding us of her presence. Kai's hands leave my hips and I pull myself off his lap. He moves across the room, opening the door and moving out into the hall.

Staying seated on the bed, I look down at the animal that is now curled up on the floor. Reaching down, I pet her soft coat of fur. A smile spreading across my face. I guess she has decided to be ours.

Kai's annoyed voice trickles through the cracked door, pulling my attention away from the sleeping beast at my feet. "He tried to have her killed,"

"He is trying to keep the kingdom safe," the king's guard argues.

Kai growls. "She is not a weapon. She is not his to take. She is mine."

"I'm sure she would love to hear you say that," the guard scoffs.

"She fucking loves it. Makes her come just thinking about me saying it," Kai retorts.

I roll my eyes. While I did love hearing him say it, he

definitely didn't need to boast. I love that he claims me as his own, while also respecting the fact that I can handle myself.

"Good goddess, Kai. You let her drink from you again?" He must have seen the fresh puncture wounds on Kai's neck.

"That's none of your business."

"Kai.. I really—"

"It is *Your Highness* or *my Prince*." He is quickly losing his patience. The patience he already had little of.

"You and *her* are requested downstairs for dinner." The only sound that follows is the guard's sword hitting his boot as he walks away.

Kai returns to the room, his hand running through his hair with a large sigh. I can see the toll everything is taking on him, and I hate that I am the one causing him so much stress.

"I come just from thinking about you staking your claim on me?" I arch a brow at him, but it does what's intended. A small smile quirks at the edge of Kai's mouth.

He sits, pulling me onto his lap. "Let him think it. In this room, we know it's you who has the claim on me. I worship you like a goddess."

"They won't be scared of me if you tell them all my secrets." I press a soft kiss against his lips.

"Between you and that dog, they will be terrified." He smiles up at me, hands holding onto my hips.

Wiggling free of his hold, I plant my boots into the carpet and head for the door. The animal looks at me for a moment before she tries to go back to sleep.

"Come," I order her. The wolf lazily rises from the floor, stretching out her body and giving a big yawn. "Are you ready? We have somewhere to be." I say, urging her out the door and down the stairs.

Kai follows with as much enthusiasm as the wolf, making me roll my eyes at them both. While some of us could lounge around all day, others would be punished for not showing up on time.

Inside the dining room, Ethan is waiting for us. I look around, confused not to see anyone else here. I would think if we were summoned, we would have guests. Taking a seat at the table, the wolf takes her own place near the fireplace behind me.

"I wanted to have a little chat," the prince says, his hands folded together in font of his mouth, elbows propped on the table.

"About?" Kai questions.

"We can't keep fighting, brother. It doesn't look well for the kingdom. With the vampire attacks on the rise, we need to show everyone we are a united front." Ethan swirls the drink in his hands, taking a sip and setting the glass on the table. His finger runs over the rim, making a high pitched hum.

"I agree." Kai winces at the harsh sound the glass is making. "I see no need to fight with you brother, but talk of Skarlette sets the bond aflame."

He is always the one good with his words. I prefer punching their lights out. I have a much shorter temper than Kai does though.

"I will try my best not to test you," Ethan says, but I can see the small glimmer in his eye, the shit stirrer in him, begging to be released.

"Great. If that's all settled, why don't we have a nice dinner?" I urge, trying to get off the topic and move on.

The silence as we eat is permeated by the thick tension in the air around us. Even though they said they would no longer fight, I can still feel the discord between the two of them. Kai stabs his steak harder than necessary, while Ethan keeps drinking the faerie wine and requesting his cup be refilled.

Chewing my food slowly, I try to ignore the tension suffocating me. I think about the my plan to burn this whole place to the ground. Finishing the morsels on my plate, I give one last scrap of meat to the dog that now lays beneath the table and look up. Both men have left, leaving me alone without so much as a see you later.

"Alright then, I guess I'm chopped liver," I mumble to myself, gathering my plates and taking them down into the kitchen.

Depositing my dishes into the sink, I dart out the side entrance and out onto the castle grounds. Outside, the wind is blowing the trees in every direction. Their limbs shake and fall as the wind howls. The doctor races up the front steps of the castle, sidestepping me as if I will lunge out and attack him. His eyes hesitate on the wolf pup that trots beside me, before ultimately choosing to ignore us.

The king deteriorates by the minute, his sickness progressing faster and faster as the final summer days drag on. I fear the state of things when he finally passes and Ethan is the one sitting upon the throne. I hate to think of all the people he will send me after when he truly has free reign to do as he pleases.

My hair whips around, it's silver strands blowing across my face. I should have taken a moment and grabbed my cloak. The hood would have kept my face from the air that dries out my eyes. I'm not really sure where I am headed this late into the evening, but I do know that I could use a stiff drink.

I'm halfway to the tavern when Janella emerges from the local bookstore. She bumps into me, her arms full of books. Several of the books tumble from the stack, and my shadows leaving me quickly, scooping them up before they fall to the ground.

"Thanks." She looks at me with a smile. "Don't tell my dad," she says with a wink before taking off towards her farm. I hate to tell her, but I think her dad might notice a huge stack of books in her arms.

Inside the tavern, my entrance makes the chatter fall silent. I realize I have just entered a busy establishment without my cloak and instantly feel too exposed. Turning my eyes down to the floor, I make my way to a table in the dark corner where I won't be so noticeable. The wood chair scrapes against the floor and creaks with protest as I take my seat. The crowd watches me for what feels like forever before returning back to their chatter.

Throwing a few coins on the table, I wait for a bar maid to bring me a pitcher of ale. I lean back in the chair, resting my legs up on the table and watch. People of all shapes and sizes sit around tables or at the bar, most of their faces filled with a gleeful happiness. Laughter flows around the patrons and to my ears. It is a pleasant sight, a sight I wish I could be a part of some day.

"Miss, it's closing time." The barkeep startles, taking several steps back when my eyes pop open. I must have fallen asleep. I let go of the cup I hold tightly to my chest, setting it on the table and rising from my seat. My feet sway underneath me as I try to make my way to the door. How much ale had I drank tonight?

Pausing for a moment in the doorway, I try to get my eyes to find one path to follow. The road that I know leads straight to the castle, has turned into two. I push off of the doorframe, determined I have found the right path towards home. I grumble drunkenly at myself for calling that place my home. I'm not welcome there. I don't have a nice warm bed. I live in the attic and sleep on the floor.

One foot falls in front of the other, tripping myself and sending me flying through the air in slow motion, straight into one of Janella's water troughs. I feel a hand grab me by the back of my shirt, lifting me from the trough as I spit and sputter. I'm coughing up lungful's of water as my ass hits the hard dirt.

"How much did you drink tonight?" My eyes move upwards, looking at the two Janella's with their hands on their hips and a stern look of disapproval on their faces.

"Since—" *Hiccup!* " when were there two of you?" I manage to say.

"Since never." Her brows rise and the unamused look on her face tells me I am making a fool of myself. "Come on." She grunts, throwing my arm over her shoulder as she tries to lift me from the ground. I push up, trying to keep my weight off of her as we stumble down the road and towards the castle.

When we arrive at the door, the guards rush to open the doors as Janella's strength weakens. We stumble inside, just in time for her to shove me off her shoulder, letting me land in a heap on the cool marble floor. I can't help the laugh that bubbles up from my chest, spewing out and echoing off the walls. I probably look like a lunatic, I know I sound like one.

Footsteps are coming slowly in our direction. My eyes look up through my brows to see Kai's approaching form. His arms are crossed and his mouth sits in a firm line. It's in that moment I realize it's eerily quiet in the castle right now. Granted, it is early morning, but still no guards walk the halls and the servants are all in their beds.

Kai's voice is gruff. "I'll take her from here, Janella." She moves closer to him, saying something I can't quite understand as she pats his upper arm.

Laying there on the floor, unmoving, I don't even want

to breathe. I can feel that I have stepped out of line and while I am used to punishment, I'm not used to *his* punishment. The way his eyes look at me with not a single ounce of warmth. The way he doesn't so much as speak as he lifts me off the floor, an arm behind my back and the other under my legs. His silence makes me squeeze my eyes shut tight. My skin feels like I have received a dozen lashings when it has all been from merely his gaze.

My neck is getting tired as we make our way up the stairs, but I refuse to lean into him. To find comfort he isn't willing to provide. He lays me down on his bed, brushing away a piece of hair I had strategically placed in front of my face so his eyes wouldn't burn my nerves so much.

"He is gone," his voice whispers.

Even in my drunken state, I can tell he is hurting. Can see the pain of his father's death written across his face. While Kai may not have liked how his father treated people, he was still his father.

Wiping a singular tear from his cheek, I brush my thumb over his skin. "I'm sorry," are the only words I can manage to say. I'm not in the right state of mind to be comforting someone, and that makes me hate myself even more. If I would have just stayed out of the tavern, I could be consoling him right now.

His body dips the mattress as he lays down next to me. I sit, propping myself up against the headboard, making it so my head doesn't spin quite so much. He rests his head against my chest and my hand plays through his hair.

Ethan will now become the King of Ruellia. When the sun rises and we leave this room, we will be under Ethan's control even more than we already were.

It is time. I need to stop messing around and actually burn this castle of villains to the ground.

# Chapter Twenty Three

## SKARLETTE

I have been dreading this night for weeks. King Serion passed last week. We quickly returned his body to the earth and the planning began. I wanted so badly to take down this castle while the king was still alive. I wish there would have been more time to ask him about what he said to me in the study that night. I wish I could have seen the disappointment in his eyes when I told him I was burning his beloved home to the ground. But time was not my friend.

The week after had passed in slow motion. The sun wasn't

even fully in the sky when a guard arrived at Kai's door, summoning us into the throne room. Ethan stood on the dais and announced his father's passing to those who had not been privy to the information. Then, he immediately began to tell us how things would work now that the king was gone. I watched as faces scrunched with confusion. A prince should be in mourning, but Prince Ethan was already planning his coronation party. A coronation party that would take place tonight, only one week after his father's passing. It was a disgrace to his father's legacy.

"Skarlette," Ethan snaps in my direction, clearing the cloud of thoughts from my mind. "Tonight, while I am being crowned king, I want you to sit right here." Ethan's finger stretches out, pointing at a spot next to the throne where a small green pad sits upon the floor.

"What—do I sit crossed legged or something?" My face twists in a look of annoyance, my arms crossing over my chest.

"Of course not. We aren't in school." His blue eyes roll, looking up at the ceiling and asking the goddess for help in dealing with me. "You will kneel."

My mouth clamps shut tightly, my nails digging into my arms—and even though I am not one to pray, I pray to the goddess that she keep him safe from me. I was about to claw his eyes out.

"She will do no such thing," Kai barks and I am grateful that everyone else has already filtered out of the room.

"She is my pet, brother. She will do as I demand. I need to show the people that they should be scared to break the laws. They should be scared of the monster I will unleash on them when they do not obey." Ethan moves around the area, making sure everything is just right for this evening's feast.

Kai's fists are white knuckled at his sides. "She is not a trophy to be paraded around."

"She is my trophy!" Ethan's voice booms, echoing off the walls. "I have control over the *Il Furfante*. I have the monster that was bred within the walls of this castle and I will use her as I please."

"She is a physical being!"

The more that they argue with one another, the louder it becomes as it echoes in the throne room. I move, taking a seat at one of the guest tables. There is no use in me interjecting when they clearly have more than enough to say about it. Maids make their way in and out of the room, their eyes darting to the side to see what all the fuss is about, but they know better than to divert their full attention from their job. If they do, Ethan will send me to their homes.

"You will not ruin this night for me, Kai!" Ethan's words end the conversation, both men fuming at one another.

I rise, causing the chair to scrape against the floor with a loud long screech. Their heads turn in my direction, remembering that I have been here the whole time.

"Well, I am glad I was able to see the show, but I have places to be." Walking past Ethan, my eyes meet Kai's and silently tell him to drop it.

If Ethan wants me to be his prize for his coronation, I would be his prize.

When I enter Kai's room, I am greeted by a completely black gown waiting for me on the bed. Holding it up to my body, I look in the full length mirror in the corner of the room. It's short, easy for me to kneel in. The bodice looks like it will hug my body and the front covers just enough cleavage for the imagination to wander. This dress is nothing like what Ethan has picked for me in the past. Maybe he wanted to go a different route tonight.

My eyes fall to the floor behind me, where the large wolf pup lets out a long sigh. Seems I won't have to worry about her while I was away tonight.

Sliding the dress on, my arms reach back to try and hook the dress closed, but I am struggling. I spin around in a circle, unable to reach. The door makes a soft click behind me as it closes and the scent of Kai envelopes me. In the mirror, I can see him coming closer, his hands reaching out to help me. He presses his lips against the bare part of my shoulder.

"You don't have to do this," he mumbles against my skin.

"It will make my revenge that much sweeter in the end." His cheek rests against my head as we look at each other through the mirror.

"Where did he even find a dress like this?" Kai mutters.

I shrug my shoulders. "I haven't seen anything like it here." Sliding on my boots, I make my way out the door. I am ready for whatever tonight will hold.

Kneeling at the bottom of the throne, I keep my hands splayed out on my lap to help me stay steady. Fae men make their way straight from the door up to the dais, their eyes roaming over me and making my skin crawl. The women look at me with jealousy in their eyes, and teenagers come to taunt me, to see if I will kill them against the new king's orders.

An older fae man with white hair and bushy eyebrows, winks at Ethan. "I bet she is a wild ride at night."

I am surprised by the grimace that crosses his face before he quickly schools it, giving the man a wicked smile before running his hand under my chin.

"She is wild indeed." His thumb rubs against my lips with a roughness I'm not fond of. The old fae chuckles before leading his wife away from us and to their seats. Even though the guests are no longer looking at us, his fingers do not let go of my chin, he holds my face in place with a tight grip.

"Why don't you smile?" Ethan says to me, finally letting go of my face before walking away to mingle with the rest of the crowd.

I grimace at his back as he moves to the other side of the room. Music from the string quartet, filters through the air and my eyes scan the crowd. Walking up through the center of the crowd, his eyes on me, is Elijah. His face is a stone, not an emotion to be found. His form towers over the guests as they part to let him through. Gasps and giggles sound from a corner of the room where a group of teenage fae girls have gathered.

The rest of the room is eerily silent. The guests whisper, some even shaking with fear of the vampire that has just stepped foot in Ruellia.

Elijah doesn't take the bait, he simply keeps walking with his sights set on me. He stops at the bottom of the dais, not daring to come any closer to me. Or maybe he just doesn't wish too.

"You disgust the vampire side of you." His voice is a harsh whisper, he must think I sit here by choice.

"I am doing what needs to be done." My head tilts sideways and up, my eyes staring into his, ready for the fight he wants to start.

"Kneeling here like his little pet." His teeth are clenched tight, baring them as he speaks. "Does his brother know this is the position you sit in when you suck the crowned prince's cock?"

"You are going to ruin everything," I say through a tight lipped smile. My eyes look, finding Ethan as he watches the display between me and Elijah.

"I hope Veron knows he wants a slut to sit on his throne," Elijah growls before walking away, my insides panicking if someone overheard our conversation. He has no right to come here and speak about those things.

Apparently, I am going to be the star of the show tonight. Kai is approaching from the left side of the room, his eyes dancing between Elijah and I.

"What was that?" He looks down at me, his brows scrunched with confusion.

"Nothing," I bite out. Apparently these men were insistent on making me look bad tonight. I will be sure to pay them back for the amount of backhands I will receive from Ethan when this is all over.

Ethan knew it too, that something is going on. He is walking our direction, ready to tell his brother to get lost. Anger resonates in Ethan's dark eyes. The closer he comes, the more I can see it, practically feel it.

"Leave," I growl at Kai.

"Whatever that was, Skarlette, it didn't look good." Kai's head turns, looking over his shoulder, his eyes following his brother's steps as he comes closer to us. The glare on Ethan's face tells me this isn't going to be good.

"Get the fuck away from her!" Ethan roars.

The entire room goes silent. Every set of eyes in this place is now pointed directly on us. We are the stars of the show. And that is exactly why Ethan was creating this scene. He is taking the attention off the vampire that just showed up, making the fae forget Elijah was here.

Kai barely looks Ethan's way. "I was only checking on our pet, brother."

Tension rises in the air, making it suffocatingly hard to breath. The onlookers are excited for a show, but I am ready to crawl in a hole and die. I like being the bad guy, but I like being a bad guy who lingers in the shadows. All this attention is too much.

"Stop it, you both—we have guests," I whisper, trying to ease the tension between them before the explosion of feelings suffocates us all.

Ethan steps up to me, taking my chin between his bony forefinger and thumb. "Did you hear that, Kai? Our little menace wants us to behave." Ethan's use of Kai's nickname for me sour's in my stomach. I dare to glance at Kai, only to find his eyes are filled with a fresh wave of anger. His hands are balled up into fists at his sides with his teeth clenched as he speaks.

"Don't you dare use my nickname for her." Ethan simply ignores his brother, placing his cold lifeless lips against my own. It's an odd sensation, for all the fae I have touched before have been warm. But Ethan is cold, unnervingly cold. Almost like a dead body, or someone who had just been pulled out of the ocean.

My eyes shoot back to Kai. I'm trying to show him something isn't right, but all he seems to see is panic. Anger flares brighter in his expression and I curse myself for even giving him a look.

"Now I know why my brother wants you. I will admit, you taste quite delectable." My stomach is doing full spins now. Sickness crawls up my throat, coming into my mouth before I swallow it back down.

Ethan laughs, letting go of my chin and wrapping an arm around his brother. "All in good fun. I hope you enjoyed the show," Ethan announces to the crowd. Music begins and conversation resumes as if nothing has happened.

My body sags against the throne, just enough to rest my legs, but not enough for anyone to really notice. I am exhausted from the events of tonight and it has only been an hour. I scan the crowd, but don't find the vampire I am looking for. Elijah is gone.

The crowd in front of me twirls and spins as they dance the night away. I am grateful that no one else comes up to see me. As the night drags on, I beg for it to be over so I can go back to my room and rest my weary legs.

The party is drawling on, midnight has long since passed and the time is now rounding into the early morning hours. Fae still linger around the room, the band has gone home and only a few young people mingle around. I haven't failed to notice a slightly peculiar fae who watches me while leaning on one of the tall pillars that rise from the floor to the ceiling.

His eyes watch me with intent. Finally finding himself bold enough, he moves closer. His legs take long and languid steps towards me, what I imagine a wolf looks like when it stalks it's prey. "My, my, what a delightful creature you are." The smile on his face makes my stomach knot with unease.

"Do I know you?" I question.

"Doubt it. I like to linger in the shadows." My own shadows stir, picking up on the unease inside of me.

"What brings you here tonight?" Trying my best to keep to small talk going, I hope someone will notice the exchange.

"A rare gem. Unlike anything the world has ever seen. I like to collect rare things." His hand twitches at his side, like he wants to reach out and touch me. The move makes my shadows flare towards him.

The smile on his face widens and the panic inside of me rises like the tides of the ocean. He knew that was going to happen. How did he know? My eyes dare not leave the mysterious man before me, but I also desperately need to make eye contact with Kai.

I rise to my feet. "Well I hope you have a good evening. If you'll excuse me." The man's hand darts out, trying to grab at me while Ethan yells in the distance.

"I did not tell you you could leave," Ethan's voice booms.

The walls feel like they are closing in on me. Ethan comes up on my right. My shadows start to darken every inch of the throne room. Fae are screaming, running out of the room as if their lives depended on it.

"Step away from her." Kai's voice calls to the men on either side of me.

"Kai, don't. She is dangerous," Kesira whines, tugging on his arm in a plea to get him to stop walking in my direction.

He growls at her. "So am I." He yanks his arm from her grasp, coming up to me swiftly. Leaning in close, his breath fans against my ear and his scent envelopes me.

"I need you to calm down. I need you to bring the shadows back to us," he whispers, placing the tiniest kiss to the soft skin behind my ear. The movement is so light, barely anyone will have noticed.

The shadows shrink slightly, coming back to us with hesitation. I lean into him, fearful of the guy standing to my left. I take a slow breath in and then out, letting my fear calm.

"That's a good girl," Kai coos as my shadows recede into nothing.

"He tried to grab me," I say to Kai through the side of my mouth.

He doesn't hesitate to demand from the man. "Who are you?"

"Your Highness," he greets with a bow. "I am simply a collector of treasure." There it is again, that sickening gleam in his eye as he gazes over me.

"Sorry, but she isn't for sale." Kai's arm wraps around my waist with possessiveness.

"That's too bad." The man's mouth is in a full downturn now. "My buyer will not be happy I have failed."

The man turns, walking out of the throne room with no more fight. Odd. I look at Kai, wondering what the hell has just happened.

"Anyone know who the fuck just tried to buy my pet?" Ethan screeches at the small group of people who still linger to watch the show.

Awkward silence permeates the room for a minute before guards come to escort the last of the party out. The room is eerily silent as Kai, Ethan, and I stand in a circle in the center of the room, waiting for one of us to say something.

"Who the fuck is trying to buy Skarlette?" Both brothers

say at the same time.

# Chapter Twenty Four

## KAI

The carriage ride to Vreilwreth is bumpy. The vampires have not been seen in some days, but I am still on high alert. I have my suspicions on who is trying to buy Skarlette for their own gain, but I really hope my conscious is wrong.

When I arrive in front of the grand, light green colored house, I take a breath. If I wrongly accuse him, it may mean I never get to see my sister again. Stepping out of the carriage, I walk up to the door. Just as my hand wraps around the knocker, the door swings open, jerking my arm with it.

Louissa's warm smile greets me and her arms wrap around my waist in a tight hug.

"Brother." She beams up at me, taking my hand and tugging me inside her home. "We weren't expecting you, so Adam isn't here right now."

I gulp down the lump of guilt in my throat. "That's okay. I thought I would surprise you." I wasn't lying necessarily, just keeping the truth of why I was here to myself.

She leads me to a brightly colored room with stark white walls and rosy pink furniture. As we take a seat across from each other, I take in her rosy cheeks and glowing skin. Something seems different about her. I can't quite put my finger on what it is though.

"I am actually very glad you came. I have some news." There is no way. I think to myself as all the signs start to click into place. I had only married my sister off to Lord Veeling two short months ago. "We are expecting."

I rise from my seat in what feels like slow motion. Wrapping my arms around my sister, I am sure I tell her that I am excited for her, all while silently panicking about what I am going to do now. I am positive Lord Veeling is the one trying to buy Skarlette. Once my menace finds out, she is going to end him for trying to own her. But now he is the father of my future niece or nephew.

The front door opens and Louissa rises quickly from the couch. My body turns as my eyes follow her to the entry way. Lord Veeling is shucking off his coat as Louissa hangs it and gives him a kiss on the cheek.

"Look who has come to see us," she smiles at him, but when his eyes land on me, I think I see him pale slightly.

"Good to see you again." I hold out my hand for him to shake in greeting, my hand squeezing his hard with a little too much force.

Louissa holds her hand above her mouth, trying to hold back the yawn from my late arrival.

"I am sorry. I was actually headed to bed when you arrived." Another yawn takes over her and I can see now the dark circles under her eyes.

"Please, it was rude of me to arrive so late. Sleep well, sister." Grabbing her hand in mine, I give it a light squeeze before she heads up the stairs to her room. The squeeze is a silent apology for what I am about to do.

With Louissa off to bed, I take a seat across from the Lord in the parlor. The glass of brandy in my hand gives me a way to keep myself from wrapping that hand around the lord's throat. Swirling the amber liquid, I wait for my chance to pounce.

"I am so sorry, you won't be able to stay long, Your

Highness. I am afraid we weren't prepared for you to arrive and we have plans the rest of the week." Ah, there it is. The, 'I'm afraid we are too busy to keep you company' trying to get me to go back home and quickly.

The lord shuffles in his seat, clearly nervous. "I should have brought her with me. She would have gotten a kick out of giving you a tongue lashing," I say before taking a drink of the liquid in my glass, letting his wide eyed expression linger as the burn settles in my throat.

"Who?" He says, his voice slightly higher pitched than before.

I drop my voice, letting him know I am not here for a friendly visit. "The woman you tried to steal from me."

He shakes his head in denial. "I don't know what you are talking about."

"So you didn't pay a man who collects rare items to come and steal away Skarlette? To collect her as if she were some prize or item you sit on your mantel?" I spit the words at him, my anger bubbling over. "You tried to take the love of my life and use her as your own personal protection."

The lord stands and I mimic his every move. I get in his face, ready to take care of this man once and for all.

He holds his hands up in a silent plea. "Please be quiet. Your sister doesn't know." His voice trembles as he looks me in my eyes.

I hiss at him and he flinches away from me. "I know she doesn't know, because my sister loves Skarlette way too much to let you try and steal her right out from under us."

"I got into some trouble with some vampires while trading my brandy, I swear! I only wanted her for protection." He's grasping at straws, trying to find excuses to make what he did right.

"Unfortunately for you, Skarlette is mine. She is my mate and she will do as she pleases." He pales even further than before at the me calling her my mate.

His voice is a whisper. "I didn't know."

"Now you do." Pulling the dagger from my belt, I make my way around him, pressing it into his back as we head outside.

Loading him into the carriage, I'm careful not to let onlookers see the knife digging between his shoulder blades. His hands fidget in his lap as the carriage takes us away down the road.

"Please—your sister is with child," the lord cries, wet tears leaking from his eyes.

"I cannot let you go unpunished for what you have tried to do." My feelings are like stone. While I did feel bad the child would be raised without a father, I would bring

Louissa home once news spread of the lord's death. We would find someone to govern Vreilwreth until the child was old enough to do it themselves.

The carriage slows, coming to a stop near the old boat house on the river's edge. The dagger weighs heavy in my hand as I hold it out, urging the lord out of the carriage and into the moonlight. We stand at the edge of the water, listening as it rushes past us and out into the ocean.

"Next time, you'll learn not to try an acquire things that ought not be bought." I push my dagger into him, sliding a bottle of Ruellia into his pocket as his knees hit the ground.

The lord falls sideways, his body falling into the water with his eyes wide. Like he hadn't expected me to kill him for trying to buy my menace. I wipe my blade clean, stuffing the blood soaked handkerchief into my pocket and replacing the dagger in my belt. Quickly, I get back in the carriage before signaling for the driver to move on.

Peeking out the window for only a moment, I watch as Vreilwreth disappears into the distance. Louissa will be disappointed when she awakes and finds out that I have already left, but she will be even more disappointed when she finds her husband is dead.

The carriage rumbles down the road as I am left with only my thoughts. This is the beginning of the end. Our world as we know it is about to change forever.

# Chapter Twenty Five

## SKARLETTE

Something strange is happening in this place. Kai left without a word four days ago, and now Ethan is telling me he wants me to sit in on a royal council meeting. I have never been asked before, so why now? I am considered, by law, the prince's assassin, even though they do not call me that. I have a right to sit at the table.

"You want me to sit in on the meeting?" My words are slow, trying to put together the pieces of what is happening.

"Yes, Skarlette," he says with clipped words. "I need you there. I have plans, and if any one of my council members wants to stand in my way, I will need you there to take care of them."

He gives me an agitated look when I still don't quite understand why he wants me there. He already has a general and many other guards at his disposal. I am used specifically to sneak up on his victims, unless he is expecting the whole council to not agree with him, then he would need me and my shadows to wipe out the entire council. If he is planning to take out the whole council, then things are turning grim already.

Ethan doesn't talk to me anymore, his hands go back to skimming through the papers on his desk and I take that as my sign to leave. His office door clicks behind me as I stand in the hall trying to figure out what is going on.

My most recent Ruellia oil purchase is burning a hole in my pocket, I need to get it into my stash before someone finds it on me. I climb the stairs two at a time, making my way quickly to my small attic room. Once inside with the door shut and locked behind me, I pop open the lid of one of the crates, digging down until I find the stash of Ruellia oil.

The purple liquid gleams in the evening sun that filters through the small attic window. I place the liquid next to the others, careful not to disturb them and ruin all my plans.

The lid to the crate closes with a soft clank as I register the sound of carriage wheels on the gravel drive. Out the window, a royal carriage with dust billowing behind it is barreling up the drive before it comes to a stop in front of the castle. It is a Ruellian carriage, meaning Kai must be back from wherever he ran off to.

Rushing out of my room and down the stairs, I arrive in the entryway just in time to see Kai shucking off his coat. A maid takes his things, humming to each of the words he says to her. When she passes me with her arms full of his stuff, she gives me a look that makes me wonder if he might be in a mood.

"You have been gone a while." My voice is chipper, trying to keep the conversation light.

"Mmhmm," he mumbles, trudging his way up the stairs.

Following closely behind, I'm prepared for him to head to his room. When he turns the opposite direction at the top of the stairs and heads for Ethan's office, it piques my interest. Where has he been? My mind ponders over the question. There is no way he knew so quickly who had offered to buy me and I had not heard anymore about the fae's plans to take out the vampires.

Kai's knuckles rap on the office door before pushing it open. He slides in, holding the door for me to follow before closing it behind us. I copy his movements, taking a seat across from Ethan and waiting for whatever he has to say.

"And where have you been, brother?" Ethan doesn't look up from his paperwork as a pair of glasses sit on the bridge of his nose, making him look about a hundred years older than he actually is.

Kai rests one leg over the other, his fingers drumming against it. "Taking care of our problem."

"I take it you figured out quickly who was trying to take her from us?"

"Yes," Kai hisses. "A lord who has been sent back to the devil."

Ethan's pen stops. "What have you done?" My brain is starting to catch up.

"She is with child. While you're busy in here signing your name and reading letters, please find time to make the child the new lord or lady of Vreilwreth."

Kai's words make the world spin around me. Lord Veeling was the one to trying to buy me? I take it Louissa hadn't known or else she may have killed the lord herself. Kai killed him. I am starting to rub off on my mate and I'm not sure that is a good thing. Something inside me wonders how he did it. My morbid curiosity begs to know if he made him suffer.

Ethan pinches the bridge of his nose. "God Kai, this is going to be a headache to explain. Who saw you?"

"No one saw me. I made it look like a drug deal gone wrong. The river washed him away." I am impressed, Kai has been taking notes.

"How did you know?" The words spill from me, interrupting their conversation and making both men turn in my direction.

"When I brought Louissa down there to marry him, I could see the obsession he had with you. Though he didn't know it was you until I brought you there when we arrested you." Kai looks at me with guilt. "I could see it in his eyes, he wanted to use you to protect Vreilwreth from the vampires."

"He underestimated us," Ethan says knowingly.

Kai nods. "He did and I showed him just how wrong he was to think he could have what is mine."

"Ah, ah, ah." Ethan wags his finger at Kai. "Brother you forget you are engaged to someone else."

That brings a scowl to Kai's face. "I forget nothing," Kai mumbles, his arms crossed over his chest as he pouts like a child.

"I have a lot of work to do now, get out of my office." Ethan grumbles, returning to the stacks of paperwork on his desk.

The door closes softly behind us. "I need a stiff drink." I sigh, beginning to head down the stairs. I halt when I notice Kai isn't following. Scanning his tired face, I take in the way his lips are turned down in a frown and the messiness of his hair.

"I think I am going to head to bed," he yawns.

"Okay." I nod before treading softly down the stairs. I'm sure having to kill someone took a lot out of him. He isn't used to it yet like I am. I still remember the first time I had to kill someone. I didn't leave my bed for a week. Even the second and third time, it hadn't gotten any easier.

In the village, the tavern is crawling with people. I barely find a seat in the far dimly lit corner. Sitting at the lone table next to the window, the sun long gone and the moon gracing us with its sliver of light, I watch the people of the tavern with rapt curiosity.

A familiar head of red hair bobs past me. At first I take a double glance. Surely she wasn't working as a barmaid in this tavern after working all day on her family's farm. But there she was, trying to buzz past me. My hand darts out, grabbing her arm and stopping her.

"What are you doing?" A corner of her mouth scrunches with embarrassment.

"Working." She lifts her finger as one of the other patrons calls for her.

"But you work all day on the family farm, and then you have to come here and work again?" My brain is really going through it today.

"Pa doesn't pay me for the work I do on the farm. He feeds me, clothes me, and puts a roof over my head. I work here so I can buy books." She gives me a sad smile.

"You should join me in the life of crime. I can get almost anything I want either through coin or from stealing." She knows I am joking, but she plays it up pretending to be ashamed.

"I could never. Stealing is bad, Skarlette. I will buy my books like the common faerie I am." We both burst into a fit of giggles. Finally having a friend after years of feeling so alone, was such a good feeling.

The tavern owner yells from his spot behind the bar. "Hey! I ain't paying ya to joke around with your friends."

"Sorry, Sam," Janella calls before leaving me a mug of ale, her body winding around tables and depositing more drinks.

The chaos of the tavern is too much for my fried brain. Today's events had left me in a whirlwind of emotions. First, Ethan requests my presence at the meeting, and then Kai comes back and tells us he killed Lord Veeling. I need to leave, to let the cool night air soak into my skin and listen to the crickets.

The small bag of coin clunks on the table. Janella would never take it if I handed it straight to her so I make sure she sees me leave it on the table before I disappear out the door. The noise of the tavern quiets when the door closes behind me. I stroll through the village, taking my time and enjoying the sights.

In a field on the edge of town, a small string band plays music with group of fae that have gathered in front of the musicians as several of them dance and sway to their melodies. Fireflies light the air around them, twinkling like tiny firelight. Something inside me pangs with jealousy at the joyous looks on their faces. They were so at peace, so happy with the life they were living.

Moving on, I leave them to their enjoyment. Further down the road, I peek inside the window of a farmhouse. A family is gathered around their table for a late night meal. Sitting on the table is a roast with potatoes and other veggies. Again, they wear smiling faces, several of the children laugh at something their father says. A small smile creeps across my face, unable to help it when I hear their giggles drift out the open window.

Leaving the smiling people, I head away from the happiness of the village and wander back to the castle of villains that looms over the village like a dark cloud. While the gardens may be filled with bright and colorful flowers and the castle made of light colored stone, the wicked people that live inside make it darker than the vampiric castle in Shadowfall.

There is a reason I call it a castle of villains. All of us inside are monsters who put other people at risk to get what we want. We care only of ourselves.

My eyes snag on a shadow sitting above me on the rooftop, it's feet dangling over the edge. It's the same moody way I have seen him sit there many times before. My hands grip onto the cool stone as I hoist myself up onto the first balcony. My feet sway beneath me, trying to balance myself so I can grab hold of the next balconies railing. I swing myself up and over, my feet landing next to him before I take seat next to him, my feet dangling over the edge as we stare out over the village.

"I remember the first time I killed." He is quiet, but I can tell he is listening. "Your brother got so mad at me when I hesitated. My hands shook, the dagger in my hand rattled to the point it almost fell on the ground. My hand shot out when he yelled at me and the deed was done."

"It wasn't my first time," he whispers.

"I have killed a hundred times and still sometimes it doesn't feel right. I save the children, I won't let him control me when it comes to them, but the others . . . I mourn them." He looks at me, surprise evident in his eyes.

"I didn't know." He holds his hand open, my own reaching for it as his fingers close around my hand.

"I like getting what I want. I like living how I want to live, but I don't like taking the lives of others for no good reason."

"I don't feel sad," he admits. "I was so angry at Veeling for trying to buy you like an inanimate object. Like a slave." His hand squeezes mine as the anger resurfaces. "I am fucking glad I killed him and that scares me."

My head falls, resting against his shoulder. I know exactly how he feels. It was my fifth kill. The man was terrible. He liked to touch young girls without permission. In fact, when I found him, he had one of the girls from the brothel in his home. He had followed her home where he stole her away. I hated the feeling after I killed him. I was happy about it. I felt like I had done something good.

I don't say that to him though, I just let his admissions linger between us.

"Kai, why don't the fireflies linger around the garden this

time of night? In fact, I never see them around the castle like I do in the village."

"To be honest, I don't know. Maybe they feel the anger and sadness inside the castle and prefer to stay as far away from that as possible. They are light and they don't want to be snuffed out by this castle's darkness." His words make sense, but something still nags in the back of my mind. Ethan's cold touch, the lack of fireflies near the castle, when I know I have seen them here before.

It is all just so strange. Something I will have to think about another time. For right now, I am relishing in the quiet.

# Chapter Twenty Six

## SKARLETTE

The table in front of me is lined with the royal council. I sit on Ethan's right while Kai sits on his left. A battle map is spread over the center of the table, and little figurines mark the landmarks on the map. The fae are going to start a war. These meetings were always a bore, but now that the fae had their sites set on taking down the vampires—that I wished to remind them they needed for trade—it was an absolute shit show.

A captain with long brown hair rises, addressing the table. His face is familiar, I have probably seen this man at least a half a dozen times, but still I can not remember his name. "They haven't met up for deliveries in two weeks."

The Keeper of Ministries tries to look at the bright side. "Maybe they're busy?" John's long gray hair was practically down to his waist at this point and his shoes were the strangest thing I had ever seen. They left his toes out to the elements.

"Maybe they just want to withhold the gold we need to take them down." Ethan flicks at invisible flecks of dirt on his jacket to keep him busy, clearly bored with the conversation.

I stay quiet, not wishing to put my two cents in on the matter. I'm not sure what is happening on the vampire's side of things, but I know they must be planning something if they haven't met up for deliveries. The fact that both sides were messing with the trading schedules would mean the people would be in for a world of hurt.

"We can't let them get away with this!" General Damien slams his fist against the table, his dark gaze landing on me before moving to Prince Ethan.

"We wait for them to come to us. If they are planning on attacking, they will come," Ethan says with utter calm, his gaze meeting the generals and daring him to speak more.

The table falls silent, looking at their prince with stunned expressions. It isn't the way. The fae don't lie in wait for the enemy to arrive on our doorstep. We go out and burn the vampires the minute they step foot on our land, but now he wants to wait? I am unsure what Ethan is planning, but even my shadows can tell it isn't good.

The door opens and a guard peeks his head inside. "Your Highness, they are ready in the throne room."

Ethan rises from his chair, bidding the council farewell and making his way out the door. I stay in my seat, waiting to hear what the men will say once the prince is gone. They really are just a table full of gossips.

"What is he thinking?" They bark at each other.

"He has no clue what he is doing."

"My brother has been training for his place as king all his life, he will be fine," Kai says over the grumbling men. He pushes back his chair and rises from his seat at the table. His eyes meet mine before he throws his head towards the door. A silent way of asking me if I am coming with him.

Leaving the gossiping table of nincompoops behind us, I can hear their voices carrying after us and out into the hall until the door closes. They could argue all day about what Ethan said before he left the meeting, but it is done. His word is final.

"Quite the diplomat you have become," I jest.

"Ah yes, what a perfect pair we make. The back up prince and the assassin." His joke falls flat.

Walking out the door we leave the castle behind us and head into the village. I sent word to Janella earlier today to meet me at the local tavern. I need a drink after that shit show of a council meeting. I wasn't expecting Kai to tag along though.

"I'm meeting Janella for drinks," I say, hoping he will take the hint and leave us to it.

"Okay." Instead of wandering off, it's like he is glued to my side as he continues to follow me all the way to the pub.

I grab us an empty table while Kai grabs a pitcher of ale. Janella enters, waving her hand in greeting as she approaches the table. Kai returns to the table at the same time Janella does and her eyes go wide with shock.

I give my shoulders a shrug and roll my eyes. "We have an extra for tonight's drinks."

"Like you two were going to have fun without me?" Kai smirks, pouring the ale into mugs.

"We were going to gossip about you." Janella lightly elbows him in the side and takes a seat across from me.

Kai sits, putting his hands under his chin and batting his eyelashes. "Don't stop on my account, tell me all the juicy gossip." I give him an incredulous look while Janella's lips upturn in a smile against her cup.

This was a nice change of pace. It almost felt like something normal friends would do. Get together over a pint of ale and talk about their lives. It gives me an escape for a few hours from the chaos that is my normal life. I hadn't seen Janella in a while with all the things going on around the castle. Louissa coming home, Kai helping his brother, it was all a big mess.

"How was the council meeting?" Janella asks quietly, making sure other patrons don't here us talking about diplomatic things .

"A shit show as always." I raise the mug to my lips, gulping down the amber liquid.

"You aren't supposed to be talking to her about that stuff." Kai narrows his eyes on me, but I can tell he isn't actually mad.

I shrug, giving him a feline smile. "I'd like to see you stop me." My gaze flicks over to Janella who looks between us with a smirk. I can already hear the crap she is going to give me later.

"Menace, I could stop you if I really wanted to." I see the look in his eyes, the inuendo to what he actually means.

"He even has a nickname for you," Janella coos, leaning over with her hand blocking her mouth as she whispers, but

Kai can still hear her every word.

I rub at the aching scar on my face, realizing I hadn't drank blood in a few days. I had just been so busy. Both of them give me a look of concern. Waving it off, I take another swig of my ale and hope it will blur the dull ache that pounds in my head.

The evening quickly bleeds into night. Janella tells us stories of her life on the farm and all the annoying clients she has to deal with. We laugh, practically to the point of tears. I haven't had a night like this in . . . well actually, I don't think I have ever had a night like this. There was that one time when me, Kai, and Louissa had played a game of truth or dare. We stayed up far too late and I was punished the next day for keeping the prince and princess up past their bedtime.

When the tears have ceased to stream from my eyes and our laughing has quieted down, I rise from my seat, giving Kai a pat on the shoulder. "I should get the prince home."

Janella nods, rising from her own chair and giving us hugs goodbye. She is too sweet for this world. She has a heart of gold and the world is the monster hiding under her bed. It will sneak from it's shadows and stab her at some point and I will dread the day that it happens.

Kai hiccups, drunk from too much ale. "I should be the

one getting you home."

"I thought I told you, I'm an independent half breed now." I laugh as Kai stumbles over a rock in the road.

Wrapping my arm around his waist, I try to hold him steady, but he is a good five inches taller than me and holds a good fifty plus pounds against me. Though it feels like I am not helping, it does seem to steady him a little. He drapes his heavy arm over my shoulder as we make our way towards the castle.

"I should have done more to protect you." He sounds distant, and when I look up, he is zoned out on the castle we approach.

"We both needed the pain we endured to make us the people we are today." He doesn't respond as we walk the rest of the way in silence. The guards open the castle door to let us in while giving me the death glare of 'what-did-you-do-to-our-prince'.

"I'm hungry," he mumbles, his feet changing our direction.

"Hey, we need to get you up to bed," I argue. His arm leaves my shoulders, grabbing my hand that is wrapped around his back and threading his fingers with mine as he tugs me towards the kitchen.

Luckily for us, the cook has long since gone to bed. If he

were to see us in his kitchen, he would have a conniption fit.

The kitchen is dark, the clouds are blocking the moon and giving us very little light. Kai is digging around in the ice box and poking through cupboards, looking for a midnight snack. Something falls, crashing to the ground.

"Shhh!" I hiss. "If cook catches us down here, he will have both of our heads.

Kai turns to me with a smile, a lemon pie from the ice box sitting in his hands. One that looks like the cook has spent all day working on it. A pie like the ones I saw as a child and would wish with my whole heart that I could have a bite, but I was never allowed.

My whisper is harsh. "Kai, put that back!"

"You want some?" he says, dipping his finger in the pie and sucking it off his finger.

"I don't know if I would like it." Crossing my arms over my chest, I try not to look at the delicious sweetness.

"Have you never had pie before?" He asks, dipping his finger in and scooping up a thick glob of lemon pie.

I lick my lips, thinking about the sour lemon taste on my tongue mixed with the sugary goodness of the merengue. "I was never allowed sweets. I tried something called chocolate in Vreilwreth, but I didn't really care for it."

Kai pushes his pie coated finger in my direction. "Taste it, Skar." His voice is husky, sending a thrill through my veins.

I look between him and the pie on his finger as it's about to drip on the floor. If we have to clean up a mess, the cook will surely know we were in hear eating his precious pie. I open my mouth and Kai sticks his finger in. My tongue glides over it as I suck off every last drop of pie.

Kai groans, his eyes dark and hooded. He takes his fingers, this time two of them, and swipes them through the pie. He holds them out, waiting for me to repeat the action. My hand grips around his wrist as my mouth closes around the two fingers covered in pie. I take my time licking up the lemony sweet dessert.

"Menace." Kai sounds like he is losing it.

My tongue slides up his fingers as I remove them from my mouth with a pop. "You were right, that was tasty." One side of my lips rises in a smile.

Kai exhales roughly, setting the pie on the counter behind us and stepping closer into my space. "You don't know what you do to me, Skar."

His lips gently brush against mine, his teeth taking my lip between them and tugging. His hands splay against my back and pull me closer as his lips dance with mine.

A sound comes from the top of the kitchen steps. "I'll be

back to bed in a moment dear! I just need to check the pie."

My eyes go wide. Kai moves quickly, throwing the rest of the pie back in the ice box. We run out the side door and out into the stable area as the chickens cluck, aggravated that we have woken them.

Kai laughs as we race our way back to the front door, up the stairs and into his room. We collapse on his bed, staring up at the midnight blue canopy.

"That was the most fun I have had in a while," he says, breathlessly.

"Tonight was the most fun I have had *ever*." I don't look at him as he props himself up on one arm. I know the pity I will see in his eyes. I don't even know why I said that.

Every time I talk, it seems to only be sadness or anger coming from me. I am not even sure I know how to talk about happy things.

"The royal name can be a lot to handle. I am sure it is the same for the *Il Furfante*." Kai's finger traces over my scar. "Are you going to tell me how this happened?"

"Are you sure you want to know?" I rest my arm behind my head, letting the other lay awkwardly between us.

"Of course I do."

"It wasn't long after I left you, actually. I had been in Vreilwreth for a few months, I found the tavern's basement fighting ring and wanted to give it a go. I was still so mad at the goddess for chaining you down to me. They all laughed when I said I wanted my name in for a fight. When they asked for the payment, I didn't have enough coin. They laughed harder. I flashed my teeth at them, my fangs usually gave people a moment to change their thoughts, but the men in this tavern didn't seem to care." The memory was so fresh, like I had just lived through it yesterday. "A kid was working the bar and gave me the last of the coin I needed to join—said he believed I would take them down."

"Jamith," Kai says with an annoyed tone.

"Yes. He gave me the coin and I entered the fight. Only problem was, they put their largest man on me. A man known to play dirty by using iron weapons. They had heard of me. The half bread that was stronger than most. The one the royal family kept as a pet. Halfway through the fight, when the fear of losing was creeping in, the man grabbed his iron axe. He swung and I ducked, but the tip of the axe gently sliced the skin on my face." I shudder as the memory brings back pain to my face.

"Drink, Skar. That's the second time you have been in pain tonight, you need to drink." He bares his neck to me, the two dots staring at me with welcome.

Kissing up from his collarbone, I hover over the sweet

spot of his neck. My fangs line up as a shiver runs down Kai's spine. I start to pull away, but Kai's hand pushes my head closer.

"Does he live?" Kai asks while I take what I need. I can feel his healing magic coursing through his blood and the pain dissipates.

"Somewhere, yes. I was not ready to hunt down my enemies then like I am now," I say when I pull away, licking my tongue over the spots on his neck.

"If we found him, would you do it, or would you like to watch me do it?" He doesn't say it out right, but I know what he means. He wants the man's blood.

"You'd sink to my level to make a man pay for the wounds he has caused me?" I gaze into his eyes, sinking into his navy orbs and unable to look away.

"I'd become the devil himself if it meant making people pay for the pain they have caused you." He places a soft kiss to my lips, then rises from the bed.

# Chapter Twenty Seven

## SKARLETTE

My eyes blink open as the sun starts to filter in through the room. My palm runs against the sheet beside me. Kai is gone and by the coolness of the bed, he has been gone for a while.

Downstairs, a commotion is brewing. "Somebody was in my kitchen! Just look at my pie!" The cook wails to the guards.

Sneaking past, I head straight out the front doors. I guess I will be getting breakfast in the village this morning. Outside, the sun is halfway in the sky, it's heat sweltering with no breeze to bring relief. Even though I am the only vampire to walk in the sun, it still brings me discomfort when it is too warm.

Inside the village, I come across a cart with fresh muffins and pastries, their smell makes my mouth water. I slide one from the cart when the baker isn't looking, taking a bite of the soft pastry, and letting the taste of sweet berry hit my taste buds. It's still warm, fresh from the baker's oven. The feeling of eyes watching me has me looking down slightly, only to see the large wolf pup sitting at my feet, and begging for a bite of my food. I guess I'm to take this as a sign that she is now my partner in crime. I hold a small bite in her direction before she wolfs it down, slobbering all over my hand in the process.

I wipe my hand along my pants as I carry on down the road and through the village. I had managed to escape the castle before Ethan could send the guards for me and I am hopeful they won't come searching as I could really use this day to myself. The only problem with that is, I am not exactly sure what I should do. The poison will take time to get more of and the night market isn't set to come back to this side of the continent for at least another week. I hate the waiting game this has become. My impatience is grating on my nerves. I want to be done with this castle and it's demands.

My feet carry me through town and along the river, black wolf pup in tow. I find a spot to sit along the bank, watching as the water flows quickly downstream. On the other side of the river, a large pack of wolves howl out. I expect the wolf pup to run off with her own, but instead, she curls up to sleep, ignoring the calls of her kind. People's voices carry as they walk the path a few feet behind us, the whole scene making me feel at peace. If I could freeze time and sit in this moment, I would.

"Skarlette," a familiar voice calls. Looking over my shoulder, I find Janella making her way towards me and I don't know what to do. Awkwardly I stand, getting myself out of my vulnerable position. The wolf pup stirs with my sudden movement, but doesn't bare her teeth at Janella like she seems to do to others.

"Janella," I regard with a nod.

"No need to be so formal, Skarlette." She gives me a playful nudge to the arm with her fist. "We are friends."

It feels so strange to have a friend. One that is actually there for me. One that I can meet in a tavern and converse over drinks. I'm not sure how to get use to this feeling or if I ever will.

Janella smiles at me, her cheeks pink from the sun on her

pale skin. The freckles on her nose and tips of her cheeks a stark contrast to the color. She takes a seat on the bank of the river, patting the ground next to her as if she wants me to sit with her.

Awkwardly, I sit down. My hands twitch in my lap when I don't know what to do with them. I opt for petting the wolf pup that has once again curled up into a ball of fluff at my side. I hate how awkward having a friend was making me. I didn't know what to say or how to act. I was so use to being on the defensive all the time. It feels like I am waiting for her to turn against me.

"Relax, Skarlette." I nod my head at her, stretching my feet out in front of me and leaning against my hands when I place them slightly behind me.

"Why are you my friend?" I ask her, concerned that maybe She doesn't realize what I am.

She shrugs her shoulders, making something out of the Ruellia flowers that grow around the area. "We all deserve at least one friend."

"No one wants to be friends with the person who hates everyone."

"You don't hate everyone. You just hate the people who don't treat you like you belong in this world," she says softly, placing a flower crown on my head and then making one for herself.

I have to speak the truth. "I hurt people, Janella."

"I know," she says, but she doesn't look at me.

We sit in silence, her fingers working away on the next flower crown. I am not sure what it is, but just the feeling of having someone who will sit in silence next to me warmed my heart.

Rising from the ground, I wipe the dirt off of my pants and turn to Janella who is also rising from her spot on the ground. "Thank you," I say softly. It's an odd thing to come off my tongue and it doesn't feel natural.

She leans in, hugging me tight and I'm not sure what exactly I should do with my arms. Do I hug her back? Do I not? If I don't, will she find me rude? Just as I am about to return the hug, she pulls away. That feeling of guilt, like I have ruined something yet again, stirs deep inside me, but I push it to the depths where it belongs. I cannot control what has happened, I must move on.

"Could I have been any weirder just now?" I mumble to the wolf dog that now chases an all white butterfly through the meadow.

I smile as the giant pups teeth chomp at the butterfly's wings, trying it's hardest to catch the winged creature before it flies away for good. Letting out a low whistle, I recall the dog to my side, ready to head back to the castle and see what I have missed out on today.

The wolf happily trots beside me as we climb the steps to the front door. A large woman passes us, tears streaming down her face as the guards escort her out. I wonder what that is all about.

Once the crying lady has been escorted through the door, I hear it. My ears perk up at the sound of several people moaning. Not moans of pleasure, but moans of pain. Following the cries, I find myself standing in front of the throne room doors.

My hand presses against the wood, gently pushing as to not make my presence known. Peaking my head inside, his eyes are already on me. He is waiting for me to get back and see what he has done. Ethan stands near his throne with crossed arms. When I step inside the room, a wicked smile turns his lips upward.

"Skarlette, I have been waiting for you." He walks slowly in my direction. Weaving his way through the bodies laid out on the floor. Two of them. A man and a woman. The woman has bite marks all over her body and the man has several fingers that have been chopped clean off.

I look at them with boredom. If he is meaning to get a reaction out of me, he won't find one. I have seen worse.

Done worse.

"See what I must resort to when my assassin runs away for the day?" His boot pushes against the man's head, making him groan.

"I was in the village, you could have sent someone to fetch me." Walking closer to the prince, I come within inches of him. He isn't as tall as his brother, so when I look up at him and his eyes stare down at me, our lips are mere inches from one another. "But I think you like it. Torturing them. Thinking about how I torture them." A sickness churns in my stomach when I see the heat light in his eyes, the way he is eating up my every word.

He leans closer, almost ready to press his lips to mine when I step away. His face falls, his eyes going cold and looking like he's been doused with a cold bucket of water. His mouth turns down into a deep frown as he watches me back away towards the door.

"Don't forget to finish what you have started. I am your assassin, not your maid, I won't clean up your mess for you." I let my words linger as I exit into the hall.

Once back in the confines of my bedroom I realize I have gone all day without any signs of Kai. It's strange, because even if we don't talk or meet up, I at least see him once in passing throughout the day. But today, it is as if he disappeared.

It has been days and still no sign of Kai.

"Hey, where did your brother go?" Ethan doesn't look up from the paperwork scattered on his desk.

"I don't know. He is a big boy. I don't always keep tabs on him, Skarlette." Ethan signs a document, flipping it over and adding it to a pile of other papers.

I can see he doesn't have the time to deal with any questions I may have. The thought crosses my mind to stay here and pester him, but I'm too focused on where the other prince might be. I leave his office, just in time to see a worn out Kai coming into the castle. "Throw him in the cellar," Kai says to the guards, but I can't see who he is talking about.

"Kai." I grab his arm, but he shoves me off.

"I'm tired, Skarlette, not right now." His tone is clipped and I reel back a little at the harshness.

"Okay," I say softly, watching as he heads to his room.

"Miss, the assassin is not allowed visitors." I can hear a guard arguing with someone at the front door.

"I am her best friend. If you don't let me in I will mess you up!" The fact Janella is threatening to mess someone up makes me laugh, for what I knew she wouldn't hurt a fly.

Coming down the stairs, I see her, arms crossed and a deep scowl pointed towards the soldier at the door. "Thank you, I will take her from here." The guard looks between me and Janella, anger and concern mixing on his face.

I loop my arm around hers, laughing when she whips her head around, looking at the rude guard and running her finger across her neck. I'm thankful for her arrival. Without the distraction, I would have been left to fester in my thoughts of Kai and his royally grumpy mood.

"I was about to whoop his ass for not letting me in."

I cackle. "I'm sure you were." Leading her up to my room, insecurity gnaws at me. What if she is disgusted by the room I am given?

She enters before me, looking around at all the old relics from the royal fae family of long ago. I chew on my lip, ready for her to tell me she wants to leave. I am a grown woman, but right now I feel like a child trying to make friends.

"You have so much cool stuff up here," she beams at me and I relax slightly.

"Yeah, but we aren't allowed to touch it." She bends

down, feeling my worn blankets.

"You following the rules?" Janella looks at me incredulously.

"You're right, let's look," I say, pulling a trunk from one of the stacks. Dust plumes across the room, sending us both into a coughing fit as we peer inside. Nothing but old gold and silver tableware.

She goes for another, but again all that's inside is some old decorations. A knock sounds on the door, making us both jump. We stuff the trunks back in their place before acting like nothing is happening.

Opening the door and I find Kai on the other side. Irritation pricks at me. What does he want? He snapped at me earlier and now he is interrupting my time with Janella.

I tap my fingers against the door. "What do you want?"

His voice is cold. "I have a surprise."

"Not a very good one if you sound like that," Janella comments from behind me.

"Leave," Kai says to her.

Looking back, I see a wide eyed Janella. She obviously isn't use to this side of Kai either. I throw my head, and try to tell her through my eyes that I will come see her later. She gives me a small smile as she slips through the door, disappearing down the hall.

"That was rude." Kai grabs my hand, pulling me down the hall and into the dungeons.

Surprise courses through me when in the dimly lit space, I see not only the man who cut my face, but Jamith. I turn on Kai, ready to chew him out, but he raises his hand, signaling for me to wait.

"But, he hasn't—" My words trail off as Kai approaches Jamith's cell.

"You want to tell her or should I?" Kai asks.

Jamith doesn't respond simply looks between me and the man staring menacingly into his cage.

"Jamith, what is he talking about?" I wrap my hands around the bars of his cell, waiting for an explanation to this nonsense.

"He is crazy!" Jamith rises, wrapping his hands around mine.

Kai's voice is lethal. "Don't touch her."

Jamith lets go of me and steps back. "Okay, fine." He takes a deep breath before continuing. "I paid on purpose!" I am so lost and confused, Jamith's complete one eighty is giving me mental whiplash. I have no idea what he is talking about. "I knew who you were when you first entered the tavern that night. I knew they would make you fight him and I paid because I knew he was going to bring in an iron weapon."

I can see the regret in his his eyes as he speaks.

"What do you mean you knew?" My voice comes out dark, like it isn't even myself that is talking.

"I wanted him to kill you. I was going to kill you." The blood in my veins turns to ice. Every time I had slept with this man, he was secretly trying to kill me. I should have known. I should have been smart enough to realize not a single soul on this earth actually wanted me here.

"Every time his cock was in you, he was secretly trying to plan the best way to take you down." Kai is shaking with anger. His knuckles are white as his grip tightens on the dagger I am surprised to see in his hand. He moves quickly, slashing the dagger towards Jamith and taking off one of his fingers.

Jamith squeals, but Kai reaches through the bars, tugging him closer. "That was for touching what is mine." Kai's teeth gleam as he growls the word *mine*. His hand grips Jamith by the throat and squeezes. "This is for trying to kill her." Jamith struggles, kicking and clawing against Kai's grip, but inevitably failing. His body slumps, falling to the ground with a thud when Kai lets go.

Then he moves to the next cell, looking at the large brute of a man sitting inside. His face is the same, large, red beard, half shaved head and sharp pointed ears. His gaze holds a look of pure and utter hatred.

"Fuck you," he spits at Kai, a glob of mucus landing just inches from his boots.

"Apparently not only does he hate you, but he also hates the patriarchy."

I shrug, an inkling of a smile playing on my face. "I can agree with him on that one."

Kai grips my chin, placing a kiss on my lips before returning his attention to the man in front of us.

"Please, I have a wife and children." He begs for his life, but it's too late, Kai has already made his decision.

"You didn't think about my own future children when you tried to kill her," he states and my head whips in his direction.

A gleam of mischief is in Kai's eyes as he unlocks the cell door. "You want to fight? Let's fight. She'll enjoy a bit of a show." Kai is menacing. I have never seen him like this. His eyes are black, no trace of navy left in them, the gold just barely glittering in the center. He licks his lips, ready to fight this man to the death for me.

Sitting in a chair at the end of the dungeon room, I watch as Kai removes his shirt, his muscles gleaming in the dim lantern light. They begin to circle each other before throwing a few good punches, each one landing a shot on the other. They grunt and stumble with each landed blow.

My shadows creep across the floor, anger surfacing as I remember the pain he brought me and the pain he now brings Kai. The shadows are begging me to go in for the kill and lash out towards the two men. This is when they scare me, when the shadows feelings over take my own. But are they their own feelings or do they just heighten my own feelings? I try to breathe and remind myself I am the one in control of them.

The redhead throws a landing punch, Kai's face snapping in my direction from the force. Blood blooms on his cheek bone and my shadows quickly ascend the redhead's legs. They hold him in place, making it so he can't move. Kai's eyes search mine for a long moment before turning towards the burly faerie.

"Do it. Finish him for me," I purr. This whole thing felt so wrong and yet so right at the same time. Kai is killing someone. For me. And something about it is making me want to jump his bones.

Kai steps up, pulling out his dagger and running it right through the man's heart. "Your payment for the pain you've caused my queen," he says as the fae man's body drops to the floor, blood pooling around him.

I was high on the sound of Kai's voice calling me his

queen. High on the adrenaline of watching him take down two people who had so much ill will towards me.

Stepping over the body, I twine my fingers with Kai's and lead him up to his room. Inside, Kai stands there, dazed from all that he has just done. Stripping my clothes off, I sit on the bed with my legs crossed.

"Kneel," I order. His eyes glass over, grazing over my bare skin as he sinks to his knees. I should be kind and let him rest. He needed to heal, even with the extra fast healing from his powers, I can still see the cut on his lip and the dark bruise on his cheek bone.

Laying back on the bed, I spread my legs. His hands answer by wrapping around my thighs with a tight grip as his lips place kisses on my inner thighs. He moves closer, closer until his tongue trails a long stroke up my center. It's warm and wet and makes my back arch against the feeling.

I cry out when his tongue does tiny circles between the long strokes. My hand reaches for him, taking fistfuls of his hair as my lower stomach winds tight. My hand pushes him into me, clamping my thighs against his head and I explode around him. Shadows black out every inch of the room around us while I scream.

Kai moves away, still kneeling before me as I sit up. "How beautiful you look splayed out on my bed. A queen completely undone."

I grab one of his tunics, throwing it on. "I'm not even officially a queen."

"To me you are," he says, rising from his knees.

"You were so mad earlier. Did I do something?" I ask, standing at his bedroom window and looking out over the courtyard.

"I was mad at myself for not trying harder to find you. For letting my brother treat you like he did. For you thinking you had to run instead of telling me that we were mates." He has so much guilt on his shoulders, guilt I have set there.

"I do not wish for you to feel guilty. My path in life was set the moment I was born. I am unwanted, but I will make them want me. They will beg for me to be their queen when we are done." He kisses the top of my forehead.

Remembrance flits it's way through my post orgasm fog. I slap Kai on the chest, his eyes looking down at me in confusion.

"You made me kick out Janella."

"I mean, I guess if you want her to watch, but I don't plan on sharing you when we are intimate."

"No, I was hanging out with her when you so rudely interrupted. You were mean to her. The poor thing was practically shaking in her bones." Janella is the sweetest person I have ever met, even Louissa isn't that nice.

"I will go apologize tomorrow after I have cleaned up the mess in the dungeon." Kai leads us to the bed where I climb under the covers as he slides in behind me. His strong arms wrap around me and instantly I feel safe. I feel at home.

# Chapter Twenty Eight

## SKARLETTE

Crawling from the bed, I let Kai's arm drop to the mattress. I have no idea how long we have slept, for the sun has long since risen and is now halfway in the sky. My feet pad along the floor, making my way to the bathing suite. Inside, I run the bath, letting the water steam into the air as I undress. I am just about to sink my toe into the water when I hear a commotion taking place outside. I quickly pull on my robe, moving to the window.

Below, guards are running in every direction. The gates are being closed and the rest of the fae army is lining up on either side. I move to the bed, violently shaking Kai awake.

"What is it?" He grumbles, his voice still thick with sleep.

"Something is happening. I think we are under attack." I trip over the large wolf curled up on the floor as I hurry to dress.

Downstairs, servants are in a state of panic, children are crying, and Louissa, who has just arrived from Vreilwreth, is trying to reassure several of them that their families will be fine. Making our way outside, we try to find anyone that will tell us what's going on, but the grounds are in turmoil. At the front of the castle, we find the general who is already shouting out orders.

"The vampires are breaching the castle!" He yells as his guards line the walls, filling in every open space behind the gates.

My mind conflicts. I'm not sure what I should do. If I am to fulfill the prophecy, I can't be seen fighting for either side. While I want to fight against the fae because of my hatred for them, I also want to fight the vampires for the fae village that lays beyond these castle walls. I can try and fight them all at once, but then I will have a man hunt on my hands, something I need to avoid if I am to unite us all.

The vampires are getting closer, my shadows flick out from underneath me, crawling across the ground. I breathe deep, willing them to go back into hiding before I hurt someone. More guards fill in around me. The doors to the castle behind me are barred shut with Ethan hiding away inside.

My eyes travel across the sea of fae military before landing on Kai. He is moving towards me, concern laced in his eyes. He stops in front of me, his hands grabbing hold of my forearms.

"You have to go," he urges. "You can't be seen fighting here if you are expected to lead these people."

"I am a villain, this is what I live for," I protest, the urge to fight surging through me. My shadows dance again, licking up his legs.

He places a soothing kiss to my forehead and instantly the shadows ease off of him. "You have to leave, Skarlette."

"I can't leave you," I whisper, the raw feeling of my words seeping out as my shadows gently caress his hands.

"You must. I will survive and meet you on the other side when the battle is over." He steps backward, dissolving himself into the army of soldiers.

I dart around the edges of the crowd. The draw bridge lowers and on the other side stand the vampires. Elijah stands front and center, his eyes narrowing when they catch sight of me, but I don't have time to deal with him right now. I need to put as much distance between me and this battle as I can. I let my shadows sprawl out, covering me in darkness. The sound of battle cries and screams come from behind me as I make my way out of the village.

I walk for ages before I reach Calix. I am tempted to enter the inn, wanting to sleep in a warm bed for the night, but if they see me here instead of in the fight that has been happening for days, everything I am working for could be ruined. The town is eerily quiet, not a single person to be seen.

When the town is but a mere speck behind me and the edge of the dark forest welcomes me, I relax. My shadows combine with the darkness the trees canopy brings, like they are happy to be home. A ways in, a tree calls to me, beckoning me with its tall roots. A perfect place for me to hide away for a while.

Crawling inside, my knees and hands become caked with dirt. I lean against one of the large roots and close my eyes, hoping for just a moments rest. I had been walking for days. My mind was practically begging for a few moments rest or at least some more blood.

My eyes burst open when the smell of of something delicious alerts my senses. In front of me, stumbling through the forest is a man. Blood is trickling down his face and arms and he looks as though he is lost. Something about the man is odd though. He has no pointed ears like the fae and he doesn't seem to be vampire either. He doesn't smell like either of our species and the blood loss seems to be getting to him.

Crawling from my hiding spot, I step directly into his pathway. He looks up at me, trying to find out who is blocking his way when his eyes suddenly fill with fear.

He stumbles over his words, his body beginning to tremble. "You . . . no . . . you aren't real."

'Where did you come from?" I question, my voice lethal. I have no idea what this creature is and if they are going to be a threat to me and my kind.

"You're a made up story. Something told to children to keep them in their beds at night," he mumbles, clearly not listening to me.

Enunciating every word, I make sure he hears me this time. "I can assure you I am very real." His face goes pale, whether from the blood loss or fear, I am unsure. "Now. Where did you come from?" I ask again.

He points to the mountains making my brows pull together in a puzzled thought. Whatever this species is, they live beyond the mountains?

"What are you?" He seems to ease a little with the more

questions I ask.

His words still tremble past his lips. "I am a human."

"Human?" What on earth was a *human?*

He seems to sense my confusion for he begins speaking. "I do not drink blood like you do. I eat food made from the earth. I also am not immortal." I take a step closer to him, sniffing in his scent.

His blood calls to me stronger than any blood besides Kai's. It beckons for me to drink from him. To taste if he is sweet or savory. His body trembles as I came closer. I reach my hand out, curious to touch him, but that makes him stumble backwards until he falls to the ground.

"Please don't hurt me," the man begs, and I love the way he sounds as he asks me to spare his life. It thrills me. Makes me feel like I am the one in control of the situation.

My shadows crawl across the forest floor towards him, circling him. His eyes follow them, eyeing my magic with both utter fear and joyful curiosity.

"You are incredible," he whispers.

"You don't know how long I have waited for someone to say that." I give him a wicked grin, right before I yell out to the guards who I know are lingering in the shadows. I can smell them, hear their breathing as they watch my interaction with this *human.*

The guards approach with a look of annoyance. "Please have him locked in a holding cell, I plan to have him for dinner." The human beside me lets out a nervous laugh, while the two vampires look between me and the strange man.

The guards tote the human man off into the castle as I lie in wait for the vampire army to come marching back through this very forest. The first person I see leading the way is Elijah.

"What the fuck was that?" I hiss at him.

"A war," he deadpans. "If you are going to be queen, you should expect to see a lot of it."

"It was an unnecessary battle. I am this close to taking down Ethan and the entire court," I argue.

"You see it as unnecessary, I see it as motivation." Walking beside him, I try to keep in step, but his legs are so long and it takes several of my steps to keep up.

My mind tries to wrap around the events, grabbing at straws for how this was even possible. "How did you guys get to the castle so quickly? I didn't even hear you coming. But besides that, if you cannot fall in line with my plans, I will have no choice but to lock you up in the dungeons,"

"You are not the queen yet. Plus, those fuckers just took out half their own army with Ruellia gas that does absolutely nothing to stop us."

I freeze at his words. The Ruellia gas was what the twins were working on for the general. The fae army was trying to take us out in mass quantities, but as always only ended up hurting the fae. I will deal with that information when I get back to Ruellia.

"We will see about that. I found a human today, but I assume you don't know anything about that?"

Elijah's barking laugh leaves me stunned. "He hasn't even told you about the humans. He is setting you up for failure. But if they have made it to the forest, I have things to attend to." He takes off down a hall, leaving me to fester with my thoughts.

He knew about the humans? The awkward feeling is like a pang in my chest. When I had been brought here and told I was the princess of the vampires, I had let myself feel a sense of belonging. It was a foolish thing to do. I didn't belong here. The king didn't even trust me with their information. Yet, here I am threatening Elijah to fall in line or get lost. Goddess, I am a fool.

# Chapter Twenty Nine

## Kai

Blood soaks the ground, it's metallic scent coating the air around me. We have been fighting for days, both of our armies dwindling as we take each other out. Fae and vampires collide, their teeth and armor clashing against one another. Villagers scream in the distance as the vampires invade their homes and shops. The hilt of my dagger bites into the palm of my hand as I clench it. I throw my hand up, listening to the crunch as it hits a redheaded vampire in the nose.

He comes at me again, his blood stained teeth inches from

my face. I spin, throwing my arm into him and sinking my dagger into his side. The vampire's cry rings in my ears. Quickly, I pull my dagger, positioning it just right and running it straight through his heart. Instantly, the heavy weight of his body falls against my arms. I drop him quickly and move on to the next.

My dagger is poised, ready to strike my next victim when a thick smoke begins to fill the area, making my eyes and lungs burn. Coughs and sputters sound out around me as the other fae breathe in the gas. Cries of agonizing pain echo across the field, overpowering the clanging of metal. What was this stuff? The vampires must have brought it with them.

In front of me, a tall, dark haired vampire is walking to me with worrying calmness. His eyes don't leave me not for a single second as the fight carries on around him. His crimson eyes are burning bright and blood drips from his chin. I hold my dagger out, ready to strike.

"There will be no need for that, Eveningglow." There is something about this vampire I recognize, but I can't quite place it.

"And you are?" I lazily say, spinning the dagger in my hand before sheathing it.

"Elijah." His hand stretches out between us, expecting me

to shake it.

When I ignore the hand, he lets it drop to his side. His face holds an annoyed look as he raises his hand high in the sky and ceases the fighting. He must be the one in charge.

"Cease this fight. I will make negotiations with your king," he says, his eyes boring into me, and making me feel like he is analyzing how best to eat me.

"I am not the king." I throw a look back to where my brother has emerged from the castle.

"Not yet, but when she becomes queen, I am sure you will be." I bristle at the mention of Skarlette. At how crass he is to talk about such things in the open. "I know it was you. I watched you two walk away."

That's where I knew him from. He was the vampire watching us in the forest. I had so many more questions for him, but my brother has arrived at my side, ready to start the negotiations.

"Come inside, we have much to discuss." Ethan holds out his arm in the direction of our castle, walking beside Elijah as they head inside.

Following close behind, I'm worried about what trouble my brother is about to cause. The dining room greats us with a fully prepared meal and places set. While we were out there fighting, Ethan was in here having the servants prepare a feast. I roll my eyes at the audacity. Our father would never. He would have been right out there fighting with us. Because he was a strong king and Ethan is weak, has always been weak.

Taking our seats, we ready for negotiations, but the words I hear come from Elijah shock me to my core.

"We want Skarlette," he says matter of fact. He leans back in the chair as if he were dining in his own house and not trying to negotiate war terms in his enemies castle.

"Not going to happen," Ethan states.

Elijah twirls his fork between his finger and the table. "You don't want her here."

"She is very useful to me." Ethan folds his arms. He won't be doing this without a fight.

"Ah yes, a simple pet used to carry out your wishes. Skarlette's powers are wasted here," Elijah bites.

"I let her use her powers as she see's fit, I don't see that as a waste" Ethan shrugs as he takes a bite of food.

He thought he was doing Skarlette a favor. Letting her give in to the dark side of herself. But really he liked how she was at his disposal. The moment she would try to go against his wishes, he would hurt her and when hurting her would no longer work, he would hurt something she loved. That is why she so badly wanted to keep me away, to not let me know of the mate bond. I was so stupid not to see it before.

"She isn't here anyway," I pipe up, and this earns me a look from the two men at the table.

"What do you mean, she isn't here?" They say in unison.

"She left when the battle started." Both men seem displeased with this answer. "Good thing too, because that gas was brutal. How did you even come up with that stuff anyway?

Elijah lays his hand on his chest. "Me? We didn't bring that. That was all you guys." My head snaps to Ethan, my anger coursing through my veins like a wildfire. He just killed a dozen of our own guards using that stuff and it didn't even have an effect on the vampires! I will be sure to take that one out on him later.

Picking up my fork, I begin to eat the food on my plate. The roast duck is cooked to perfection and the potatoes are creamy. I can feel their eyes still staring at me as I eat every last speck of food on my plate. Elijah wants to see me and Ethan fight. Ethan wants to fight. And I am not going to give either of them the satisfaction.

Rising from the table, the wood chair rumbles against the stone floor. "This was a wonderful dinner, but I must be returning to my room. Gentleman." I bid them farewell.

I pretend to head to my room, slipping down the hall and through the secret entrance that leads into the gardens. I need to find Skarlette before either of them do. I need to find her quick.

Outside, the warm summer air clings to my skin. Summer bugs litter the sky above me and the crickets chirp in high succession. A crow caws over head. Apparently I wasn't the only one out for a late night stroll.

A few people still linger over the burning fires. Fires made from the debris of their homes. The bodies of their loved ones. Tomorrow the village will start to rebuild the small sections that were torn down in the heat of battle, but I won't be here to see it.

I make quick work of bartering for a horse in the village. If I am going to catch up, I will need it.

# Chapter Thirty

## SKARLETTE

Standing in front of the tall window, I look out across the expanse of land before me, my eyes glued to the mountains and to what lies beyond them.

"They have been there this whole time?" I ask Veron.

"Yes. We have done trade with them for many centuries. We send a team of fae and vampires to trade with the humans. The team is sworn to secrecy, or they die. It is this way to protect the people." He walks closer, coming to stand next to me. His robe drags on the floor behind him, it's dark onyx color making his crimson eyes glow in the reflection of the window.

My head whips in his direction, anger burning through me. "And you weren't going to tell me?"

"I would have told you before I ceased to exist, but it wasn't the right time when I first saw you. I had already changed your world, I didn't need to add a whole new species into the mix." Veron's hand squeezes my shoulder lovingly. "They send us sacrifices in trade for gold and Ruellia."

"And what do the fae get out of this agreement?" I question.

"Iron."

A part of me hates how much he is starting to feel like a father to me. I know he will be gone from this world come winter, but I desperately want him to stay. How I wish he would have stolen me away from the fae and taken me in as his own. I loathe him for casting me aside all those years, but part of me is finding it in myself to love him.

"How am I supposed to run this world when I don't know everything about it," I say more to myself than him.

"You have been chosen Skarlette. You will lead the world as you know how and learn with the mistakes and successes you make." With that, Veron leaves, the back of his robe billowing behind him.

My attention returns to the land beyond the window, watching as the top leaves of the trees blow in the wind. My mind flits back to Callum, the poor human that still sits down in the dungeons. I'm not cruel enough to keep him from food and water, but he came here to steal from us, even if he gave me information, he tried to use it as a weakness. But they will learn, I am far from weak.

I need to find out why the humans have been hidden from us all this time. They sound weaker than us, so why would they be hidden from us? At this point, I feel like I have more questions than answers anymore.

Making my way through the large castle, I let the marble floors lead me to the deepest and darkest parts. I need to find the library. There will certainly be books that mention humans. There has to be. At the end of a long hallway,  A large set of double doors call to me. My fingers close around the cold gold door handle, turning it until I hear it give. I push open the door just enough to slide my body in and shut it behind me.

Books line three of the walls, floor to ceiling. Rolling ladders that rise the full length, lean against each wall, waiting to help someone find the book they need. I let my fingers feel over the spines, reading as I go. Vampires, more vampires, fae. The list of creatures goes on and on, but so far no humans. My fingers stumble when one of the books is quite a bit smaller than the others. It's a plain brown journal with black letters. Hard to read unless you have vampire eyesight.

*Jacoby*

I slide the journal from its spot between the large tomes. In the center of the room is a large table with chairs sitting around it. I pick a seat and flip through the pages.

*You would never believe the creatures I have found on the other side of the mountains. They look a lot like the fae, but they have no pointed ears. Very unfortunately, they do not survive like those of us on this side of the mountain range. I drank far too much and the poor thing practically wilted in my hands.*

The words in the journal only seem to add to my confusion. Why have we not taken out this weak species sooner?

*They work so hard and only live a mere eighty years at best.*

I skip ahead several pages.

*I have been here for almost a month now and am in awe of this life the humans live. Though they live such a short time, it makes them live so thoroughly. They enjoy almost every moment of it. Oh how I wish the fae and vampires could live like them.*

A snort escapes me. Obviously my father had been quite the romantic. Here he was, romanticizing the life of these weak beings, while I was suffering at the hands of the fae royal family.

*I have met with their king. He promises the use of his best scientists if I provide him with gold from our mines. I am not sure what I would ever need a scientist for, but I assured him I would make good on our deal.*

The next page greets me with dread.

*I am slowly dying. I am far too young for this. I may need that scientist now.*

I can't get myself to look at the last few pages, I know that they will spell out the last few days of my father's life. Closing the journal, I shove it under my arm and hope I will not be caught with it. I quickly and quietly making my way down the halls and back to the room they say is mine. Turning the corner, I freeze when I come face to face with a faerie servant.

"Mom?" My voice croaks. I had only ever seen pictures of her, but there is no mistaking that it is her. The golden blond hair and eyes to match. The eyes of a healer. The way her nose is just like the one I see every morning in the mirror.

The woman looks at me with shock. Her head shakes no, clearly not pleased to see me. At first I am not sure what to say, but then anger roars its ugly head. My mother has been alive this whole time and she didn't bother to come see me? I needed to calm down, my shadows were going haywire in the hallway. Maybe she had an explanation? Maybe they kept me from her?

More questions I obviously am not getting answers to because the woman before me spins on her heel and takes off down the hallway. I try to chase after her, letting my shadows hide me from view as I run after her. I lose her for a moment, circling back around and heading down another hallway. Doors line the hall on either side, solid black doors that stand out against the red and white of the floor and walls.

Towards the end, a door is cracked open and I can hear hushed whispers coming from the other side. I pull my shadows in close, sticking to the darkest part of the hall and getting as close as I can to the open door without being seen.

"What is she doing here?" My mother doesn't sound sad, she sounds angry.

"Who, Candella?" A woman's voice asks.

"That half breed mutt I left back in Ruellia," Candella spits.

I hate the stab of pain I feel in my chest. The way it cracks at the sound of her words. I hate the weak feeling of not being enough. I turned off the emotion of hope a long time ago, but when I saw her, I had hoped a mother's love would be enough. A tiny part of me remembered the way the queen used to treat Louissa, and that part of me ignited with the hope my own mother would treat me the same. But I was wrong.

"Your child?" I can here the surprise in the other woman's voice.

"It's no child of mine. I was so stupid back then, getting lost in a vampire. I would have never given myself to him, but they said vampires couldn't breed." They said that because it is so rare. That's what King Veron had told me.

The voice mumbles. "I hear she is to be our queen."

"I cannot live here with that thing!" Candella screeches.

The knife in my chest twists deeper. I have to get out of here, I can't listen to another second of this. I flee the hall, tucking my father's journal so tightly against my chest that it might bruise my skin. I speed past my room, down the stairs and out the castle doors.

Outside, I take in a long breath of fresh air. Fog hangs low around the castle and sweeps in through the forest. I slow my pace, but keep walking. For the first time in a long time, I let the tears free fall down my face, flowing as if I am trying to fill a river.

I am used to the pain other's give me. A royal family who took me in, but treated me like garbage? Fine. The school children in the village? Fine. The people who try to break me before I dispatch them? Fine. A mother who is supposed to have a special bond with me, who is supposed to love me unconditionally? I find myself broken.

Stealing a horse from the local tavern in Calix, I ride several days to get home to Ruellia. I don't sleep. I carefully take small amounts of blood from the horse, to keep myself sane.

Crickets chirp around me as I let my horse walk for a while. I can't keep pushing it at the rate we are going or I am going to have a dead horse on my hands. Several yards ahead I can see the outline of someone approaching on horse back. Instantly my shadows ready themselves. My right hand reaches for the dagger while my left hold the reins steady.

"Skarlette?" The figure asks and instantly my shadows fall. I sheath the dagger back in my boot.

"Kai." If I could jump from my horse and into his arms, I would, but right now I need to get back to Ruellia.

"There is so much we need to talk about." We say at the same time, making each other laugh.

"When we get back to Ruellia." Riding side by side, I hold my hand out which he happily takes.

Throwing my leg over before the horse has even fully stopped, I throw it's reins towards the stable boys. I take a small moment, pressing my forehead against the horses.

"Thank you for your service," I say to him in a hushed whisper. The last thing I need is people thinking I am soft.

"Make sure it makes it back to Calix." My voice is muffled by my hood, but they nod their heads in understanding.

Leaving Kai to talk with the guards near the front door, I take the stairs up to my room two at a time. I make it to my room in record time, stashing away my father's journal in a secret compartment before anyone can see. My body jumps, my heart rate picking up at the sound of knocks on my door.

"Just a minute." I hurry, throwing my cape on the chair and walking to the door. The cold knob turns roughly and I have to yank to get the attic door open.

Ethan is standing on the other side. His eyes travel around the inside of the room, but he doesn't come in.

"Where have you been?" He swipes a finger through a layer of dust on the dresser closest to the door.

"On business." One hand holds the door, while I set the

other on my hip. I try to hide my nervousness, make sure my eyes don't dart to where I just hid the journal.

"Well now that you are back, we have business to attend to." He spins on his heal, barely giving me time to close the door and catch up to him.

"It's the middle of the night. What could we possibly have to do right now?"

"Are you questioning your king?" His gaze slides to me from the corner of his eye.

"Of course not, Your Majesty."

"Good, cause tonight we have a guest." The way he says it makes dread fill my stomach. If he is happy about the late night guest and coming to get me, it could only mean one thing.

My mother has come here thinking I stayed back in Shadowfall.

We enter the throne room to see a woman standing in the center. Her gaze sets on me and she scowls.

"What can we do for you, Candella?" Ethan says as he climbs the dais and takes a seat on his throne. I stay in the corner, closest to the doors, easier for a quick escape.

"I was hoping to come here for sanctuary, but it seems no matter where I go, she is there." The way she says it, the disgust that rolls off her tongue at the mere mention of me.

This is bad, so, so bad. My mother is going to tell Ethan about my staying in Shadowfall. Me and Everything I am working for is going to be ruined.

My eyes meet hers, my lips in a thin line as I contemplate what to do. The smirk on her face tells me everything I need to know.

I blurt, unable to stop the words that spill from my mouth, but I need to protect myself. "This woman cannot be trusted, Your Majesty. She has been living with the vampires. I was there on business earlier this weak. She lives inside their castle."

"She was the one in Shadowfall, Your Majesty. Ask her what she was doing there," Candella screeches. She wasn't expecting me to speak up.

The smile on Ethan's face tells me he is enjoying the show. "You expect me to believe a liar over my trusted assassin?"

"I—well, yes."

Ethan rises from his throne, walking in a predatory way towards the woman who birthed me. He circles her, looking her up and down. "Seeing as I am grateful to you for leaving your half bread child here to use at my disposal, I guess I could give you a job."

Candella spits in my direction. "And what of the mutt?" Standing here with my arms folded and my feet a shoulder width apart, I stare at her with fury that I hope she can feel in her soul.

"Oh, she stays. She also has permission to order you around as she see's fit." A smirk ghosts my lips, but I quickly shut it down.

Something flashes in her eyes. Is it fear or determination to make my life a living hell? I can't be sure, but I am sure that I hold no sympathy for her. I hold no emotion, really.

Ethan snaps at one of the guards. "Take miss Candella to the servants quarters."

"I can't wait to see how you punish her." Ethan's smile is wide as he passes me, leaving the throne room.

His words make me at war with myself. I want to treat her like she treated me, but Ethan wants a show and I don't want to give him one. I have too much on my mind.

"Get out of my sight." Spit flies from my mouth with the force of my words.

Candela looks between Ethan and I, her eyes wide with shock. But Ethan is unamused, I did exactly the opposite of what he wanted.

Candela scrambles, but the guards stop her before she can get far, making her way out of the room with a guard hanging on to each of her arms without so much as a passing glance. My hand goes to my forehead, rubbing at my temple, trying to ease some of the chaos inside my mind.

Ethan's voice carries towards me as I try to leave. "Where do you think you're going?"

"To my room."

He stops inches from me, his hand moving between us before wrapping around my throat.

"Why were you in Shadowfall, Skarlette?" His hand is like stone around my throat. His grip is punishing and I can barely breathe. My hands reach up, trying to help ease his tight hold.

"I…wasn't," I choke out.

"Are you planning against me, monster?" His teeth gleam, inches from my face.

"No." I say, but I want to laugh in his face. If only he knew the downfall I am planning for him and this castle.

He eases his grip on my throat, his cold hand still wrapped around it, but with less pressure. "She says you were in Shadowfall. You tell me she is lying?"

"Yes. She obviously hates me and will do anything to get me in trouble. Why would you believe her over your most trusted assassin?" I hope my lies are enough to keep him from knowing, that he might forget I admitted to being in Shadowfall only a few minutes ago.

"Get out of my sight." He shoves me back before letting go of my throat, making me fall to the floor.

A hand reaches under my arm and tries to help me up, I cry with relief when I see Kai standing behind me.

"I take it that is what we have to talk about." He mumbles into my hair as he pulls me in to a tight hug and leads me back to our room.

My head nods against his chest. There is no one to see me here and I feel the urge to let myself be vulnerable. To let the villain hide away for a moment while I lay my heart out.

# Chapter Thirty One

## SKARLETTE

Fall is approaching faster than I have prepared for. Before I know it, the first frost will hit Ruellia and I will be queen. In front of me the ground is littered with leaves from the trees, their vibrant reds and oranges bringing color to the muddy ground. It rained all through the night, leaving puddles along the road to the village. A village still trying to recoup after the loss of so many during battle.

My mind still spins with thoughts of the other night. Kai listened while I told him of what happened in Shadowfall, yet my tongue didn't seem to let it be known about my father's journal. Some things still stayed secret.

I was abhorred when he told me of what Ethan did with the lethal gas he let loose. Killing so many fae in an attempt to wipe out the vampires isn't a good look for him.

A wagon passes me, splashing in one of the puddles and drenching my clothes. Gritting my teeth together with annoyance, I look down at my now wet clothes that are splattered with mud. Brown speckles my hair, forcing me to put it up. It's probably for the best anyway, I won't want it in the way for what I am about to do. I throw the braid over my shoulder, letting it sway against my back as I walk and hope my clothes dry some before I reach my destination.

Today, I am going to get a semblance of revenge.

I look down at the large black wolf dog that bounces next to me as she keeps up with my pace. We follow the village road, past the meadow that is still trying to regrow itself from my most recent tantrum, and into one of the more densely populated areas.

The small townhome, with it's brown body and green shutters looks quaint. If only the person that lived inside was the same. I knock on the door softly, listening as her feet shuffle across the floor. Her face greets me when she opens the door, looking at me with a small smile that instantly drops with recognition.

"What do you want?" She grumbles. Her wrinkled face looks at me with disgust and her hand shakes against the knob as she tries to hold open the door.

"What do *I* want? Everything. What did I need? Love and compassion. I was a child who needed someone to stand up to the king and queen for how they treated me. And instead, I got a nurse maid who thought I would be better off dead." Her already pale skin, grows paler.

"Killing me won't bring you any of that."

"Oh I know it won't, but I am a villain and revenge brings me a sense of. . . peace." Bella growls as I smile at the woman.

The swirling fear in her eyes, dances between the wolf pup and myself.

"It will be easier if you just let this happen. You are almost to the end of your life anyway." She tries to close the door, but my boot is quicker as I wedge it between the door and the frame.

I shove the door open making it bang into the wall behind it. Bella stalks towards our prey, her teeth bared as she pushes the woman towards her chair.

"You don't deserve the kindness of a quick death. Not only did you treat me like garbage, but you did Prince Kai as well. You constantly belittled him and referred to him as the *'back up prince'*. You are scum."

Her shriveled lips turn up into a smile, a wicked smile that I have seen many times before. "You too are perfect for each other. Neither of you are worthy of the life you live. The king and queen were stupid to give you both a home. If only the queen was here to see what her son has become, what he is chained to." I'm slightly taken aback by the fact she knows about our mate bond.

The anger I feel pumping in my veins trumps everything. I walk behind her chair, look down at the hate that resonates so deeply within myself and drag my blade across her throat. Quickly, I leave before I can be overwhelmed by the scent of her blood. I wanted so badly to drag that out longer, but the anger was red hot and blinded my every thought.

Outside the house, I double over, my hands leaning against my thighs as I take deep breathes. Something about the way she knew everything makes me wonder who else knows about the bond between Kai and myself. Who is watching us from the corners of rooms and the tops of trees?

Stopping at the meadow on our way back to the castle, I watch, looking in every direction for whatever spies Ethan has hovering over me while the wolf pup gets a drink of water. I hate the feeling of always being watched. That no matter what I do, someone will be there to tell me if I did it right or wrong. That's the freedom I crave. The freedom to do what I want, when I want, and not be judged on how well I do it.

Once I am back at the castle, I start to look for Kai. I need to ask him if he knows anything about the spies following me. I'm starting to feel a little crazy with how far my mind is spiraling.

I halt when I hear a familiar name coming from the throne room. Creeping closer to the side entrance door, I push it open just enough to see what is going on. Inside, Janella's father is on his knees, begging the prince for something.

"Please. Please marry my daughter. I promise she is good. She will supply you with many heirs." The hairs on my neck bristle at the fact he is trying to marry off Janella to Ethan.

"I will do no such thing." Ethan clearly dismisses him, but Jon doesn't take it well.

"If you won't marry her, I will send her here to be friends with your assassin and convince her to get you drunk. She listens to me, and if I tell her to impregnate herself with the king's sperm, then she will." He rose to his feet, spitting the words with anger.

Bile is rising in my throat, burning it with stomach acid. How could he say those things about Janella? I couldn't stomach to listen any further. I have to leave and I still need to find Kai.

Arriving in front of his room, I can see the door is cracked. Kesira's whining voice filters through making my ears stay on alert. Kai and I have been so entangled with one another lately, I had almost forgotten his brother had betrothed him.

"You have to stop. You're practically flaunting her around," Kesira complains.

Kai is pacing in his room, my ears pick up on his footsteps shuffling against the carpet and I can hear his long sigh. "I thought you already knew, I'm not marrying you."

"I did not know. Your brother said we are to get married. He is now the king." Her whiny voice grates against every nerve ending in my brain. Bella, lets out a low growl as if she is sharing my exact sentiments.

"She is the love of my life and my mate. You think you ever stood a chance against her?" He lets out a harsh laugh, sending Kesira into hysterics.

"Your brother promised," she sobs.

"My brother is a fool. Now get out." Kai is harsh, harsher than necessary in my opinion. His actions reminded me of something I would do. Be mean to someone even if they didn't necessarily deserve it.

The door bursts open, making me stumble back as Kesira barrels through. She stops, giving me an ice cold glare before her eyes catch on the dog next to me and she wails again, running down the hall to get away from us.

The wolf pup trots ahead, pushing into Kai's room like she owns the place. Her tail wags as her body bumps against the furniture. A lamp almost knocks to the floor before my shadows can grab ahold of it and place it back in it's spot.

Looking around, I am ready to let the dog sleep while I attend to some things. But he reaches out for my hand, squeezing it with a loving touch.

I know what he wants and I know the implications. "Kai—"

"Just stay." He takes my hand, rubbing his thumb against my skin. The dog on the floor bristles. "I'm not going to hurt her," he reassures her.

I climb into the bed beside him, but it feels off. Laying next to him in this plush bed is amazing, but he just sent his fiancé away. It feels like I am lying in someone else's spot. Like I don't deserve to be here. It doesn't take long before Kai's breathing evens out next to me and I know that he has fallen asleep. I lay there for a long time, letting the silence sink into me before deciding to rise, and tiptoeing to the window where I take a seat on the alcove.

The village below is dark, fires lighting several spots where people are on night watch or still awake to work.

From this high up in the castle, the guards wandering below look like ants. I can still make out where people are trying to rebuild and guilt instantly fills me. I hadn't checked on Janella after the fight. Life has been pushing me in every direction but hers. I curl my legs to my chest, wrapping my arms around them and resting my chin on my knees. I would have to check on her as soon as possible for now I watch the land below as it rises and flows.

The pack of wolves are still on the other side of the river, taking down a cow and it reminds me that I will need to ask the cook for some meat. Bella would be hungry soon. The only con to letting her sleep in the castle, was she didn't hunt as much as she did when she was wild.

The view out the window keeps me occupied until the sun begins to rise. A beautiful glow casting over the valley as the suns rays peak over the mountain. I hear Kai yawn, and my head turns just in time to see him run his hand over the bed in search of me. He sit's up quickly when he realizes I am gone. A small smile plays on my lips while watching him panic for a moment.

"Good morning," I murmur.

His eyes are glazed with sleep, his hair a ruffled mess. "Good morning," he responds with a lazy grin, relaxing when he realizes I haven't up and left in the middle of the night.

The wolf at the end of the bed stirs, her yawn wide enough to fit someone's head. She shakes the sleep out of her fur before coming up to me to rest her head on my arm.

Kai points to Bella. "I think it's hungry and probably needs to relieve itself."

"I named her Bella." Leaving the beautiful morning sunrise, I get to my feet. Putting on my corset, Kai helps tighten it until I can't breathe. I twist back the front of my hair, pulling it away from my face and pin it. The long ends flow past my shoulders in curling waves.

"Beautiful," Kai says, his lips connecting with my shoulder.

I smile at his reflection. It feels so normal to be here with him. It doesn't feel like we are planning the take down of our home. I call to Bella and head out the door, ready to destroy the day.

# Chapter Thirty Two

## SKARLETTE

People falter as I walk past with my large guard dog. If people were scared of me before, they are terrified of me now. The cook gave Bella enough meat to get her started this morning, but suggested I take her to hunt for the rest. Ethan sent us off with a list of two names. I hesitate slightly as I read them over. Both names on the list were going to put me in for a world of hurt today.

Elijah's name is scribbled in the king's hand on the yellowing parchment of paper. The second is Jon and there is no need for the last name, I already know who it is. Having seen the names, I crumple the paper, tossing it into the fire as I pass the blacksmith's stables. Elijah has done it now. How am I supposed to kill him? Maybe Ethan is testing me after Candella spilled my secrets.

"How he thinks I am going to accomplish that without starting an all out war is beyond me," I mumble to myself, kicking a lone rock with my foot and watching it sputter down the alleyway.

The edge of the forest with it's tall trees that sway in the wind, approaches as I send Bella off to hunt while I take care of the second name on the paper. This one is going to hurt.

I rap my hand on the door three times. My knuckles pounding the same spot they do every time I come here. I can't get myself to look at the door, instead I focus on the dying flowers in a pot near the window, their leaves drooping from not enough water.

Janella's sister stands in the doorway, her eyes filled with worry and I know she knows why I am actually here. "Oh—sorry, Janella isn't here right now."

"That's okay. It's better that she isn't." Stepping into the house, my eyes take a look around the small area. The sink is full of dishes and several small children play on the floor.

"Would you like some tea?" She asks, her voice trembling with fear.

"I would take them to the bakery, get them some treats and find Janella." I hold out the small, leather bag of coin. "Where is he?"

She points down the hallway to what I assume is a back bedroom. I walk slowly, giving her time to wrangle the kids and head into the village. When I reach the last door down the hallway, I kick it open, but he doesn't stir. The large man with gray hair and bushy eyebrows sleeps, his snore vibrating in the small room. A bottle of rum hangs from his hand, spilling onto the floor below.

Oh how easy it would be to snuff Jon out while he slept. But he doesn't deserve to go easy. I wonder if Janella knows how disgusting this man really is. Offering his daughters up as whores for the king, all while wanting royal treatment by selling off his own kin for money. Money he would surely use to buy himself more drinks and more whores.

Creeping close, I use my shadows to muffle the sound of my boots on the wood floor. I put my face close to his, baring my teeth and wrapping my hand around his throat. His eyes pop open, going wide with shock.

"Hello, Jon," I purr, digging my nails into his fleshy skin.

"Please," he chokes out.

Letting go of him, I take several steps back, but keep myself between him and the door. He sits up, coughing from the pressure that was just previously on his windpipe.

"You see, Jon . . . when I saw your name on the list, I was confused. How could my sweet friend's father do something to annoy my prince and have his name end up on my list? But then I remembered the conversation I heard the other night. How you begged on your knees and then threatened him." His face is paling with every word I speak. I guess the truth of what he has done is even too much for him.

"Does Janella know?" He squeaks.

I lean against the door. "I haven't told her."

"I-I was only doing what was best for my family. The farm is struggling," he stutters, trying to find excuses for his abhorrent decisions.

"The farm Janella works day in and day out to keep running, while your frequenting the local taverns and whorehouses running up bills you can't pay back. Offering to marry off your daughter to pay back your debts." I pause for a moment. "Oh sorry, no you didn't offer to marry her off. When the king denied a marriage, you threatened to send Janella up to the castle while visiting me and throw herself on the king so that she would become pregnant with an heir."

Shame fills his face, but I don't hesitate at others guilt. It's not how I was raised.

"She is going to hate you for killing me." He tries to find a guilty conscience in me. Grasping at the frayed ends of his metaphorical noose. But it will do him no good.

"She will hate me for a moment, but she will feel more betrayed by you than me. You pretended to be kind and to love her. But she has always known I am the villain." I push off the door and stalk to him. He rises from his bed, his body swaying as he tries to stand up and fight me.

"I won't go willingly!" Spit flies from his mouth, landing on my face.

"I was hoping you wouldn't. I do love a good fight. Makes it feel more worth it." My smile is wicked and my shadows thrum with the excitement of work.

He tries to throw a punch, but misses when I duck quickly. I grab his hand twisting it around. His cry is like music to my ears. "I don't know why people like you think that you can get away with things and not be punished," I growl.

I shove him hard, making his body fly backwards, and his head bounce off the floor from the force. He lays there unmoving, staring up at me with so much fear that I can smell the piss as he soaks his pants. I can't help the laugh that escapes me as I shake my head at the ridiculousness of it all. He is disgusting.

"They deserve so much better than you could have ever

given them." The shadows crawl from all the dark corners of the room, circling around his body. They twist like vines around him, squeezing tighter and tighter. I pull the dagger from my boot, stabbing him in the chest several times before I feel his body go limp.

I'll have to send someone to clean up before Janella and her siblings return. I would hate for them to have to see the carnage I'm leaving behind. Exiting the house, I leave the farm and head to my next name.

It takes days for me to get to Shadowfall even on horseback. It's what had amused me the most when I saw his name on the list. Ethan is willingly sending me away from the castle for days on end to meet with the very people he thinks I'm conspiring with. It doesn't make a whole lot of sense.

Shadowfall's castle looms in front of me under the dark cloud covered sky, the ominous black stone castle setting the mood for a sour visit. I'm not even sure what I am going to say to Elijah or my uncle. In fact, I didn't even want to come in the first place. It is far too close to the end of my uncle's reign and I know he is waiting for me to tell him the news.

The closer I come to the throne room, the more I pick up on voices. Elijah and my uncle's tones carry their heated discussion out into the hall. My body is paralyzed by the door, waiting for it to quiet down before making my presence known. I'm not scared of much until it comes to telling people what I want, and then it is like the earth might explode.

"What do you need?" It takes me a moment to realize Elijah's words are pointed at me.

"We have a problem." He looks at me, not the least bit worried about whatever problem we might be having.

They both stare patiently, waiting for me to continue speaking. "Your name was on my list this morning."

Elijah barks out a laugh. "And what exactly do you plan to do about it?" His arms are crossed and a smug smile is on his face. He knew I wasn't here to kill him, but the fact he acted like I wouldn't, irritated me.

Making quick work of the distance between us, I get right in his face. My shadows pull the dagger from my boot and place it in my hand. I press the tip of the blade into the side of his throat, my teeth bared.

"I was going to let you live, but now I am rethinking that decision," I growl in frustration. He isn't taking me seriously.

His smirk stays, his eyes daring me to do it. I drop my dagger, letting my hand fall to my side and then pushing the dagger back into my boot.

"Stay off the fae lands. I need Ethan to trust me if I am going to try and take him down. I need this . . ." I pause for a moment. "If I am going to become queen of all the lands."

My uncle's hands clap, a smile of joy on his face now that I have said it out loud.

"What makes a villain good for the throne?" Elijah's face is clearly not enthused with me deciding to stay.

"What makes a villain unable to see the line between right and wrong? The only difference between me and the hero is that I know I am doing bad things to get what I want. The heroes hide behind a mask of pureness, saying they are doing evil for the greater good. The difference is I am willing to do the bad things to keep my peace and destroy those who threaten to take it from me."

Elijah's face is stone cold. I turn, heading for the throne doors that open as I come closer. "Oh, and Elijah," I call over my shoulder "I'm serious, I don't want to see you in the fae lands again. If you do, I will be forced to take action against you." I make my way out into the hall.

Behind me, I can hear my uncle's voice. "She is your

queen and that is an order." A giddy smile spreads across my face as I hear Elijah curse. A door in the distance slams before the throne room doors softly click shut behind me.

I head to the room that uncle Veron had called mine. Inside was dark, with crimson and black curtains, but the bed in the center now has a navy blue comforter with gold swirls. It reminds me of Kai's eyes and makes my chest ache with longing.

I don't need to rest before heading back to Ruellia, but I decide I want the break. In front of the window is a small cushioned seat, that connects to two large book cases sitting on either side of the window frame. Another thing in this room that reminds me of Kai. From this spot in my room, I can see the entire vampire village. Because the sky is turning purple, the sun now behind the mountains, vampires begin to come out. They linger on the edges of the forest, hunting prey and visiting with friends.

In the village, lights flicker to life, brightening store windows and shining against the dark mountainside. Both sides of Aurenda were beautiful in their own ways. Ruellia was best in the spring and summer, with the sun shining bright on it's meadows and rivers. While Shadowfall's best time was at night, with it's dark themes and vibrant nightlife.

I wish everyone could see it for all it's beauty and not just one side or the other, but that is a fight I will endure when I am crowned queen of Aurenda.

332

# Chapter Thirty Three

## SKARLETTE

Ruellia's streets welcome me home after my almost two weeks away. It feels like I have been gone forever while also feeling like I have been gone for only a few hours. Time is a strange thing.

Trotting up the road in my direction is a large black ball of fur. A strange feeling of happiness courses through me at the sight of her and it's what I imagine a mother feels like when they see their child. I reach down from my saddle, scratching the large mutt on her head.

"Bella, where the hell have you been?" I haven't seen her

since I left her to hunt nine days ago. She nuzzles her wet nose against my arm.

When we finally arrive back home, I trudge my way up the stairs. My feet feel heavy after so many days in the saddle and I haven't drank very much blood. I didn't even manage to eat the entire time I was gone.

Bella trots in front of me, nosing her way into Kai's open bedroom. Someone grabs ahold of my left arm, twisting me to look at them. My shadows respond quickly, pulling my dagger from my boot and placing it into my hand.

I press the blade against my attacker's throat. Looking up, I see Kai giving me a lopsided smile. Returning the smile, I shake my head. I had been only a few seconds from slicing my dagger through his neck and here he is smiling at me. He leans into my dagger, pursing his lips towards me and waiting for a kiss.

I give him a quick peck, my dagger still poised between us. After one more quick touch of our lips, I drop my weapon before sheathing it back in my boot. I scrub my hand against my face, willing the exhaustion to wait.

"I'm sorry. I am exhausted. Janella's dad was on my list and then I was gone for several days." My arms hang at my sides limply. It isn't often I show someone my weaknesses, but with him it seems to be happening more and more.

Kai's arm wraps around me, leading me into his room. "I have food in my room and you can drink from me before we sleep," he speaks into my hair.

His promises sound heavenly. I still haven't faced Janella and it is something I am going to have to do sooner or later. As soon as we cross the threshold into his room I can smell the lamb stew. My mouth waters and all thoughts of dealing with my actions slips from my mind, put on the backburner until later.

Eating the delicious fresh warm stew, I throw a few bites of meat in Bella's direction. She greedily chomps at them, licking her lips and staring at me for more.

"So, you had to kill your best friends dad," He says around a mouthful of food.

Shrugging my shoulders, I finish off the last of my plate. "Honestly, I was bummed for Janella when I saw it, but after I heard him talking to Ethan in the throne room, I didn't care."

Kai leaves the table, moving to the bath where he turns on the steaming water. It pours from the faucet, filling up the gold tub. The water splashes onto the floor as I sink in, heating my bones, warming my muscles, and sending my body into a relaxed state. My eyes close, on the verge of falling asleep.

"You need blood, Skar." He holds his wrist out in front of me. "My menace needs to replenish."

Looking deep into his navy blue and gold flecked irises that I have come to love so much, I wait for them to show me he hates all this. The feeding me when I won't feed myself. The looking after me when I inevitably do the wrong thing. But in his eyes, all I see is love. He looks at me expectantly, waiting for me to sink my fangs in his skin and take what I need.

"You really shouldn't be so willing," I say to him.

"Why not?" He shrugs his shoulders, shoving his wrist closer to my mouth. "You need it and my blood heals you when you drink it."

Placing a soft kiss to the sensitive skin on his wrist, I smile when he hisses. I sink my fangs in, his delicious spice flavored blood hitting my tongue and instantly making me feel energized. Despite my body urging for more, I only take a little, dropping his hand and sinking deeper into the bath water. Kai leaves the room and I sink further beneath the water. I hold my breath, letting them burn and ache for the relief that oxygen would bring.

Sometimes I wonder what it would be like to forget the world. To let the darkness and silence take over. But then Kai's smiling face is there in my mind and Janella's melodic voice and I can't help but want to stay earth side.

Breaking through the surface of the water, I take in lungful's of air. My eyes land on Kai as he returns to the bathing chamber, his shirt is gone and he has a dark look in his eyes. I realize now that enough water has splashed from the tub making it so my breasts are no longer covered, they are bare and the coolness of the air against them has made my nipples into hard peaks.

Kai kneels next to the tub, his hand slipping into the water and getting dangerously close to the spot between my thighs. He runs his fingers up and down my legs with featherlight touches that make my head fall back against the tub as shivers crawl up my spine.

"Kai," I breathe, and even though I didn't think it was possible, his eyes darken further. His fingers whisp over my center before he withdraws his hand from the tub.

I frown, looking at Kai with betrayal. "You're gonna just tease me like that?"

"You are tired and in need of rest," he says, helping me out of the tub and placing a kiss against my forehead. He leads me to bed, curling up against me as we drift off.

I wake a few hours later with a groan. I had forgotten to report back to Ethan. Crawling from my comfortable spot on the bed, I throw on a fresh set of clothes. I really hope

Ethan doesn't know I'm back yet. But I am sure the guards went and told him of my arrival, just as he has instructed them to do.

Ethan's office is empty, same with his room. I find him seated at the dining table, eating dinner alone. The servant at the far end of the room brings an extra plate and silverware set to the table, signaling my arrival.

"Ah, Skarlette. How lovely it is you finally come to see me." The words are so simple, like he is greeting me after a long time, but I can hear the subtle accusation in his tone.

"I am sorry I did not come sooner. I was exhausted after the journey." I take a seat in the chair, filling the plate in front of me with a small amount of food, still full from the lunch and blood.

"I take it the vampire is taken care of then?" Ethan sips at the hot dark liquid, something called coffee that just made it's way to us. They didn't say from where, but I could put the pieces together. It had come from the human lands.

My eyes focus in on Ethan. Something is off. His skin looks paler than before. He doesn't really seem sick. He acts as though nothing is wrong and I have no gossip from the servants about him being seen by the royal physician.

I nod, chewing on a mouthful of eggs. "It is."

"Such a good little pet you are." He smiles, but again

something doesn't light up in his eyes. It's almost as if I am looking at a dead person. A talking one.

I shake off the feeling of unease, not wanting my shadows to make an appearance. Finishing off the items on my plate, I take notice that he hasn't touched a single drop of his own food.

"If you'll excuse me, I am afraid I am still in need of rest." My legs push the chair back as I rise, bowing to him before I leave.

Once out in the hall, I press myself against the wall, calling to my shadows, and using them to hide me in the shadows behind the door. Waiting, I listen to find out what exactly is going on with the new king.

The teacup in Ethan's hands clatter to the table, a curse slipping from his lips as the servant rushes over to help him clean it up.

"I need the scientist. Get him here now. Whatever he has done to me, it's not working." The servant trembles with fear as they scoop up the pieces of the broken cup. I can hear the clatter of the broken pieces as they walk away.

"Your Majesty." The royal guard's voice is shaky as he steps up to the table.

"I don't care. I need this done now. I will be the one to fulfill this prophecy not her." The shadows around me grow cold as the realization hits.

The guard said they were trying to create something that had only been born once. Ethan talked about the prophecy. He knows that I am meant to unite the two kingdoms. He knows about everything and that is why he is trying to keep me on a leash. Though I have not been the only half breed to be born. There is the other who Ethan must have had killed to keep from learning the prophecy.

In my moment of frozen thought processing, I almost miss when they escort Ethan out of the room. I follow them up the stairs, keeping enough distance between us to not to be seen. Just as they get him to his office, they shut the door before I can slip in.

This is not good. Ethan is trying to turn himself into a half breed like myself. He is going to try and control the entire continent of Aurenda.

# Chapter Thirty Four

## SKARLETTE

My countdown is starting to dwindle. The first frost is coming to Ruellia quickly. Every morning when I wake, the temperatures are cooler than the morning before. My time is running out to take down the royal family before my coronation. If I fail to complete my last job before the first frost, an unimaginable war will be coming to for the entire continent of Aurenda.

Pilfering through my box of hidden Ruellia oil, I grab one of the smaller bottles. Sneaking down into the kitchen, I find the king's plate, adding a dash of the purple liquid.

Not enough to kill him yet, but enough to make him sick. Hopefully before he is able to turn himself. I need him weak and this was my chance now that the royal taste testers are gone. I want him to watch helplessly as I burn his castle to the ground. He needs to know before he dies, that I have won.

I make myself scarce, leaving the castle in search of Janella. I need to talk with her. I can't put off what I had done any longer and I need to make sure that she isn't too mad at me. I have been avoiding her for too long. I still haven't even asked her how she is doing after the fight against the vampires. I am being a terrible friend.

The farmhouse comes into view. Janella is sitting on the porch, a needle in one hand, shirt in the other as she sews up a hole. Her head rises when she hears me approach. I'm not sure what to do with the look on her face, she looks sad, but also something like relief lingers in the deep recesses of her eyes.

"I wont apologize." My tone is abrupt, but I won't be sorry for taking down the man who tried to sell her and then use her like a weapon.

"I know." She looks back down, continuing to sew.

"When you are ready to hear it, I will tell you why." I begin to walk away when I hear her call for me.

"What did he do this time?" She knew then, some of what lead to her father's fall, but not all of it.

"He was going to sell you to the king and when the king said no, he threatened to have you impregnate yourself with the king's heir." I can see the tear that drips from Janella's eyes and splatters against the brown fabric in her hands.

"Did you make him suffer?" Her voice is cold.

I nod. "Enough."

The sound of footsteps behind me makes me turn my head, surprise ignites inside me when I see Kai walking towards us. He places a hand on Janella's shoulder, giving it a loving squeeze.

"When I had found out what he had tried to do to you, it was no longer Ethan's revenge I was doling out, it was for my own pure hatred. My anger was stronger." Janella rises from her seat, her arms wrapping around my body and giving me a tight hug.

"I have some meat in the ice box for that mutt of yours. Keep her away from my sheep." The corners of her mouth quirk up in a small smile and I know she is changing the subject, cause she can't bare to hear anymore.

My eyes scan the farm, making sure everything is in place after the fight. I know Janella is done with talking about sad things for one day, so I don't bring up the vampires or the fight.

"Thank you." I take the meat, leaving Janella to her sewing and feeling better about what I have done. Knowing that she isn't mad at me makes me feel relieved. It's not that I feel guilty for killing him, I feel guilty for not being the one to tell her.

Taking Kai with me, I find the little bookshop in the center of the village with it's stacks of books lining the windows. Inside, it's like a maze with stacks of books on either side of the small pathways. Off to the left sit's a counter where a man with glasses that hang on his nose, reads a book that looks like it is a million years old. A black cat meows, walking up to me, it's nose cold as it sniffs my hand before hissing.

Turning my head to where the cat's eyes have wandered, I look back at the huge wolf pup behind me. "You better wait outside." Pushing her out the door, I close it. She lets out a whine, her wet nose pushed against the glass as we walk away from her.

Kai follows me deeper into the musty store, the smell of inked parchment mixed with wet wood fills the air around us. My fingers run across the spines of books I've never even dreamed of reading. While I do know how, I'm not the most fluent. The village teacher didn't take kindly to me asking questions when I was growing up, leading to my dislike of learning. While I could read notes and papers, I haven't sat down and read a book since I was a child.

He gives me a curious glance. "What are we looking for?"

"Janella loves books," I whisper to him, making sure the shop keeper can't overhear our conversation. "A few weeks ago, I saw her carrying a stack of them out of here. I wish she could see the library in Shadowfall."

I can't tell him the other reason we are here. While I am looking for a new book for Janella, I am also looking for a book about the humans. My dad's journal provided me with a lot of insight, but I need more. My curiosity about these creatures cannot be quenched. Something in me tells me they are so much more than my father let on.

We scour every inch of the shop, finding a couple of books for Janella, but I see nothing about humans. Disappointment blooms inside of me. I was really hoping for anything, even a small journal of information about who and what they are.

"I'll pay if you want to go make sure Bella is still out there and not causing chaos," I say to Kai over my shoulder as I approach the counter.

Once Kai is out the door, the shop keeper puts their book down, staring at me with an intensity that makes me wonder if I left the castle this morning with dirt on my face.

The man's voice crackles, like he hasn't spoken in a long time. "I have what you need."

"I'm sorry?" The shopkeeper is already moving, sliding a book across the counter in my direction. The book is old, it's edges torn and bent after years of use. Dust sits in a thick layer on the cover. I blow against it, watching the dust plume across the room.

*Humans: The Complete History.*

This is it. But how had the shopkeeper known I was looking for this? I look up, ready to thank him, but there is no one in sight.

Stacking the books, I put my copy on the bottom and tuck them tightly under my arm. Outside the shop, Kai is trying to wrangle Bella from chasing after a group of kids playing tag. He hangs from her neck, yelling at her to stop chasing. I watch with amusement as she practically drags him around.

My lips purse, letting out a low whistle. The dog stops dead in her tracks, sending Kai flying forward and landing on his butt on the ground. I laugh, a loud giggling laugh that has me doubling over.

"You really couldn't just listen to me for once?" Kai grumbles to the dog. Another chuckle leaves me when the wolf narrows her eyes at him.

"I have some stuff to do. I will see you later, okay?" Kai places a kiss to my temple, leaving me on my own.

Depositing the books I bought for Janella with her sister, I make quick work to get up to my attic room where I can look at my own book without prying eyes. Bella curls up on my small blanket bed while I take a seat at my desk, opening up the old book and flitting through the pages.

*Humans came from somewhere across the ocean. They first came to us with curiosity and kindness. We let them stay in our towns and villages, learning about us, but then they used our weaknesses to take over our land. They may be mere mortals, but they have strong minds. We made a deal with the humans and the vampires that we would all stay in our designated areas on the land.*

*Peace was kept for years before one of the vampires traveled to their lands. They managed to convince him of their kindness and trade began between the lands. Though the full scope of trade stays between the royals, we know that they meet in secret, sure to keep the existence of humans a secret. The fae king was too scared of what had happened before. Too worried the humans would take over our lands again. The fae king said they had weapons, weapons unlike anything he had ever heard of or seen before. Weapons that made him cower in his castle.*

The information is almost too much. Closing the book, I

shove it into a desk drawer and look out at the sky. Evening is coming, the sun is starting to dip in the sky. I need time to digest all that I have learned. Life seems to keep throwing more and more at me, like I can handle all the secrets everyone has been keeping without exploding.

I open the door, halting when I see Kai's fist raised, and ready to knock. "I was coming to see you."

"I was just heading out, but you are welcome to come along if you and the dog can behave. Also, you'll need to keep what you see between the two of us." He nods, letting me lead the way out of the castle.

The night market is crawling with people, making it hard to stick to the shadows, especially when I have Kai and my large pup following me. I draw my hood closer around my face, keeping my eyes to the ground. I weave through the tents of the night market, but my favorite vendor is nowhere to be seen, making my anxiety swirl like bad meat in my stomach. I need large amounts of Ruellia to pull this off and I don't know if I trust anyone else to get me it.

"*Il Furfante*," someone calls out. I probably shouldn't stop. It could be a trap after all, but when they call it out again, whispering the name for only me to hear, I decide to chase my curiosity.

"I have what you need," the woman says when I approach

a smaller orange tent.

"Do we trust her?" Kai says beside me. I shrug in response, not sure if I should trust someone calling me by a mythical name.

"And what is it exactly you think I need?" I don't want to give away what I'm looking for. I'm still cautious that she isn't actually trying to harm me.

"Vido sent me. He was caught and managed to pass this particular crate off to me, making me swear I would get it to the *Il Furfante*." Her eyes nervously dart around the area, looking for any royal guards who may have decided to check up on our little market. They land on Kai and go wide.

"Show me the crate. He is with me." I urge her inside the tent and away from the prying eyes of the night market patrons. Kai stays at the entrance, standing watch.

Inside sits a small crate. When I pry the lid off with the edge of my dagger, a smile spreads across my face. Inside the crate amongst the straw, sits dozens of bottles of concentrated Ruellia, enough to light a whole fucking castle on fire.

"Thank you. If you speak a word of this to anyone, I will send my shadows to your home." A bag of coins plops down on the table from behind me. The lady nods in agreement, scooping up the bag and tucking it away.

I spin as my eyes narrow on Kai. "I can pay for it myself."

"No need, Menace. It's my pleasure." He holds my hand, letting me wrap us in my shadows as we make our way back to the castle.

I quickly make it to my room, depositing the crate next to the other, making it seem like it has belonged here the whole time. Tomorrow, I will really up my efforts on getting the Ruellia oil in it's designated spots.

I need to hurry. The first frost is only a few weeks away and I need to make sure Ethan is taken care of before he successfully changes himself into a hybrid.

"Kai, I have to tell you what your brother is trying to do." I spent all night last night thinking of how I would break this news to him. "He is trying to change himself. There is so much that you don't know . . . "

"Take your time." He takes a seat at my desk.

The words fly from my mouth without stopping. All the information I have kept bottle in my brain, trying to unravel their mysteries on my own, now out in the open. "Okay, well first of all, there are people completely unlike us that live on the other side of the mountain range. They have strange, un-pointed ears, and they only live like seventy years. Well, they have these people they call scientists, and

I overheard Ethan talking about them changing him."

He leans forward, resting his elbows on his thighs. "Wow. That's uh . . . a lot."

"I know, and I am sorry for not telling you sooner. I'm just so used to handling everything myself." I curl my arms around his head as he leans it against my stomach. My finger traces the tip of his fae ear, causing bumps to pebble across his skin.

His hands splay across my back as he looks up at me. "I am here, Skarlette. I can help you hold the burden of your thoughts. I have always been here. It's me and you against the world, Menace."

His fingers move, unlacing my corset and letting it fall to the floor between us. My hands curl around the edges of my shirt, lifting it over my head and letting it join my corset on the floor. Excitement courses through my veins. I just told him how fucked up life is and he is here wanting to worship my body. His hands pull me closer, his lips placing kisses on the skin above my heart. His thumbs hook in the waist band of my pants, pulling them off with excruciating slowness.

I straddle his lap, placing a leg on either side of his hips. My knees dig into the chair, threatening to slip off the small space. Kai's hands grab hold of my thighs, keeping my legs planted on the chair as my lips mesh with his, dancing against his with the same slowness he provided me.

"Skar, I need you," he groans when I let one of my fangs nick his lip, taking a small amount of blood before it heals.

"Show me." I stand, letting him drop his own pants. My tongue darts out, swiping across my lips with hunger when I see his cock spring free. My stomach tightens with need. "Bring me my salvation."

He grabs my hand, tugging me back to him. He guides me, helping me to seat myself just right, so the minute I sit down, I sink onto him, burying him deep inside of me.

Our foreheads meet, our groans tangling with each other as I rock against him. If I die before I manage to pull of my plan, at least I will have this. I will have felt love and ecstasy. I will have felt what it was like to have someone in your corner no matter what.

My shadows slither from the corners of the room, wrapping around my arms and holding them to the arms of the chair. Kai's hands grab my hips, moving me faster, his eyes searing into mine until we both come undone.

The minute I have come down from my orgasm induced high, the shadows slither away, letting go of my wrists and making their way back into the corners.

"I didn't summon those," I say with slight panic.

"I know." Kai's grin is huge. "I did."

"What?" I'm thoroughly confused. How is that even possible?

"I was thinking about how handy it would be if I was the one with shadow powers, and then I saw them slithering their way across the room. My father mentioned it briefly when he told us about fae mating, but he wasn't one to spend much time talking about that kind of stuff." He pushes me from his lap, grabbing my clothes and helping me dress as he continues speaking. "All I had to do was think about what I wanted them to do and they did it. Though, I can only channel them when we are connected deeply like this."

Goddess, I know nothing of this world I live in. Everyday I learn something new, something I never thought was possible.

# Chapter Thirty Five

## SKARLETTE

I'm placing the fifth bottle of Ruellia in the throne room when I hear footsteps on the other side of the door. I duck into the corner as two guards patrol the room. Ethan is out on official royal business, making today the perfect opportunity to plant his demise.

"I can't believe the king lets her have pretty much free reign of this place." One of the guards says to the other.

"Yeah, if I was the king, I would have had my way with her and then dumped her in vampire territory. Let them deal with the abomination that she is." They are talking about me, nausea rises in waves, making my stomach churn.

I am about to do something I can never come back from if they don't stop talking.

"She is beautiful though. Those tits . . . gorgeous."

"Too bad the weak prince is the one who got her."

"Yeah, what even is that? He did some training and now thinks he is all badass."

My teeth are gritted together, practically breaking from the force. Anger is burning it's way through me, blinding me with red hot rage. I have no control over what my shadows begin to do. They wrap around the guards feet, dragging them to the floor and slamming them against the stone wall. The shadows retreat, letting the guards drop from the air and onto the floor with two loud thuds. They let the guards feel safe, like they have disappeared and decided to let the guards live, but then they return, wrapping around their necks. The room echoes with the snaps from their necks. I stare at them for a long moment. This is what I was scared of, the inability to control my rage and now look at what my magic has done.

I flee, running through the halls, and not caring one bit about who see's me. I need to get out of here. When people see the guards, they will know who is responsible, there is no hiding it. My time in Ruellia is over, it is now time to go home. To Shadowfall.

Bursting through the door to Kai's room, I hope he is in here and can help me get out of here as quickly as possible, but I come to an abrupt stop when I see someone near the fireplace.

The maid startles, rising to her feet and getting ready to bow when she realizes it's me. She straightens, her face looking at me with discontent.

I stare at my mother, at her sullen skin and sunken eyes. The dark circles that create half moons underneath her bottom lashes. Her face is covered in soot from the fireplace. I should feel something, right? I should feel sorry for the fact that my mother is withering away while she works for the royal faerie family. But I feel nothing. I can't muster up even an ounce of sympathy for her.

Her eyes stare into mine with a hatred that fills my soul. Tears begin to streak down her face as her dry lips tremble with anger. She tries to throw her words at me like daggers, but they fall flat. "You ruined everything for me. I was a maid here, a respected one who even warmed the king's bed when his wife wouldn't. Then I got pregnant with you and the bastard cast me away to that vampire hell hole. But even there, I had friends. People who loved me."

Ignoring her whining, I begin to tell her my own story.

"I used to dream of what my life would have been like had you survived. I dreamt of a mom that brushed my long hair and gave me hugs when I was feeling down. A mom who brought me warm food after the prince had hit me once again. I cried and begged the goddess for someone to love me, anyone. So excuse me for not feeling sorry for you."

Kicking over bucket of dirty mop water in front of me, I watch as she lunges to keep it from spilling on the floor, but she misses. The contents of the bucket are everywhere and the floor she just spent an hour cleaning will now need to be cleaned again.

"You brat!" She hisses.

"Call me what you want. You are a part of what made me this way. Every person who ever turned the other way, every person who sneered. They made me what I am today and I won't be sorry for it. I love myself for the person I have become. You see me as a villain, but I see myself as strong. I don't take people's shit anymore."

She mops aggressively, trying to ignore my words. My shadows reach out to grab her head, forcing her to look at me. "Don't worry. When I am finished with this place, you will burn right along with it. You will go down with those who threatened to control my life, to use me for their own gain. I will not mourn for you either, for I have no feelings towards you, and that's on you."

"Why would I want some half breed mutt to mourn me?" I can feel the betrayal growing inside me, bubbling up like a volcano getting ready to burst. The shadows grip her tighter and it takes everything in me not to let them take her out now, but I want her to suffer. Need her to feel some sort of emotion for leaving a baby to fend for themselves in a castle of villains.

But when I look into my mothers eyes, I see nothing. They hold no emotion for me. The small piece of myself, the little girl who always dreamed of having a loving mother, floats away into nothing. The last of my humanity is hanging by a single thread that leads to Kai. He is the only thing holding me together from using my shadows to wipe this earth of everything, including myself.

I let the shadows fall, turning away from the maid and heading out the door. I will not waste another second demanding love from someone who does not wish to give it.

I need to find Kai, I need to outrun the damage I have done.

Looking everywhere, I finally finding him in the training ring on the side of the castle.

"Finally, I have been begging you to train with me for

weeks," he teases.

"I don't need to train. I'm a goddess created weapon, but Kai. . ." I don't have time for this. I need to get out of here, get away from the damage I have caused.

He motions for me to come closer. "It never hurts to train."

Pushing my body off the wall, I walk towards him. Fine. He wants me to train? I will train. Maybe it will help me ease the anxiety of what I have just done. Maybe it will keep people from suspecting that the guards are dead by my doing.

I get close, swinging my leg out and kicking him right in the shin. He grunts but moves towards me, reaching out and grabbing my arms. I try to wiggle from his grasp, but his hands are stronger than I imagined. I jump, managing to wrap my legs around his hips. A smirk spreads across his face, and I can feel the growing need between us. I drop my legs, letting them fall to the ground, and he responds by letting go of my arms.

But I'm not done. I spin, my arms going behind me and wrapping around the back of his neck, I pull with all my body weight. Flipping him over my shoulder and lying him out flat on the ground.

Smiling down at him with victory, I hold my hand out in

an offering to help him up. His hand is hot as it envelopes mine. Just when I start to pull him up, he yanks me down. I fall, landing on top of him, my face mere centimeters from his.

His hand grabs the back of my neck, closing the rest of the space between us before he places his lips to mine. For a small moment the world around us disappears. The dead guards, my mother, it all slips from my mind. But then I hear a commotion and all of my betrayals and hurt rush to the surface.

"This was fun, but now I need us to be serious. I need help." The smile drops from his face, concern etching into every line.

"What is it." We rise from the ground, my eyes darting around to make sure the guards aren't on their way to find me.

"I couldn't stop the shadows. I was so mad. I killed two of the guards." My eyes plead with him to help me flee.

"You get Bella and meet me in the courtyard in fifteen minutes. I'll have horses ready to go." We split up, ready to flee this castle once and for all.

The ride to Shadowfall is usually four days on horseback, we barely stop, taking a short minute to let Bella rest and change horses in Calix. We manage to make it to Shadowfall in two and a half days. My legs ache with soreness from riding so long. It was an awful ride that had me looking over my shoulder every few minutes to make sure we weren't being followed.

Standing on the steps to Shadowfall's castle stands Elijah, his face is solemn and I know that something is wrong. I can feel it in the magic that pulses inside me.

I rush to him, worried that my world is going to crumble around me. "What is it?"

"It is time." He turns away from me, heading into the castle. I knew what that meant. It was time.

I follow him inside, up the stairs and down the hall. We stall in front of large white double doors and I can see how much this is hurting him. Elijah knocks before one of the doors swings open. Inside, the room is dark, a bed with red curtains around it sits on the farthest wall. No windows grace the walls of this room and in the bed lies a frail old man. It takes me far too long to realize the man is my uncle Veron, the vampire king.

"What's wrong with him?" I ask Elijah, taking my uncle's hand in my own.

"He has refused to drink blood for weeks, at this point it is severely aging him as if he were a mere human. Soon he will turn to ash." I can tell it is painful for Elijah to watch his father deteriorate like this.

"Sit with him, Elijah. I will take care of things," I say softly, rising from the bedside chair.

"There are vampires here who still aren't sure you are the right fit to rule," Elijah tries to argue.

Placing my hand on his shoulder, I give it a loving squeeze. "I will take care of it. You deserve to spend this last few moments with him." I leave Elijah with his father, deciding it best to get cleaned up after our long ride here before attending to any vampiric matters.

The smooth stone of my throne is cold against my bare ass. When I decided to come down here after my bath I expected to be lost in my own thoughts and quickly head to bed after. But now, Kai is stalking towards me. Determination in his eyes as they run up my bare legs and up to where my nipples peak, pushing the fabric of my robe up. He stops a few feet from the bottom of the dais, waiting for me to give him orders.

Lifting my hand, I crook my finger and motion for him to come closer. He climbs the steps of the dais, coming to stand directly in front of me.

My voice is commanding, like I am talking to an army. "Kneel."

It doesn't surprise me when he does as I say. His head bows, looking down at the floor as I put my leg on his shoulder. He looks up at me and I can see the desire in his eyes. His lips meet my skin as he places kisses all the way up my leg, stopping at my knee. The gentle touch of his warm lips to my cool skin, sends tingling sensations all through my body. I let my leg drop back down to the floor and watch with my own hunger and excitement as he rises. He wraps his arm around me, flipping me around so my knees now sit on the seat of my throne.

"Grab the back." he growls and I hear his pants hit the floor behind me. My hands fist around the two spindles at the top of my throne. Anxiously awaiting his touch.

Kai slides into me, slowly, luxuriously. Like we have all the time in the world. Pleasure soars through me each time he slides in and out. My head falls forward coming to rest on the back of the golden throne.

"Kai," I pant as his thrusts become quicker.

"You look so fucking beautiful bent over your throne." I can feel it coming, feel the small waves of my orgasm as the larger ones build. His hand reaches forward, taking my nipple between his fingers and that's all I need. My undoing crashes through me at the same time his does.

I hiss when he slides out, the friction too much to handle so soon. He fixes his clothes and takes the steps down. Turning to look at me, he holds out his hand, ready for us to go back to bed. Tonight will be a night I replay in my mind for years to come.

It makes me feel powerful and weak all at the same time. It is my throne, but he made me come completely undone upon it. I am the ruler of this kingdom and he is my worshipper, but he is also my salvation. He will save me from the monster that lays deep inside me. The one who tells me I'm not enough and that I can't do this. For Kai and I are two parts of a whole.

Inside our room is sweltering. Kai's body radiates an unnatural amount of heat. Probably because of the healing powers. I cross to the window in our bedroom, pushing and pulling until it finally opens with a loud creak. Dust billows from the window sill, making me cough, but the breeze that enters through the window is welcomed. Kai shifts in his sleep, murmuring something about injustice and it makes me wonder what he dreams of.

The sheets bring me comfort as I climb back in beside him, the fabric cool from the air. The need to sleep evades me after just having drank Kai's blood. It seems to keep me rejuvenated for days. It is amazing the effect it has on me, but it is also like a drug which is why I will only drink it sparingly. I may be a villain, but Kai is the exception, he will always be the exception. Which is why I would never let myself overindulge.

I awake the next morning with the crows. Moving to the window, I look out over the land. Shadowfall is covered in a thick layer of frost. The first frost of the year is here. I will now be the queen of Shadowfall and soon to be the entirety of Aurenda.

I dress, sliding into my tight leather pants and a long sleeve black shirt, cinching my corset as tight as it will go before putting my daggers in their hiding spots. I look to the bed, the bed where Kai had fallen asleep with me last night, but where he no longer rests this morning. He was gone before the sun had even graced the horizon. I hate that he had to leave so soon, but I understood why. He has his own kingdom to care for while I plan out how we were going to end an entire monarchy.

"Good morning," my maid, Amelia greets.

"Good morning." Taking my tea from the tray she sets on the table, I blow the steam away and sip the hot liquid. The food here is so strangely different from that of Ruellia.

I am expecting the warm vanilla flavor of our morning tea, I'm not expecting the hint of blood that lingers with it. All the food is like that here. Soups and stews are made with blood broth. Tea and wine, mixed with blood. In fact, so much food is mixed with blood, it shows me how they keep themselves so strong.

After my tea, I take breakfast in the quiet dining room. I suppose since most vampires don't need to eat actual meals, I was the first to use this room regularly. While they added the blood to the food, most vampires seem to prefer drinking their blood straight from the tap, resorting to the food only when necessary. A curse of my half faerie blood was the need for both blood and food. I wish Kai was here to eat with me. I did enjoy talking to people. Maybe I could send my guards to get Janella for me? A thought that both made me happy and worried. How would the other vampires do with seeing her here? Would she be safe?

A servant is standing in the corner of the room near the door. He seems to be trying to hide himself behind a houseplant, but is failing. His auburn hair doesn't blend well with the green of the foliage. His fae pointed ears tell me he is probably in servitude for committing a crime against the vampires. I debate for a long moment if I want to ask a favor of him. His eyes shift around the room, landing on me for a moment before looking away again. He is afraid of what I might to do him should he displease me. Good. He should be scared. I can be villainous.

"Ask them to send guards to Janella Odeam. She lives in the fae village, but tell them to ask nicely," I order, remembering that I am the queen of this castle.

Kai enters the dining room, grumbling under his breath, and clearly in pain. My eyes narrow in on the chain digging into his arm. The skin red and angry from the iron.

"Who did this to you?" I try to keep calm, my hands aching as I peel the iron chain from Kai's arm.

"Doesn't matter." He grunts as the chain finally releases it's hold on him and falls to the floor.

"It does." My chair falls backward from the force of me rising from the table. I grab a napkin from the table, dampening it with water from the pitcher and begin to tenderly pat at the angry skin. His healing powers come in full action, the skin is already looking like a white scar where it heals.

"Just some stupid vampires," he mumbles like a child who is in trouble for fighting.

I grit my teeth. "They have no right to harm you."

"I don't need you to fight my battles for me!" Kai bellows. "I spent three years without you, fighting and getting stronger." The agitation in his voice cracks my core.

"I didn't…." I start to say, but my voice falls. I will protect him for all that it costs, the same way he will protect me, but I don't want him to feel less for fighting the people who wrong him. I know that he can take care of himself. I am just so use to fighting everyone's battles for them and I am going to have to learn how to let him fight them on his own.

"They decided I needed a little lesson after I dispatched the wretched thing that kidnapped you and brought you here." Realization is slowly crawling through my brain.

"You didn't." He also has no right to go killing vampires while he is here.

"He kidnapped you," he says it slow like I am stupid.

"I cannot win over the small group of vampires who believe I don't belong here if you are out there killing them," I hiss.

"I need to go back to Ruellia." I don't want him to leave mad, but I can't stand that he would go behind my back like that.

"I think that's for the best." I will have to fix all the chaos Kai has managed to cause while I slept in.

# Chapter Thirty Six

## KAI

The guards are waiting for me when I arrive back in Ruellia. Dismounting from my horse, my arm aches slightly from the iron chain that the vampires had used to try and chain me. A small glimmer of guilt accompanies the ache. I shouldn't have done that. I should have talked with Skarlette first. But I saw him, standing there, sneering at me and boasting to his friends about kidnapping the queen. I couldn't help myself for what I did next.

I feel bad for leaving things the way I did with Skarlette. I don't want her to think that I am weak. That I can't handle myself when inevitably I am supposed to be at her side.

The guards escort me to the throne room where Ethan is waiting for me.

"Where the fuck have you been and where is my monster?" My brother growls.

"I have no idea where Skarlette is. I was out dealing with some vampire sightings," I lie, hoping he can't tell, but I see the way his eyes narrow. He is trying to use his powers on me.

"You know where she is, you just don't want to tell me." Ethan's hand holds a dagger, the tip digging into the throne as he twirls it.

"I can try and help you find her," I offer.

"And have you leading my men on a wild goose chase?" My brother unfolds himself, rising from the throne and walking towards me. "I think not." He stops in front of me, bringing the dagger up and holding it against my throat. I can feel the blade's cold metal delicately touching my skin.

"Come now, brother," I offer with a small smile.

"She thinks I don't know she has been conspiring against me. She thinks I don't know she has been sneaking off to Shadowfall for months now." I gulp against the blade, worry lacing through me at just how much my brother knows. "I have always had eyes on her. I know of her prophecy and I am so close to taking her place in it before she can. I would have been successful sooner, If only she hadn't had you to help her fight off that guard."

"Does Skarlette know about all of this?" My brother laughs, digging the dagger into my throat more.

"Stop pretending. She has known for months. I also know just how strong she gets when she is able to drink from you." Fear drops like water into the bucket that is my stomach. He knows everything. "Guards, I think it is time my brother sees his new room."

The guards grab hold of my arms, dragging me out of the throne room and down into the dungeons. I kick my feet, using my strength to twist myself free of their arms, but one of the guards is ready. He pulls something out of his pocket, digging the needle into my flesh and making the room spin around me.

I fall to the floor, darkness clouding the edges of my vision and then there is nothing. No sound, no light, just darkness.

My eyes open, blinking away the blurriness and scanning over my new cell. Through the small window, I can see it is dark outside, meaning I have been asleep all day. I look around, but no food has been left for me.

Days pass. The only food I am brought is bread every other day, enough to keep me alive, but slowly starving. I startle when the iron bars behind me rattle. It's dark and my eyes can barely see the person shimmying the lock. The door flies open and the person's arm reaches out for me.

"Come on!" Hisses Janella.

I scramble to my feet, dizziness taking over me at the lack of nutrients. Janella's hand wraps around my own, pulling me up the stairs and down the halls. I can barely keep up with her. I'm so tired and my stomach grumbles with hunger. We dart to the right, into the kitchen and out the side entrance door where we pause for a moment, hiding behind one of the large bushes lining the garden.

Two guards pass us, too busy talking to notice where we are hiding. Janella moves, quick but quiet to get us outside the gate and into the village before anyone notices.

"Hey! Wait! The prisoner has escaped." A guard yells just as Janella throws a set of reins in my direction.

I hesitate, looking back at the guards. "Come on, what are you waiting for?" Janella is already up on her horse, ready for me to follow.

Climbing into the saddle, I stuff my feet into the stirrups and take one last glance back at what used to be my home. Standing there on the balcony is my brother with his arms behind his back. His eyes are cold as he watches me ride off into the night.

Janella and I ride all day and night, pushing our horses past their breaking point to make it to Shadowfall in two and a half days. We don't dare stop anywhere now that we are fugitives to the crown. Even the protection of Skarlette can't help us when she is all the way in her castle.

"That was exciting and crazy." Janella shoots me a smile over her shoulder.

"Thanks for getting me, but how did you know I was there?" We stop near a river on the edge of the dark forest, letting the horses drink.

"I was here at the castle and Skarlette was so worried about how you guys left things. She was chewing her lip raw." She shook her head. "I offered to talk to you when I came back. Problem was, when I got back, you were no where to be found. Lucky for me, I overheard two guards talking about throwing you in the brig." She rolls her eyes. "I swear, faeries are the biggest gossips."

"You are seriously bad ass, Janella." Her cheeks turn bright pink with the compliment.

"Ah, it's nothing. You and Skar are my friends. I would do anything for you guys." We click our tongues, making the horses move and take us the rest of the way to Shadowfall.

We reach the castle an hour later. Standing on the steps with her arms wrapped tightly around her, is my beautiful menace. Her hair is down, hanging over her shoulders and brows pinched with worry.

I dismount before my horse is even stopped, running to her and wrapping my arms around her. I squeeze her tight, not wanting to let go of her. Her palms push against me, pushing me away from her.

"I am so glad you made it here. I had spies, but I had to pull them out, we had no idea you were in prison or I would have come myself. Janella sent word before she saved you." Tears are streaming down Skarlette's cheeks and I know she doesn't want everyone seeing her like this.

"Come on, lets get inside." I wrap my arm around her shoulders, leading her into the castle.

She sniffles, wiping her nose with her sleeve. "You must be hungry."

When the door is closed, I stop walking, turning to face her and taking her head in my hands. Janella walks past us, heading into the dining room and leaving us to have a moment alone.

"I am home now, Skarlette." Her lips are wet with tears as I kiss her.

She smiles, wiping the last of the tears from her eyes. But I can see the worry in them as she takes in my slim form. "Come now. Let's get some food into you."

"As long as it isn't blood flavored, I'm good," I joke.

I'm amazed when I enter the dining room to see the table covered in all sorts of faerie food. Janella already has a plate full. My mouth is watering from the delicious smell. Roast duck, spit fired boar, potatoes and soup. All the food I could have ever asked for is on this table, waiting for me to devour it.

With my plate piled high, I sit across from Janella. Skarlette sits at the head of the table, drinking a goblet of something. I watch her wipe the blood from her lips and feel the jealousy as it winds its way around my my chest.

"Menace," I say with surprising calmness, "are you drinking someone else's blood?"

The corners of her sweet mouth turn up slightly. "And if I am?"

I rise from my seat, standing before her. My hand reaches between us, wrapping around her pretty throat. "You will only drink from me, or I will have to punish you."

My eyes follow her tongue as she licks her lips. "I look forward to it," she purrs, and I almost lose control right there, but Janella clears her throat, reminding me we aren't alone.

"That's great, but could we at least wait until I am done eating?" Skarlette and I laugh, returning to our food.

I didn't realize how alone I felt in that cell until I was back here with Skarlette and Janella. Our laughter and small talk, filled my heart and made me angry with myself and how I had left here.

I am about to apologize when Skarlette talks. "Janella I have something to show you if you guys are done eating."

Janella buzzes with excitement the entire way down the hall. We come to stand in front of two large, dark doors. Skarlette unlocks them, pushing them open to reveal a massive library. Janella spins in the center of the room, looking at the thousands of books that sit among the dark wood shelves.

"Skar, this is amazing," her friend gushes, enclosing Skarlette in a hug.

Leaving the two of them in the library, I'm too tired from

the last few weeks to stay upright another minute longer. I crawl into Skarlette's bed, closing my eyes, only to be met with awful nightmares.

*Ethan's eyes are red like Skarlette's. When he laughs, fangs descend from his gums. The throne room is full of bodies, Louissa's being one of them. Tears are streaming down my face, as I hold my sister's lifeless body.*

*"What have you done," I cry and he laughs.*

*"I will rule it all. It's all mine." He yanks on a chain, dragging someone to the floor.*

*Skarlette is in a slump, an iron collar wrapped around her neck that is attached to the chain. I drop my sister's body, trudging through the lifeless bodies that are piled across the floor, trying to make my way to her, but it's like a sea. The bodies keep pulling me down as Skarlette and my brother get farther and farther away from me.*

I wake up with sweat pouring from my face. Skarlette is laying next to me, her breathing soft as she sleeps. Shaking away the dream from my mind, I wrap my arms around Skarlette, holding her close and letting sleep take me once more.

# Chapter Thirty Seven

## SKARLETTE

"The vampires aren't taking well to your ruling." Elijah walks beside me down the hall. It has been a hard transition, I will give him that. A lot of vampires still hate seeing a half breed on their throne.

A commotion is coming from the dining hall, a ruckus that sounds far too hostile for me not to be included. I round the corner, coming into the hall and watch as a vampire drinks from Janella's neck. A group of vampires surround the room as her arms go limp. He digs in deeper, completely draining her of all of her blood.

A scream echoes of the walls, piercing our ears. My hand flies up to my mouth, realizing that it's my scream we are hearing. My shadows swirl at my feet, feeding off the anger and hurt coursing through my body.

"Xander!" Elijah barks and the vampire whips his head in our direction. When he sees the fallen look on my face, a wicked smile spreads across his own. He knew exactly the pain he would cause, he knew that it would hit me if he killed her and that is my fault for letting them see her as my weakness.

Janella's body lays at my feet, splayed out on the floor. Her beautiful navy blue eyes, lifeless. She is gone. The one person besides Kai to truly show me friendship and kindness and she has slipped through my fingers before I could tell her how much I appreciated her. The tears threaten to come, but I push them down, letting them fuel my anger.

I stare at the vampire in front of me as shadows lash out towards him like whips. "You killed my friend."

The smile on his face drops when my shadows grab his arms, pulling him closer to me. I growl at him. "I don't have many friends in this life and you just killed one." My arm snaps out, grabbing him by the throat.

"I didn't know," he says, the cockiness from earlier completely gone, replaced with raw fear.

"A mistake you will have to remember in your next life." Grabbing a torch from the wall, I let my shadows carry the vampire out of the castle. In the square, the shadows drop him in a heap on the ground. He tries to scramble away, but I am quicker. I set the torch to his clothes, watching as they light up like the wick of a candle. His screams carry through the air, telling the other villagers what happens when they kill someone I love.

My shadows hide from the flames of fire, retreating back to wherever they come from. I don't wait around long. I would rather take care of Janella's lifeless body than sit here and watch this disgrace of a vampire turn into ash.

Making my way back into the castle, I find it hard to enter the room. I know I will see her there and wish that she would come back to life. I linger at the door for a long time before entering the dining hall. Crouching down beside my friend, a singular tear slips from my eye and onto her pale skin.

"The world is too cruel." I sniff. "They took you before you could even make your dreams a reality."

Kai rushes in, dropping down beside me and closing Janella's eyes. His hand smooths over my back, trying to provide me comfort, but I don't want it. The pain inside me is raw and ugly and I would give anything for someone to take it away, but they can't. It wasn't her time to go. She had dreams that needed to be fulfilled.

My fist pounds against the red and white marble floor, the impact splitting the stone from my force. I let out a growl that turns into a scream.

I look back up, at a crowd that has formed around us, staring at the sight unfolding in front of their eyes. They watch like hyenas ready to pounce when I am distraught.

"You dare take the things I love from me? You question if I am the rightful queen?" My shadows dart towards the vampires as they stagger away.

Kai stands, moving away from me, letting me exact the my vengeance.

"You dare question what King Veron set in motion before he returned to the earth?" My voice is louder than I ever thought possible, the walls shake as my shadows climb them.

"Show me the ones who thought this was a good idea. Show me the ones who dare defy me." Tendrils of my shadows push three men and a woman in my direction. I don't hesitate not even for a moment, before my shadows wrap around them and stab them straight through the heart. They weren't the ones to drink from her, but they were the ones who cheered him on. They are the ones that planned with him on how they would make me hurt.

Their bodies crumble to the floor in heaps as my shadows return to my side before scooping up Janella and carrying her out of the room with me. I walk all the way down and into our crypt where my shadows lay Janella's body on a smooth stone in the center. The utter stillness of her body makes me cry. I am expecting her to pop up and tell me it is all some prank to try and get me to lighten up, but she doesn't move.

Down here, away from the prying eyes of all those who must see me as strong, I let the tears flow in waves. They run down my cheeks and splatter to the floor. Leaning my head against her cold arm that is crossed over her chest, I choke on my sobs. I can't breathe and my lungs are aching for air, but still the tears flow.

"I loved you so much. You were the best friend a villain could ask for," I whisper.

I quickly dry my tears when I hear footsteps padding down the stairs. Poising myself, I'm ready to tackle what comes next. When Kai's soft navy and gold flecked eyes peak around the corner, I let out a shaky sigh.

"How are we supposed to do this without her?" I ask him softly.

"Exactly how you survived before you found out she was

your friend. We will be sad and we will wish to turn to her when we are in need, but she won't be there anymore. She will be watching us from somewhere beyond this place. Somewhere we know nothing about. Let us hope it is somewhere the goddess or the devil, whoever they may be, is watching over her." I nod, his words running deep in my soul.

I laugh a little, thinking about how Janella would have responded to this situation. "Only a week in our new home and you have already killed five people," I say, mimicking Janella's voice and Kai laughs too. "I guess I am predictable." I chuckle, snuggling into Kai's embrace.

"The Aurendian people will learn to love you. Just give it time." He places a kiss on my forehead before letting me go.

I sleep away the rest of the day. When I wake that night, the tears once again flow freely down my face. My friend is gone. I need her here. I need her laugh and her sunny optimism. She was the sunshine to my darkness. While Kai helped, he is the other half of my soul. She was well, my opposite.

Sitting in the window, I am numb and unable to cry anymore. The sun is rising over the mountains, and I have work to do while the other vampires sleep. It is hard. Life goes on for me. I am expected to rule Shadowfall and take over Ruellia even though my friend's life is over. I am expected to act as if everything is okay. As if a part of my life hasn't just been ripped away from me yet again.

Today, the vampires will learn just how cruel I can be.

Elijah greets me in the hall. "Good morning." He nods his head and is surprisingly pleasant this morning. "I take it you will be taking some time for mourning?" His voice sounds so sure, but there is a hint of question in it.

"No, I would like to see the vampires in the castle this evening, just after sunset. I am going to make sure they know me and my plans for us." Elijah's face turns up in a scowl, but quickly he hides it, smoothing out his expression.

"I will pass along the news." He bows, leaving me to sit in the dining room alone.

The food on my plate doesn't call to me. I push the eggs and links of sausage around. My stomach twists anytime the food so much as touches my tongue. It is all so strange. Even though I saw her die, I still feel like any moment now she will pop her head into the dining room and join me for breakfast.

But she never comes.

# Chapter Thirty Eight

## SKARLETTE

Ruellia's castle looks awful, weeds grow from the garden and no guards protect the entrance. It sits dark, with overcast skies hanging above it. I heard through my spies, that the scientist had managed to turn Ethan, but no blood could quench his thirst. He drank and drank from everyone in the house and still it wasn't enough. Now he is the King of decay. They say he sits on his throne, surrounded by the pile of bodies he used to try and fill the ache of hunger inside himself. The scientist must have seen the evil that Ethan was and without even knowing it, helped me to end the rein of this villain.

Inside, the castle is desolate. The trinkets and vases that sit on tables are lined with dust. The maids were obviously the first to be feasted upon. The doors to the throne room sit ajar, squeaking loudly when I finish pushing it open to enter. Sitting there on the throne is Ethan, his crown hanging sideways on his head, his eyes sunken into his skull and his skin hanging off his bones. A shiver snakes down my spine at the mere sight of him.

Ignoring the large pile of bones that sits on either side of the throne and the living pile of bones sitting on the throne, I move around the room, spilling the vials of Ruellia oil and grabbing a torch that hangs from the wall. My eyes catch on a familiar face that lays motionless on the floor. Kai's fiancé lays there, her body filled with tiny dots from where Ethan continued to drink from her. He must have used her, kept her alive to help try and curb the bloodlust, but inevitably the hunger was too strong and he consumed her as well.

Holding the torch with an iron grip, I look at the pitiful man in front of me. "You underestimated me. You thought you could keep me chained, keep me under control. But I have news for you. You didn't create a weapon for you to use at will. You created a monster hell bent on destroying the very people who threatened to use her for themselves."

Moving to the corner of the room, I light the first puddle of Ruellia concentrate, watching with delight as the flames lick up the curtains.

His voice is strained, the poison I had been slipping in his food and the lack of blood taking it's toll. "I saw it. I saw the villain you were becoming. When I couldn't manage to kill you, I hoped we would do all this together. I didn't however see your plan to burn me alive."

"You were too blinded by power. Too blinded by your own agenda to see the plans I was carrying out right underneath your nose." I move to the next corner, lighting the next spot.

The heat licks against my skin as the fire grows, taking every curtain and dried wilted flower with it. My shadows dance around my body, trying their hardest to keep me safe from the heat of the flames. Smoke fills the room, making it hard to catch my breath. I can hear Ethan struggling to breathe as well, but I keep going. When the last fire is lit, I drop the torch.

"Remember—" He takes a sharp inhale of breath. "That I made you this way." Another sharp inhale "Every time you destroy someone . . . remember it was I who taught you to be cruel."

"I won't remember you. Your memory will fade away

into nothing." Those are the last words I speak before I leave the castle. As I cross the threshold, the memory of my mother surfaces, I didn't see her in the pile of new bodies, so I only assume she was one of the first to be feasted upon and now her bones will turn to ash with the rest of them.

At the entrance to the village, Kai stands there with crossed arms, waiting for me to join him. A mix of emotions swirls in his eyes as he watches the smoke begin to swirl from the windows of his home.

"Everyone make it out okay?" I ask, mostly concerned for the very pregnant Louissa.

"She is on her way to Shadowfall as we speak." His gaze doesn't meet mine, he simply looks at the burning castle, watching as all of our childhood hopes and dreams burn to the ground. Every memory of our childhood drifting up in the embers and floating away into nothing but ash.

"I had to, I couldn't bare to see it stand another minute and you know he had to go with it." He drops his gaze to look at me.

"I have never once questioned it and I won't be starting now." His forefinger and thumb take hold of my chin, tilting my head and kissing me with a force that takes my breath away.

Taking Kai's hand in mine, we walk away as the castle

that was once our home burns behind us. We have done it. We have killed the king and any hold he had over us is now gone. We are free to be the very villains we had become. There will be no turning back from this. The fae will see us as the monsters we are and the vampires will continue to hate the fae who sits on the throne.

When we arrive back at the vampiric castle a few days later, I immediately go to the window. I watch as the last remnants of the fae castle smolder to the ground in the far distance. It is now nothing but a pile of rocks. Something in me is gleeful to see the destruction, but a small part of me pangs with grief. It was full of memories, but also full of heartbreak. That castle had been my prison, but it had also been home. A place to keep me from the weather. A place where I met my deepest fears and my greatest friends.

Kai approaches, his hand resting on the small of my back. The featherlight touch of his thumb rubbing against my back, making me feel more comfort than I have ever felt. This is it. We were home.

"It's bitter sweet to see it gone," he says, his voice thick with melancholy.

"Maybe we can rebuild some day, make it a summer home?" I suggest.

"That would be nice." His lips meet the side of my head

in a small kiss as we watch the last of the embers float away.

Leaving my side, he crosses the room and picks up a small box. He holds it out to me, offering for me take it. The box is smooth in my hands, a beautiful black velvet container.

"Open it," he urges.

My fingers pull off the lid, looking inside to see the most beautiful crown of gold with sparkling blood red rubies encrusted all over it. My breath leaves me as I pull the crown from it's box. The firelight from the candles in my room glint off the dark red rubies.

"Kai, it's perfect." I breathe.

"A crown fit for my villainous queen."

The crown falters slightly in my grasp. "What makes me any better than him?"

"You are villainous when you need to be and just when they deserve it. He was a monster who made you kill people he didn't like." He grabs hold of my hand, making sure I understand that Ethan and I are not the same. "It's time for you to get ready." He takes the crown from my grasp, placing it back in its box before tucking it under his arm. "I will make sure we have this when they crown you our queen." He pecks me on the cheek, leaving me to dress for my coronation.

The castle hall is lit with thousands of candles. I had a large chandelier added to the center of the room that holds five hundred candles itself. I had to make accommodations to the castle if I wanted the fae to feel included. People file in, cramming the space with both fae and vampire, but the divide between them is obvious. Right down the center of the room is where they split, fae on one side and vampires on the other.

Only time will tell if this is going to work. If we can come together, two creatures that are so different, while also being the same and make a life as one.

Standing before them in a beautiful black dress, I address my people.

"Thank you all for coming," I announce. Nervousness swirls around in my stomach, crawling up my throat and making it hard to speak. Something about having the eyes of two entire kingdoms on me was nerve racking. Like at any moment I could say something stupid and have a full out war on my hands.

Kai gives me a reassuring whisper through the side of his mouth. "You're doing great."

"I hope to unite the kingdoms as one. Nothing will change and we will trade the way we always have. It will be your choice to live where you please, but know that I will be as villainous as I need to be. If you are kind, I will give you kindness, if you are cruel, I will be crueler." I wait for a long moment, letting my words sink into the minds of my people.

I'm about to turn away, decide this whole announcement thing was pointless, when slowly they start to kneel, bowing to me. They lower themselves like a wave, chanting words that will begin our new life as one.

Kneeling before Kai, I let him place the crown upon my head. I smile up at him before rising to my feet and watching to the crowd as they continue to chant.

"Our Villainous Queen!"

The End

# Acknowledgements

I want to give a huge shout out to my family. You guys always cheer me on even on the days when I feel down. You guys are my cheerleaders and I wouldn't know what to do in this life without you guys.

Also, to all my readers. You guys keep me going even when I want to throw in the towel. I love creating these stories for you all and I hope you all know how special you are.

Special shout out to three ladies who I met on Booktok. Maria, Megan, and Lorenza I am beyond lucky to have found you all when I did ARCS for COLAL. You are the best readers a girl can ask for.

# About the Author

L. N. Reagan loves writing fantasy romance. From a young age L. N. Reagan enjoyed reading books and getting lost in a story. Living in the PNW many days are filled with rain which means many hours spent at home curled up with a good book. L. N. Reagan is a mom who loves taking her kids on adventures as well as curling up at home with all of her pets. She hopes her stories bring as much joy to her readers as others books bring to her.

# *Also by*

Also by Author L. N. Reagan

The Nights Revenge

The Crowns of Love Duology